"Do you believe?" he asked sternly.

It was the first time they both really saw each other's full faces in the parlor's subdued room light. And it was the first time they looked directly at each other's eyes, and into them—

"I believe in what I see. Not what I don't," Janek replied in a soft-spoken tone, as if already knowing the answer to the question.

Lancelot took a small step back into the room's shadows.

"But what if what you don't see actually sees you?"

Janek smiled as he answered, "The Spirits of the dead?"

"Seeing is believing." Lancelot moved one open hand into the space around him, pointing out the answer.

"So, you don't believe." Janek's eyes seemed to twinkle in delight as though he knew something that his adversary didn't.

Lancelot chuckled. "In foolish folktales made up by writers such as us? No. I don't believe."

"Then what about the ghost behind you?"

GHOSTS

you'll believe

by

JOE JANOWICZ

Cover: Megan J. Parker

Editing: Elly Stevens

Formatting: Suzanne Blessing

Printed in the United States of America
by NewField Publications

ISBN 978-1-08801105-8

https://www.joejanowiczauthor.com

Chapter 1

"Noooooo!"

Her bloodcurdling scream cut through the star-filled midnight sky and echoed off the surrounding castle's gray and crumbling rock walls. Her terror-stricken voice was loud enough to wake the dead. But the "dead" was clearly alive in front of her, struggling with someone who was about to die—her husband.

She watched as the man-monster held her loved one by the throat, strangling the last breath out of him while he flailed and made futile attempts to break free. The predator smiled sardonically in anticipation of the kill he was to carry out. And there was nothing she could do to stop him. As her eyes widened in horror, the demon slowly turned to face her and opened his mouth wide and hissed, barring his long, sharp fangs.

Trapped at the edge of the castle's stone balcony, there was no place for her to run, as this hellish six-hundred-year-old creature and her dying husband blocked the only way in and out. Moments earlier, the couple, exploring the darkened castle, found the long, winding, empty corridor with the hope that it would lead to a way out. But the castle's lone occupant knew where it led, which made it all the more easier for him to trap his prey.

Behind her was air—a sky full of air, heavy with an approaching storm that grumbled like an older man clearing his throat before spitting out bolts of bright yellow lightning. Beneath the balcony, a hundred feet, two hundred feet, or maybe three hundred feet below was the ocean, its angry waves crashing on the giant jagged rocks that jutted out from the swirling, dark blue water, beckoning the storm's approach. Surviving a fall from that height would be a miracle but escaping the monster's wrath was an impossibility. Death was the inevitable answer. And death was what she faced. But death did not become her this night. Not tonight. It was their honeymoon, and she would not allow an infernal creature in an abandoned historic castle in a foreign land ruin her vacation, let alone end her life.

"Noooo!" she screamed again, as the monster sunk his sharp teeth into her husband's throat.

His glistening fangs went deep into the man's exhausted body—deep into the arteries that held his precious blood, which this nightmare-come-to-life creature now claimed for himself. Her husband's battered and beaten body was limp and dying. It was his end. His alone. Not hers. Yet.

"Noooo!" she screamed again, no longer out of fear of dying next, nor the horror of the spectacle of death she was part of.

"Noooo!" Her voice was louder than the sudden sound of clapping thunder, as her tears became mixed with falling raindrops. Her unleashed rage filled her very soul with a trembling anger—anger that consumed her body and gave her the strength and reason to react.

"Hell hath no fury" when this woman's love was at stake. And that was the answer.

The wooden stake.

The wooden stake her husband had dropped on the stone floor when they were suddenly attacked by this hell-spawned creature of the night.

The wooden stake that they found next to the empty open coffin in the lower part of the castle they explored, leaving the other tour members of the historic castle behind.

The wooden stake that they had "taken" as a souvenir and unique prized possession with their devil-may-care attitude and laughter.

The wooden stake that he dropped in the struggle to protect her from this undead demon.

The wooden stake that lay alone in the shadows of the moonlight mere inches away from where she stood.

It was there now—for her to pick up and use as the only possible weapon against this blood-thirsty creature. And she would.

And she did.

Dropping his dead prey, now drained of all life and blood, the vampire turned to face her. Her. His feasting was not yet over.

His fangs dripped with the blood of her husband, as he slowly licked his lips, savoring her husband's taste. And in that horrific moment, a full moon broke through the surrounding clouds before heaven opened its gate to hell. And in that moment, she thrust the wooden stake into the vampire's bare chest, using her full body weight to push it deeper and deeper until it could go no further, as its splintered, sharp point pierced his black, rotting heart. Punctured it enough to make him scream louder than any of her earlier screams. Louder than the full fury of death unleashed.

But it wasn't deep enough to kill him.

The vampire backed away, a foot or two, maybe three or four, in shock, pain, and his own seething anger. His dark red eyes focused on her as his screams went silent. And then he smiled. Smiled wider than he had smiled at her before, and his mouth was filled with blood, not only her dead husband's but his, as well. And his fangs glistened in that brief moment of remaining moonlight as he slowly withdrew the wooden stake from his chest and slowly dropped it to the floor next to her dead husband's body.

This thing, this monster, would not die—it could not die—for it was already among the dead.

She knew the choices she had left. There were only two. To submit to him and become the vampire's bride, or to...

And she made her choice.

It really was the only janoice.

She knew that there would never be a second honeymoon in her life with this ungodly creature's desire to possess her. Her love began with the commitment she made to her childhood sweetheart, the commitment they made as young children who were best friends, best friends who became best lovers, and finally husband and wife. Their commitment with the words spoken to each other in front of the eyes of the Lord, *"Till death do us part."* And that was her choice.

With the vampire's blood-filled mouth opening wider and wider, she stood quietly as he approached, almost waiting, and smiled back. Without tears, without words, she made her choice.

Turning silently and without pause, she stepped off the ledge of the balcony, through the broken, crumbling, short wall railing and into the hot summer air and surrounding deep darkness of night. One hundred feet, two hundred feet, she fell with her arms outstretched like an angel in flight, ready to embrace the outcome. How far she fell, how long she fell, it didn't matter. Nothing mattered. Her choice was to be with the one she loved, yesterday, today, and for all the never-to-come tomorrows. And she would.

After what seemed like an eternity, she entered the waiting sea, swallowing her whole, creating a final resting place for her lifeless young body. The crashing waves on the jutting rocks covered her as she disappeared from sight, leaving the shocked monster far behind.

From the castle above, the howling shriek of a tormented soul in the undead body of a six-centuries-old vampire pierced the sky. His lust denied.

But she couldn't hear the monster's agony. Nor could she see the demon as she looked upwards through the swirling water into the darkened sky above her. As she sank deeper, and further, into the chilling waiting water, her dying smile grew wider. A peaceful smile. A loving smile. A lasting smile. Death did become her. Finally, and forever.

The End.

Silence.

Complete, absolute silence.

In the semi-darkness of the auditorium, countless watery, tear-filled eyes stared silently. Hearts and heads, filled with emotions from the just-spoken words of the voice reading by the author who stood on stage alone at the podium, remained in shock and wonderment as he closed his book and waited for what he knew would come next.

Applause.

Thunderous applause, as all two hundred fans, listeners, admirers, and everyone else in between, packed into a totally filled room came to their feet as one. Clapping as loudly as the thunder in his story. Roaring as loudly as the heroine screamed in the story he had written. Cheering as loudly as the waves had crashed on her final moment, as she disappeared forever into her water-filled grave.

They loved his story. They loved his new book that they had waited impatiently for nearly a year since his last book, which they loved, too. They loved all his books. And they loved him.

Lancelot Strong, at 30 years old, was the world's best-selling author of romance vampire horror stories. Since his first book was published ten years ago, each new book was more successful than the previous. He had sold more books than any other author of any genre in any period of recorded bookselling history. He was the king of gothic romantic horror and his fans reveled in the characters and images he created. At six foot two, with long blonde, perfect-looking hair that fell to his shoulders and moved so sexily with the turn of his head and punctuated with steel-blue eyes that melted the heart of every woman who looked into them, he was more than just handsome. He was every woman's fantasy come true. Even the artwork on his book covers seemed to resemble his image and bring it to life, as if he were the actual vampire in the story. And his stories were written with words that cast a spell on the reader and woven with feelings that brought a new definition of gothic eroticism. Stories that, when he did a book reading, seemed so natural, so real, you would almost believe "he believed" he lived them himself. But of course, that's impossible, and makes for good press releases. Yet, that's what writers do, and he was a "Master" of that. He created images and fantasies that all his many female readers and fans wanted to live in, unrestricted by the real and mundane world they actually lived in. And his reading tonight did just that as it had done so many times before. It was *spellbinding*.

Lancelot Strong was on top of his writing game. He was rich, famous, and handsome, and he could and would sleep with any fan who desired to be with him. After all, their desires were his desires, and their obsessions were never ending. Not only was he a great writer, but he was also a great lover. He had it all. Everyone said that about him, "He has it all."

Almost.

Lancelot Strong, writer extraordinaire, certainly had "all the fame and all the glory." But unfortunately, just one "thing" was missing in his life. One comparatively small, but to him, one very important thing. One thing he craved far more than the money, the fame, and all the women he had bedded and would also bed later this night. Although he enjoyed those things, too. For his entire writing career, something was missing in his otherwise perfect life. One thing. The most important thing he wanted. A good review. Just one. How simple was that?

Every fan worldwide loved him. Every woman worldwide desired him. Every publisher worldwide wanted him as their author, and, of course, their ever-constant money-making machine. Put "every" in front of "everything," and that was his definition by everyone. Everyone, but himself. In his make-believe world which existed in his real world, one word drove him to near madness; one word drove him to complete sadness; one word mocked him; one word he never wanted the word "every" in front of, one word alone: Critic. Every critic hated his work. Hated it, laughed at it, scorned it. The world's bestselling, greatest selling, richest author in modern times, Lancelot Strong, had it all, almost. He wanted, needed, desired and maybe would have killed for, just one good review. Just one. But even after tonight's success—tonight's introduction of his soon-to-be bestselling novel ever, there would be none. None to add to all the previous "nones." In his turmoiled mind, he was a failure. He didn't see all his success; he only felt his personal failure. But things were going to change. Things that he himself would never anticipate, nor ever would believe. But soon he would, in a way he would never expect.

Chapter 2

A strange clanging sound finally broke the silence. It was expected. It was loud. Very loud. It sounded like an old metal pipe being hit with another piece of metal, leaving a diminishing echo while another clang followed, and then another, and another. Then, as suddenly as the other sound had begun, a new high-pitched buzzing noise started and stopped. And then began again. If this were a science-fiction movie, the sounds might be from a high-tech ray gun, blasting in spurts, followed by a metal sword fight. But this wasn't a movie; this was real.

The mixture of sounds continued for a minute, maybe two, but to the person experiencing it, there was no time reference. It was all encompassing. And then it stopped.

A brief silence was followed by an electronic whirring sound as if something was being moved. And it was. A body. An older man's body rested on a flat platform covered in stark, bright linen. A half-moon-shaped chamber of bright lights surrounded him. His breathing, which, based on everything that was happening, should have been exaggerated, but instead was quietly relaxed, and extremely controlled.

Normal, as if there were any such word to describe his state.

"Are you comfortable, Mr. Janek?" a young male voice floated across the open air and bounced off the limited space enclosing the older man.

"Yes." A simple reply came without emotion.

"Good. Then we'll continue the next series of tests. More of the same sounds. Some a little longer; some a little shorter," the voice continued.

There was no verbal or visual answer from the older man lying on the platform. No thumbs up or happy waving of his hand. There was no arm movement whatsoever from him, not that he couldn't. But he knew he shouldn't, and most definitely at this time, wouldn't. Lying perfectly still was important, very important to the results. Each arm had its own IV attached to it, one above the wrist area and one in the vein at the crook of the arm. One solution carried saline to prevent dehydration. The other injected a series of intermittent dyes. Both were important and part of the procedure. Everything was serious, as much as the reason for his being there, being tested, was serious.

The clanging began again.

Passing electricity pulsed through large gradient coils, which also caused the machine's inner coils to vibrate creating a magnetic field and producing the knocking sound inside the scanner. Janek knew all about this. His doctor had taken the time to explain the function of the equipment he was placed into, but it was Janek's own inquisitiveness that made him learn more about it, especially since this was his first time in one. An MRI, the layman's quick pronouncement of a magnetic resonance imaging scanner, contained two powerful magnets hidden inside its internal plastic walls. Those were the most important parts of this giant body-encasing machine.

Janek already knew that the human body is largely made of water molecules, which are comprised of hydrogen and oxygen atoms. He also knew that at the center of each atom is an even smaller particle, called a proton, which serves as a magnet and is sensitive to any magnetic field. Normally, the water molecules in the body are randomly arranged, but what he was told before entering the MRI scanner was that the first magnet causes the water molecules to align in one direction, either north or south.

The second magnetic field is then turned on and off in a series of quick pulses, causing each hydrogen atom to change its alignment when switched on and then quickly changed back to its original relaxed state when switched off. Although he could not feel these changes, the scanner detects them and, in conjunction with a computer, creates a detailed cross-sectional image for the radiologist and attending medical staff to view. That's all he knew; that's all he was told, except that the results would be forthcoming shortly after the thirty-minute procedure.

Vladamir Janek, 75, a tall, thin, Eastern European with handsomely chiseled features, closed his mind to block the continuing sounds. His eyes were already covered with a surgical eye mask as bright lights continually filled the machine's bore, which he was lying in. His body remained still while the machine did its work. More clanging, more banging, more electrical-sounding impulses resonated over and over and throughout his body—sounds that most people are frightened by, especially while in an "uninviting-looking" chamber that was the primary make-up of this giant machine, and one that created a claustrophobic effect. But not to him. It didn't matter that it looked almost like an open coffin; he actually found it rather interesting, especially in the field of work he was in. It didn't bother him in the least. Throughout the continuing noises, his creative, or maybe demented mind was somewhere else— somewhere else in a writer's world he created, owned, and lived. He controlled the sounds and blocked them, just as much as he controlled his personal life and blocked it off from the outside world. Only he knew the truth about himself, a truth that was as secretive as his life.

Most people knew that he was the world's most critically acclaimed horror author, perhaps the greatest of all time. He was great in telling stories— stories defining a thin line in both the psychological terror and horror of the human mind. His words painted pictures that were both romantic and chilling, with a crisscrossing of boundaries between disturbing and loving. His theme was always simple, yet forever haunting. He wrote of men turning into monsters— monsters who took the form of giant wolves, werewolves, and monstrous beasts spawned from between the depths of insanity or maybe a distorted reality of a man's mind gone mad. It was always about one's struggle with madness—complete unbridled madness. But there was something more in his writing, something perhaps poetic, or something perhaps horrific. He combined medieval and modern stories, stories that touched the nerves of the reader no matter what era they took place in. His monsters, his mental demons, his characters who became werewolves were so realistically written that they seemed to come to life and off the page. So compelling and tragic, they created a mesmerizing effect that stayed in the reader's mind long after his books were read—forever becoming a part of each reader's memory. Stories the reader would actually believe. Stories that critics salivated over and praised in all their media forms, but alas, stories that didn't click with today's younger discerning book-buying fans who loved blood and gore, with a lot more gore and blood in between.

Even with such major critical recognition, he had never become a bestselling author. Never.

He was prolific, a genius, gifted with an IQ that was probably higher than anyone could imagine. A revered writer with god-like fame, yet poor, like a beggar's son. There was no peace in his mind, only chaos. His life mirrored his stories. His stories mirrored his life. He, himself, didn't care if he were a success or a failure. All that mattered were his stories. And with each new story he wrote, he grew further away from the real world, if even his mind could comprehend a real world, as such. Vladamir Janek was a man of many secrets—secrets that were hidden in a brain that was filled with each character's insanity. And maybe, his own.

Now, today, on this not-so-comfortable table, which was assembled to make him feel comfortable, he knew time was running out. At his age, and in his situation, with all the many horror stories that still lived in his head, he knew only a few more would be able to find a way out and onto a completed page to be read. He realized that from the way his body was changing—changing or collapsing—from the inside out.

Janek was unafraid of what the procedure would tell him and most likely confirm. He already knew. Maybe it was his writer's sixth sense. Whatever it was, it was. He expected the answer before it was given. Simply put, he was dying. Dying from a rare unexplainable anomaly in his brain. At first, his doctors thought it was cancer, but no cancer looked like this.

It was like his brain was being taken over by an unknown, undiagnosable entity, like a pitch-black shadow moving across the once fertile land and now forever covering it in darkness.

Although he could not feel these changes in himself, he had sensed them for a long time. Because he was private, he hid the truth in his mind and his life for as long as he could. But he could no longer hide that truth. The scanner would detect the problem and, in conjunction with a computer, would create a detailed cross-sectional image for the radiologist to study, a so-called medical roadmap to help answer how much time he had left. "How much time left" was really the only question he wanted answered. And the only reason he did this test.

As suddenly as the loud clanging had begun, the clanging ended, as the procedure was complete.

"Mr. Janek, we're done." The same familiar voice he heard before now communicated these words to him through the machine's intercom speakers. "The table will move out of the bore now. Remain as you are until we remove the IVs. Your doctor will give you the results soon."

Throughout the entire procedure, with all the giant machine's electronic noises, Vladamir Janek heard nothing. No sounds, no clanging, no banging, nor the words from the technician that the MRI was over. Throughout it all, his mind stayed silent, closed off from the real world, but in between his imagination and realities, he thought of and heard, "Death."

Not his, but of others he had already killed, and those that he still had to kill. But no one there in the examination room—the radiologist, the technicians, his concerned attending doctor—no one heard what he had heard and still did. To Vladamir Janek, the machine's sound had been a cacophony of screams— silent screams that he feasted on and enjoyed while he reposed in the long chamber, which, to him, resembled an endless tomb, a tomb that he once wrote about where people were trapped and dying, killing each other as they sought to escape. In that story, no one escaped, and now, neither would Vladamir Janek. As the greatest horror author of all time, he alone understood the reason why his words killed people. Now, in his time left, he knew he had to finish what he started as a writer. And now, he was more convinced than ever, he had to do it soon.

As his frail and dying body moved quietly out of the machine's long, shiny, silver chamber, his only expression was a small, but visible, haunting smile. He knew he had to kill again, but not in his words. This time in real life.

Chapter 3

Her naked shadow danced up and down across the white hotel wall as her real-life body felt the pleasure of their lovemaking. She was seemingly in control. Seemingly. He liked it that way. He liked to feel sexually dominated by his partners. It gave him great pleasure. It also gave him a greater voyeuristic view as he watched her soft round breasts above him move rhythmically with her body's every motion. He liked to watch.

He held her tight by the waist as she moaned softly. Her moans grew louder with each of their combined movements. As he thrust upwards, she came downwards. His fingers reached backwards and slightly dug into the warm flesh of her tightly toned backside. Her moans were either from the extreme pleasure she was receiving, or maybe from the fact that she was having sex with a celebrity. After all, he was.

Lancelot Strong smiled to himself as he pleasured himself, and her, too. It was just another over-sexed fan of his who was being bedded in a reoccurring ritual he was so used to after a book-reading or book-signing appearance. Or any appearance, if that really mattered. Women threw themselves at him, and not just for an autograph. And he was more than willing to help them fulfill their fantasy as it also fulfilled his insatiable desire. He liked sex, a lot. Plus, it was another "notch" in his proverbial sexual gun. In the seven years of his worldwide best-selling romantic vampire books, he had sex with hundreds of fawning and willing women. All types of women, all types of sex, even weird and kinky sex. There were no boundaries in his wanton desires. During sex he also bit quite a few of them, or maybe just nibbled on them. They liked it, so did he. Sometimes they even screamed a little, just a little, whether it was their way of showing pleasure, or maybe showing a little bit of fear. Just a little, but he enjoyed hearing the screams. So did his innermost demons.

Maybe they thought he was a real-life vampire like in his books. How wrong they were; how right they almost were. It was his secret of what he really was, just one of the many he had. We all have secrets and sometimes "secret" lives.

Lancelot Strong had a lot of secrets.

Some secrets he expressed in his writing or displayed in his daily lifestyle. Some he kept compartmentalized for use in his future storylines. Some stayed hidden from both public knowledge and kept to himself for good reason. Writers always have "lots" of secrets. But secrets aren't always as secret as one would think or hope to keep. And sometimes secrets can't be buried like the dead.

It was no secret that not only were the critics unkind to him, and he to them, but so were the tabloids. He was a popular target with whispers and innuendos. Sordid stories claimed he was "bad in bed"—wrong!—or that "he liked male lovers"—well, almost wrong—and he had someone else write his novels...a "ghost writer" or...

Lancelot Strong really didn't care about rumors. All he cared about was the money he made, the fame he achieved, and the many women he bedded. And this was what made him smile the most. He loved himself first and foremost. And it was right now he loved himself even more as he gave his new sexual conquest probably the best orgasm of her young life. He didn't even know her name. Not that he cared, or that it even mattered. It was all about him. Always about him. He smiled as he completed his orgasm, too.

As they lay in bed in the hotel suite that had been provided to him as part of his speaking fee arrangement, he didn't think of the attractive naked young woman next to him and the pleasure they just shared. Not at all. He only thought of how well the reading had gone earlier that night and the feeling of power he always exhibited. A power that began with his good looks and transcended his audience with his hypnotic romantic and chilling words. Every word he spoke, every sentence he read, every scene he described, the audience embraced almost lustfully, willingly, and wantingly. He even imagined, or knew, that some of the women in tonight's audience, which was mostly women, may have even orgasmed during his read. Maybe. Probably. For Lancelot Strong, it was all about him and his power. Besides loving himself, he loved his power.

The sudden pulsating sound of his cell phone on the end table next to his bed broke his train of thought. Forgetting to put it in silent mode, it now jumped to life, breaking the silence of two first-time lovers catching their breath. He really hated getting late-night calls, especially when he knew he was going to have sex but, here at midnight, he was getting a text, and it had to be important, as not a lot of people had access to his private cell number.

"Shit," he muttered half to himself, half to the phone sound.

It was a short text, but an important text. *"L. Return to NY tomorrow but come directly to my office for an important, very impt meeting at 5. A game changer. Rhonda. P.S. Get rid of the girl in bed, tabloids snooping."*

He placed the phone down without replying. He half-smiled smugly. He didn't want to let his agent know she was right, as usual. She was always right; that's what made her such a good agent to him and his work. But she wasn't right about his getting rid of this nameless girl in bed with him tonight. He was unconcerned about being seen with his new girl "toy" by some snooping photographer. Bad press, good press, it was all another way to sell his books, not that he needed press, but it was something that drove his ego. His power-drunk ego. And there was something else. Something "strangely" else. He had other plans for her.

As he silently slipped out of the large bed, he picked up his half-empty, half-filled glass of champagne that waited for him on the nightstand. It was just one of the many drinks they had shared on top of the other drinks they had at the hotel bar earlier where they met after his reading. He met a lot of women that way. At his readings or signings, he would always mention where he was staying, as a sexual innuendo roadmap to find him. And they always would. And then he would do a pick from the so-called waiting "litter" of women. Sometimes, based on how he felt, and how they looked, and how and what they wanted, he would pick more than one. It added to his feeling of power. Voyeurism and power combined together.

Standing naked, proudly showing a reflection of his finely chiseled athletic body in the subdued lighting of the full-length-room's balcony window, he looked out at the city below, and beyond. It seemed to beckon him. He sipped on his half-empty, half-filled glass, as he looked at the thousands upon thousands of miniature-sized twinkling lights of snake-like streets mixed with odd-shaped buildings and old city homes. They were just another backdrop to his fast-paced life. So many appearances, so many signings, so many cities, so many hotel rooms. They didn't matter, except for the "so many" women he shared them with.

Staring into the outside nighttime world, trapped in his inside daily world of being who he was and knowing what he would soon become, he was intrigued by the words in the text "game changer." He almost wanted to text his agent back and question what that meant. But he didn't, and he wouldn't. He had a more important game to play now, a sort of personal "game changer" in and of itself, and the reply text could wait. He had a game that was part of the many "secrets" he kept to himself. A very private and special game.

He finished his drink, leaving the glass now fully empty. Lowering his hand with the glass slowly downward, almost hesitating, past his nude waist, he let it finally drop, falling onto the thickly carpeted hotel-suite floor. It didn't break but rolled back and forth in a half circle. Back and forth. He watched it as if it were a metaphor of his unusual life. Back and forth, until it stopped, maybe wishing he could also.

With a long deep sigh that held a thousand previous sighs, he slowly turned, looking back at the young woman in bed. He feasted his eyes on her naked young body. How flawless, how perfect, so very perfect. Moonlight from the window quietly broke through the cloudy outside night and cast a sensual shadow across her. She was asleep. Sound asleep. The sex had been very satisfying and very tiring. Satisfying and tiring. Back and forth. Again, and again.

It's true; he didn't even know her name, or maybe he never even asked her what her name was. It didn't matter to him. It never did. If he did know it, or even remembered it, he would maybe find a way to use her name in one of his books. Usually as a victim. Usually as someone he would kill in the story. Usually. After all he did like to kill. He even jokingly told people he met for the first time, who didn't recognize him as a horror writer, that his profession "was to kill people"...in his books. Usually. But only he knew the truth. Always.

The truth was his secret, alone.

Lancelot Strong's eyes remained fixated on her, as his right hand next to his side started to open and close into a fist, slowly, again and again. Tighter and tighter. Again, and again.

At the same time, his body began to rock on his naked heels, back and forth. Back and forth.

Again, and again.

As the bright moonlight, freed from the once-encompassing clouds, now fully illuminated the suite's bedroom, he saw a new shadow on the wall. This time, not dancing like hers had earlier; this time, seeming to slowly twist in shape and transform into a bizarre, hideous image. An image seemingly growing larger and more distorted with each passing moment. Rocking back and forth. Again and again.

Secrets. Yes, Lancelot Strong had secrets. We all have secrets, but none of us had a secret as horrific as his.

Chapter 4

She was early. He was late. He was always late. She was always early. But it really didn't matter. Rhonda Austin was a patient woman. For her, it was a part of her professional makeup, and she was used to waiting for him. It bothered her, but she knew it was just him being himself. But she was also a tough businesswoman; that's what made her a great agent, and that's why he always apologized when he was late.

Rhonda casually looked at the watch he had recently given her as a gift of appreciation for all she did for him. It was ten minutes past five. Mickey's white-gloved hands pointed at the number five and the number ten. She loved Mickey Mouse. She loved the whole Disney "thing," as she laughingly referred to it. She loved going to the theme parks and she loved the characters who lived there to make everyone's dreams come true. And she loved her new Mickey Mouse watch. It made her smile while she waited. And she didn't smile that often. Today was just another endlessly busy day in her busy life, but with the interesting news she had to share, she felt it was a good day, a really good day.

She took a sip from her drink and looked at Mickey again. He seemed to smile back at her. As she did to him.

My Office was "their office," sort of—a trendy mid-sized millennial bar and restaurant tucked in between the towering skyscrapers of New York City. This place was the "latest" place to meet and be seen and was fast becoming a famous watering hole with eclectic food choices for the discerning celebrity-type guests. It was also a perfect place for them to meet, since she lived in nearby Connecticut and he lived in a glass-enclosed penthouse of a skyscraper with a view to kill, or at least a view that cost him a cool million-plus dollars. She had never been there; she could only imagine it, not that she wanted to—she was afraid of heights. My Office, as a first-floor meeting place, kept her feet firmly where she wanted them. On the ground.

She took another sip from her drink and looked at Mickey again. This time he didn't seem to smile. Neither did she.

"Hey, I'm sorry I'm late," a familiar voice broke through the noisy surrounding guests' conversations. As if making a planned grand entrance, Lancelot Strong came hurriedly through the packed after-work crowd, and over to the booth she sat in.

Rhonda leaned forward to receive his apologetic and simultaneous "Hello, I'm here" kiss on her soft cheek. She smiled. Mickey probably smiled, too.

Lance slid into the leather-cushioned booth, close to her, but still leaving some space between them. He knew she wanted it that way. And she did, sort of. She still carried a torch for him as they were once lovers a long time ago. They had met in college, became friends first, then more than friends, and shared in the dreams of someday making it big together. He was already getting a growing college fan following with his short stories that were published and read on campus, and she was learning how to promote and manage him. But he was too much for one woman to manage or, let alone, handle.

After college, their relationship became a revolving door for his many sexcapades with other women, while she looked forward to any time he would share with her. Their relationship eventually evolved, and they created a business partnership. He was the hot-looking, bestselling horror novelist and she was the tough-as-nails business promoter and agent. Actually, one of the best in the literary field. At age 33, she was on top of her game, and so was he. But being lovers and co-workers wasn't always the easiest thing to do, or the best kept secret either, especially when pleasure got in the way of business. She still had feelings for him. She knew he still had some feelings for her also, just some. Unfortunately for her, and all the many other women he constantly bedded, his feelings were mostly for himself. Maybe that's part of what made him so alluring. His devil-may-care attitude, his do-as-he-pleased, say-as-he-wanted lifestyle. Maybe. But he was also so "fucking" handsome; that's what made him even more desirable. But no matter what her, his, or their feelings were, that was then, and this was now. And now was all about business.

She spoke first. "So, how was the reading?"

"The usual. It went well. Sold a lot of books," he replied without any enthusiasm, just a "matter of fact" while he looked for the roving waitress to catch her attention and order a drink.

"Did you get to see much of Syracuse?"

"Didn't have much time." He finally caught the waitress's eye.

"But you did have time to have sex with another fan," Rhonda remarked sarcastically to get his attention.

He finally turned to her. He smiled with his reply.

"Just another city."

"Did you get rid of her as I asked?" she asked sternly, as though she were a parent scolding a child who had done something wrong and deserved to know it was wrong.

He smiled again. A different smile.

"Yes, long gone; it's like she never really existed."

She paused at his words and smirked in response.

"Hmm. Must make them feel real special."

He paused at her words and smirked in response.

"Yes, real special."

He licked the lower part of his lip, either losing himself in some secret thought or maybe hiding a forbidden pleasure.

"Drink?" A female voice interrupted his private thoughts. It was one of the female waitresses—young, cute, and probably harboring a secret desire to be with him.

"The usual." Lance nodded with more than just a smile.

"So, your message said our meeting was important?" He returned his attention to Rhonda.

"Yes, very important." Rhonda began the business at hand.

"And?" Lance wanted to know more, especially since receiving her mysterious text at midnight.

"Your publisher called me. They came up with an idea—an interesting idea that I think you're going to like," she continued, almost teasing him as sometimes young children or even old-time lovers would do to each other.

"An idea? Publishers don't know shit about ideas; they just publish books," Lance responded, almost disappointed. Almost.

"Well, let's just say it was an idea that I shared with them and now it has become their idea. You know how the business works," Rhonda added to calm his impatience.

"Yeah, the business. I just love the "no-nonsense" business. So, what's the idea?" he inquired, once again in an inquisitive tone.

"What's the one thing missing in your life? The one thing you always wanted and still haven't gotten?" She dangled the proverbial carrot in front of him as if this were a guessing game they liked to play.

He looked at her, answering without speaking.

Rhonda continued, knowing him so well that he didn't have to reply.

"A good review. Your work has never gotten a good review. Lancelot Strong, Author Extraordinaire. Loved by millions but disliked by 'all' the critics who control the closed circle of literary acceptance and write the most important reviews."

"Damn the reviews," he quipped in a personal annoyance.

"Right. Damn the reviews. But we both know the reviews damn you. Actually, they haunt you. Don't they?"

"*Kiss of the Vampire* will outsell all my books. You and I both know it's great. So do my fans. Fuck the reviewers." He was becoming more annoyed.

"Right, just someone else to fuck?" Rhonda's reply had a ring of truth to it.

There was a pause between them as Lance finished his drink quickly as if washing away his anger.

"What if I could guarantee you a good review, maybe a great review, maybe the greatest review of a horror book ever written?" she continued, getting his attention again.

"Sure, so tell me what you want me to write."

"Not what, but with whom," she responded smugly, then sat back against the booth, waiting to see and hear his reaction.

"Who?" he replied with a tone of unexpected shock.

"Yes, who. Specifically..." She took a deep breath and slowly let it out, "...Vladamir Janek."

The name bit at his soul. He hated Janek. He hated his work. He hated the fact that Janek was favored by the critics, all the critics. He could write shit and they would still adore him. In his mind, he did write shit. His own books were filled with exciting stories and electric, mesmerizing moments wrapped around romantic and chilling words. Janek's books were boring, dull, long, drawn-out and...

"Janek?" he finally replied aloud. "Why would I waste my time writing with him? I despise him."

"You don't know him. You never even met him. You may say you despise him, but you really envy him." Rhonda stated a fact that even he could not deny.

"He envies me," Lance blurted out. Words that rang hollow. It was a reasonless defense. They had never met, and he had never heard any interviews where Janek included or mentioned him in any way— good or bad. He wasn't even sure that Janek knew he existed. All he knew is that they were literary competitors. He was the king of sales, and Janek was...

"Maybe." Rhonda broke his train of thought by answering for him and continuing her agent-to-client pitch. "But all that matters is that your publisher, and his publisher, me, your agent, and his agent, have all agreed that it would be the perfect collaboration. The world's two greatest horror writers working together to create what will become the greatest horror story ever written."

Lancelot paused to mull it over.

The young barmaid came back over and interrupted his thoughts.

"Another?" She smiled seductively.

He nodded with his head as his eyes locked on her and her eyes seemed to smile back at him. He knew she wanted to be with him, and he knew it would be easy to have sex with her. Very easy. *"Maybe later,"* he thought to himself as he watched her tight ass in her skintight dress as she turned to go to the bar. And then the thought of her disappeared.

"And he agreed to this?" Lance looked back directly at Rhonda.

"Yes."

"Why?" His one word held more than just a question. It opened a door to a lot of questions. "He doesn't know me. He probably doesn't even know my work; he probably hasn't read a word of my books."

"Perhaps; perhaps not. What matters is that he is critically acclaimed, and you are the greatest selling horror author of all time. Putting you both together, away from all sorts of disturbances; someplace filled with no distractions, a place of solitude to create a masterpiece together—just think of what you both could do. Think of it, Lance. It's an opportunity to get you that elusive golden ring on the carousel ride of book reviews. It's a once-in-a-million opportunity. Just think of the press, publicity, the new-found fame for you, and the critical acclaim you want and deserve and will most likely receive. It will be the crowning achievement of your young career. And perhaps the greatest best-selling horror novel of all time. And maybe ever!"

She sat back in the booth, but not far enough away from having her bare leg from beneath her leather skirt purposely touch his leg

"Hmmm. Intriguing, but...where do we do this collaboration? In some publisher's boring conference room?"

"No, not at all. We came up with the idea of something a little more you, and a little more him."

"His place? My place?" he asked tentatively.

"Let's just say, the perfect place," Rhonda replied, then paused before revealing the answer. "Actually...a haunted house."

"What?" Lance sat straight up in the booth, taken aback from what she just said.

"Yes, an actual haunted house, secluded in the Hampshire White Mountains, away from everything. You will both live there together for a week. No distractions, no phones, no communication to the outside world! You will both be driven there, dropped off, and left there. Just the two of you. You'll have all the food and living accommodations you'll need while you work. You'll be far away from any nearby towns or other nearby houses. No one to bother you; no one for you to bother. It's very remote, and not well known or an advertised vacation spot. Actually, it's never been for rent since..."

She paused, maybe to leave him wondering why, or to wonder if she should really tell him what she knew about this place.

"Since?" He questioned her pause. He questioned her comment.

"Well, let's just say that it's a very old Victorian-styled house with a bit of history. Just the perfect setting for the two of you.

"A haunted house?" He mulled the words over, speaking aloud to himself and maybe to her.

"Yes, a real haunted house."

He laughed, maybe to hide his true feelings; maybe because he didn't believe. Maybe.

"Sounds boring. Can I invite a few guests?" he asked with a sly smile.

"Well...yes and no," Rhonda replied in a serious tone.

His eyes narrowed as he was caught by surprise and intrigued by her reply. He finished his drink and waited for her next words.

"No, you can't invite guests, and yes, you will probably have guests."

It was her turn to finish her drink and wait for his reply.

"Who?"

There was a pause between them. And then she replied—

"Ghosts."

As her one word sunk into his mind, something undefinable also chilled his heart. Ghosts.

He frowned.

She smiled.

Mickey covered his eyes in fear.

Chapter 5

Everyone loves Candyland. It's fun, colorful, exciting, and a fantasyland game for children of all ages to play. Everyone loves Candyland. Well, just about everyone.

Certainly, Arianna Jones did as a young 5-year-old girl playing it over and over with her two not much older sisters. She was the youngest of six children, and growing up in a small, subsidized apartment in Harlem didn't leave room for a lot of games. Actually, there was very little family money to even be spent on *any* games. This game was a hand-me-down from some family relative her mother knew, just like most of the clothes she wore. Hand-me-downs. In addition to having no money to buy children's games, there was also no money to buy new clothes. But in her young mind, she felt that someday she would escape this world of poverty she lived and grew up in and enjoy a better world of luxury and riches. It was her dream. It was the dream of a lot of young naïve girls. Someday, a real-life Candyland.

And now, years later, for Arianna Jones, that someday, that dream, finally came true, sort of.

She recently left her family's too-small-to-stay-in-anymore apartment to begin a new life. A way to make a quick buck to finally get all those many things she wanted. Tonight, as she did most nights in the past year, she stepped out into the streets of her very own Candyland. Actually, "Candy Lane"—a small, mostly neon-lit, rundown city street tucked into the lower part of New York's Bowery, not far from the richness of Wall Street, the one true "Candyland."

Candy Lane was well known as "the street" for its easy-to-secure prostitutes and drugs, or "candy," as referred to by its nightly clients. And there she was, all grown up, at a fabricated age of 22, but really years younger. "Sweet Chocolate" she called herself. A made-up name with a made-up age, as she became the real-life candy to the male customers who came looking for a young, sweet girl and more. Her customers gave her cash for the sweet treats she gave them in return.

Tonight was supposed to be like most of her recent other nights. Show some leg, attract a customer, get in a car, give some "candy," get some cash, get out of the car, and start all over again. Again and again. But tonight wasn't going to be all "gumdrops" and "lollipops." Tonight, just like in the Candyland game, there would be winners and losers. And, tonight, she would arrive at the "finish line" sooner than she expected.

As the evening closed in on the witching hour of midnight, it was starting to drizzle. Just lightly. A steady, soft rain splashed in a dance-like pattern in the growing street puddles. Dirty puddles reflected and distorted the surrounding neon signs from the late-night bars and cheap all-night eateries. The rain would bring more customers in cars, according to her pimp, who was also her boyfriend. More customers in cars meant that it would save time from back-and-forth trips to nearby small, sleazy, cheap hotel rooms. She never liked those dreary rooms, but it was part of her job. But not tonight. Tonight, with the rain, all she had to do was just hop in and hop out, after performing a quick oral trick, which she laughingly called a "lollipop delight."

As it started to rain harder, she knew it was just a matter of time for her to find another ride. It would be her fourth of the night. Just another one or two customers and she could go home, if you call it that. A two-room, 3rd floor walk-up apartment filled with dirty clothes and dirty dishes and a dirty boyfriend who snorted coke and played expensive video games. But she liked him—maybe loved him—and would do anything for him. And, in return, he did mostly nothing for her, except set nightly quotas. Had to get more money to buy more video games. She didn't realize he even played her life like a video game. And tonight, being rainy, and leaving a bit of an early Fall chill, she wanted to find that ride soon enough to fill her quota, and so she did.

Out of the narrow street's darkness, a shiny black stretch limo came and slowed down close to where she stood. She watched it, as she knew someone inside watched her. It was how the game was played. Everyone checked out the players. And everyone was a player, of sorts. Stopping beside her, it remained running with its windshield wipers making a rhythmic sound, almost a beckoning sound, which she understood was for her, and her alone.

A side passenger door of the limo opened outwards. Dim lighting from inside the car's doorway and deep interior was the only invitation she received to enter. From her angle, she could see someone seated alone, inside, surrounded by dark shadows. Someone, hidden enough in the dark to prevent her, or anyone else, from seeing who it really was. Soft music, nothing popular, nothing well known, floated in the air from the inside to the outside. Inviting, yet, uninviting. But inviting enough to make her feel safe to go inside.

As she sat on the limo's leather couch-like seat across from where she entered, the door closed on its own, and the car slowly moved through the rainy street. It was warm inside. Very warm. The limo was very long and, from where she sat, with a quick look-see, she could discern that she was alone with the person in the dark. For a long moment, nothing was said by either. Only the music filled the space between them.

The limo ride was smooth; it hardly seemed to be moving, but she knew it was. She was first to speak and break the silence.

"I can't really see you over there in the dark."

There was only a short pause, which maybe was a long pause, before the shadowed person replied.

"You can come closer. I don't bite."

It seemed to be a reassuring voice, not a

concerning one. A man's voice. Not a gruff voice, but a gentle voice. She wasn't sure if it was a younger man's voice or an older man's voice. She had heard a lot of different voices and understood a lot of different replies in all the men she favored This one occmcd different. Confident, alluring, maybe playful, and definitely with a touch of the mysterious. Definitely different.

"Well, maybe *I* bite," she replied half-jokingly or at least trying to make a joke of what he just said.

"And maybe you should," he responded with no emotion, or at least anything she could perceive as to what he actually meant.

Arianna was used to word games with her customers. Sometimes they were shy and didn't want to come right out and say what they wanted. Sometimes they didn't know what they wanted till she told them what she offered. It was "all" a game to her. She performed what they asked for, and her dirty deeds resulted in her being rewarded with all the winnings. Winnings which meant money, lots of money, that was split between her and her boyfriend— a boyfriend who waited night after night in their small apartment blocks away for her eventual return, snorting coke and playing his video games while she played her games. It was all about the winnings and, of course, the different games they each played.

"You a cop?" she asked, as she always asked with every ride she took.

"Do cops have cars like this?" he answered back, again with no emotion, but with a reassuring tone that made her believe him.

"Are you a celeb?" she asked curiously.

"Aren't we all?" he replied smugly.

She felt comfortable enough with his answers to start the business transaction.

"Okay. One-hundred bucks for a blow job; two hundred for more," Arianna replied, as she had replied so many times before.

He didn't answer. From where she sat, she saw that he already had money in his hand. Through the dim lighting of the limo's interior that hid most of his face, she saw a gentle smile. Nothing monstrous, nothing scary. A smile that seemed inviting. A comfortable smile that caused her to make the worst mistake of her life. She smiled back.

Without hesitation, Arianna slid across the long, winding leather seat and moved closer to the stranger. Close enough to reach out her hand and take the money from his hand, but still not close enough to see his entire face. Shadows seemed to always hug him, to protect his identity, as the limo continued its ride through the dismal rain.

"Whew," she exclaimed as she saw the money was all in hundred-dollar bills. "$500!"

"That includes your tip." His emotionless voice came from the surrounding darkness that hid his face.

"Okay. Thanks," she replied, quickly tucking the money inside her bra.

"The guy up front watching?" Arianna asked, while turning her head to the front of the inside limo. She could see a dark glass built-in sliding window, separating them from the driver.

"No. Should he?" It was a playful reply.

"Don't matter, as long as he keeps his eyes on the road. Wouldn't want you to have an accident in this big, badass limo," she stated matter of factly, as if repeating another line, a line she used many times before.

There was no reply from the stranger. Only the soft, endless stream of piped-in music and the faint sound of falling rain on the limo rooftop broke the silence.

Without hesitation, Arianna slid across the remaining space that separated them. She immediately knelt between his legs and quickly began her job.

Arianna was good at this. She could unzip a man's pants faster than you could say the words "Let the game begin!" And she did, quickly opening her mouth to start her work, which was also her pleasure. She liked sex, and especially doing oral. Whenever she did this, which was every night, she always let her mind drift back to the first one she gave a few years back. One of her older sisters' boyfriends came around when no one else was home except her. She was bored, babysitting another baby her mother recently had on top of all the others. He invited himself in and she didn't resist. She "sort of" liked him; maybe had a crush, maybe an infatuation. He had only one thought in his mind and it was apparent as he came on to her. Being a virgin, she didn't quite know what to do, or how to do it. But she knew she wanted it, too. She submitted quickly, and easily, and even enjoyed it. She enjoyed it a lot. What she did that day made her feel grown up, like her older sisters. It also gave her a feeling of power as she heard him moan with pleasure the faster her head moved on him. She liked it a lot; so did he.

Arianna always remembered that first time, and then the memory always morphed into the hundreds of times since. For her, it was like her childhood game of Candyland. A real-life game she now played over and over and enjoyed every time. Tonight, like all the previous nights, she got paid to play. Pleasure and money. What better way to make a living; what better game to play, so she thought.

As her head moved up and down on him, she tried to look up at his face. It was something she always did to see the pleasure she was bringing to her customer. As before, as now, his face remained hidden throughout the entire time she was in the limo. From what she did see in the moving shadows of the car, he looked handsome. But she couldn't really tell for certain. Or maybe he looked older, but she really wasn't sure. It really didn't matter, really. All that mattered was the money. But something else suddenly mattered. Something she didn't expect. It was his eyes. In the many shadows that covered his identity, she could see his eyes, and they seemed to glow a strange color. A very unusual color. Almost a bright blood-red color. Like nothing she had ever seen before in all the many eyes she looked at while she performed her work.

Maybe it was just an illusion from the mixture of changing colored lights inside the limo. It had to be; it couldn't be anything else. Maybe, or maybe not.

His eyes locked on hers as they both watched each other. His red eyes grew brighter by the moment, sending a chill through her, which almost made her stop. But she didn't. Maybe it was just her imagination. It had to be. Maybe. Sometimes her eyes played tricks on her, especially after a long night of her head going up and down, as if bobbing for apples. And it had been a long night, and she was very tired. But, no matter what she thought, or how she felt, his eyes were red. Very red.

Arianna's eyes closed to block out his. All that mattered now was to get the job done quickly, take her money, and go off to the next "opportunity," as she had done so many times before to so many faceless, nameless customers.

But her thoughts of finishing quickly weren't quick enough.

Without words, he suddenly put his hands on her head gently, letting his fingers touch her hair and go through it, gently, not messing it, mostly caressing it. He played with her hair, as she played with him. They were now both players in a sex game. A game that would soon "come" to an end. She knew she was giving him pleasure, as he stiffened his body even more to get closer to his climax. It wouldn't be much longer now. She knew this from her past experiences. She knew how to read a man's pleasure, even a spooky man like the one she knelt before. This excited her, too. It made the whole sex game more fun, more exciting. Pleasure and Money. Money and Pleasure.

Then something happened.

The game changed.

Without warning, his hands suddenly and forcibly pushed her head fully down onto his exposed groin area. Deep into her throat he went. Deeper than anyone had ever been. Deep enough to cause her to suddenly gag. From her experiences, she knew it was sometimes just a momentary part of the sex ritual. Going deep. Sometimes. Men came in many different ways. But this wasn't momentary. Not this time. Something was different. Very different.

He held her head tight, too tight, for too long, not allowing her to move her head back up and breathe through her nose or even her mouth. Simultaneously, his hands pushed tighter on the sides of her head as he forced her to remain impaled by his member. Her face was pressed fully against his naked skin. She couldn't breathe. She couldn't bite. And she began to gag more, to choke, to panic.

She struggled futilely, trying to pull her head back upward to breathe. But she couldn't. He was too strong. His hands pushed her face forward even more into him, but there was no more space to go. Her nose seemed to bend forward, blocking her nostrils completely. Her windpipe was blocked, too. She couldn't breathe at all. She was choking. She was choking to death.

Arianna struggled even more as she fought for the

air she so desperately needed. His hands shifted and now pressed harder into the sides of her face. Her gagging continued, making strange, distorted sounds. Traces of drool came from either her compressed and closed mouth, or through what was now a broken nose. Blood rolled down her face, mixed with the tears from the fear and horror in her eyes. His strength was overpowering. There seemed to be no escape. None. She looked at him, her eyes begging, pleading for her very life, or what little life she had left.

She pounded her fists against the man's legs and side of his waist. Faster and faster. Then slower and slower, as her strength gave out. She was becoming limp. Without air, she had no energy. Without energy, she had no further willpower to fight.

Her hands stopped hitting him and now started twitching in a weird uncontrollable dance-like spasm. Her whole body did as well. It was a lonely and seemingly endless dance of death, kneeling on the floor of a very expensive stretch limo, in puddles of her own drool and blood. With the pressure of his strong hands still pushing hard on her face, Arianna's eyes barely opened and closed, seeming to bulge from her head. Bulging as if they were ready to pop right out. Death was knocking on her doorstep, waiting for the final end.

Slowly, he leaned forward from the interior limo's shadows, and she finally saw his face. The face of a grinning monster. A face with way too many teeth, sharp, blood-dripping teeth that appeared ready to devour her. A face that made her want to scream, and maybe she did, in her mind, and in her soul.

A long, silent, scream of death.

From outside the moving limo, if one could, they would clearly hear the faint sound of an animal growling inside. Or maybe something that was not an animal; maybe something that wasn't human.

And then the sounds ended.

An eerie silence remained as the car's moving tires caressed the dark and dirty pavement beneath.

The limo never stopped as its side door suddenly opened—the same door Arianna had entered a short time before—and her lifeless body was pushed out onto the wet street.

Her body tumbled and rolled several times, splashing over and over in the wet street's puddles. Face down, partially sideways, it finally stopped in a rain-filled gutter next to a broken and crumbling concrete curb. It lay there, alone, abandoned—arms and legs broken and bent from the sudden impact on the road. Blood gushed and covered her face, both from the hard pavement it struck and from the pushed-in sides of a what appeared to be a partially crushed head. Her wide-open eyes "bugged outwards," staring neither at heaven nor hell. Staring at the street she walked so many nights before but would never walk again. Staring, as if they were barely held in her smashed skull by a long, loose string tucked inside the pushed-in, misshapen head.

It was late, and the crooked and worn sidewalks were empty. Mostly everyone had long gone home.

Rain gently fell on what was once a beautiful body,

licking at her horrific wounds. Deep red blood mixed with the collected muddy and dirty street water and flowed towards the closest sewer, disappearing forever into the drainpipes below.

As the limo sped away into the darkness of the night, Arianna who was sweet sixteen, pretending to be 22, remained behind, alone in the garbage-strewn street of Candy Lane.

Her Candyland was now a memory lost with her final heartbeat. Arianna was dead. So were her dreams.

Game over.

Chapter 6

It started the same way every day—every day, for as long as he could remember—and his memory was filled with a lot of time passed, and with little time ahead.

Vladamir Janek stirred his cup of tea tentatively. Very tentatively, but with purpose. It was a special tea from a special mixture. An assortment of strange-sounding herbs and minerals, not the typical store-bought kind but, rather, a family recipe which was passed from generation to generation. Maybe it helped keep him healthy and alive for all these years. All these long years that now filled and clouded his tortured mind. Years that seemed to blend together and hide so many secrets. Although he was 70-some years old, he felt a lot older. Perhaps he was. Perhaps he wasn't. After all, age is just a number, isn't it?

His spoon moved the dark black tea in a slow swirling manner, mixing in a white powder that created strange patterns within the liquid's circular motion. Patterns that resembled parts of faces. Faces that swirled and slowly began to come together, and in focus. Faces with mouths and eyes that seemed to open and close with the tea's movement, as if crying out in pain. Crying out for help. Or maybe just crying for forgiveness. Faces that looked strangely familiar. Faces that looked like his through all the years. Through all the many, many years.

As he stirred his tea, it looked the same way every day. Every day for as long as he could remember. If he even wanted to.

Holding the wet silver spoon in front of his eyes, he could see himself. A small reflection, yet a telling one. A reflection that wasn't sad; a reflection that wasn't happy. A reflection that was somewhere between being at war and at peace within himself. Somewhere. Somewhere between. Somewhere within. It didn't really matter, though, it was just a reflection, albeit somewhat distorted, and reflections don't always tell the truth.

Sipping at his tea, his thoughts drifted to yesterday—the medical procedure he endured, the results that he already knew, and the prognosis he was told. Simply put, and without all the doctors' medical mumbo-jumbo, the abnormality in his brain was getting worse. It was an anomaly, and uniquely unpredictable in why and how it was happening. But what was certain was the diagnosis. He was dying. And he was told it was just a matter of time. He thought about the words, "Just a matter of time," and briefly smiled to himself. Time, such an elusive thing. An unknown quantity with a quality of its very own. You can't touch it, hold it, stop it; you just watch it, or it watches you. Time, which can define a person's life, or time, which can be used to bury unforgiving moments. He again looked at the tea. Only one face looked back at his. His own, laughing.

The ringing sound of the hotel room phone caught his attention. It was the car service calling, as arranged yesterday for his pickup today. It was on time. That was important to him. He always understood the value of time, of punctuality and of using time to one's advantage. And he did. Time played an important part in his life as his life played an important part in time. He had a long life, an experienced life, a life that no one would, or could, really understand if he told the truth or shared his past. A long-storied life that held many, if not too many haunting memories. Memories that kept themselves hidden, but every once in a while, played an unwanted game of "peek-a-boo" with him. That was most annoying to him. Most annoying. No matter how hard he tried, or how many times he failed, he couldn't change one thing. Vladamir Janek was more than a writer, he was a...

The phone rang again; this time it was his agent.

"Just wanted to check in with any last-minute questions regarding your trip." It was an older male voice. A business voice, not a friend.

Janek held onto a private thought for a moment before answering.

"Everything seems fine. The car is here and I'm assuming it will take me there as planned, and then return for me in a week?"

"Yes, next Sunday, as discussed. Noon. Easy to remember. Time enough to pack and say your goodbyes."

"To my fellow writer, or to all the ghosts?"

"Maybe both," the agent's voice on the phone replied in a cross between a "matter-of-fact" tone and maybe something more.

Janek didn't smile at his words, nor laugh. In all the years they worked together, Janek never showed or shared much emotion. To him it was all business, just business. Even now, especially since he was told of the location for the writing collaboration. He really didn't care. It's not that he didn't believe in houses being haunted, or any type of paranormal activity that was said to have once taken place there, it's just that he didn't care. So it seemed.

"The advance money we agreed on will be deposited in the account I requested?"

"Publisher transferred it yesterday. Still not sure why you wanted most of it upfront; you could have made a lot more after the expected sales."

"You mean *you* could have," Janek added wryly.

"Well, honestly yes, we both could have. But it's really not about the money is it? It's about him, isn't it?"

Janek gave no reply. Sometimes he did that. And when he did, it was his way of replying. And people would understand, or at least try to understand his silence.

His agent continued.

"You suggested the idea to work with Strong. Well…be as it may, you're getting what you wanted. But from what I know about this guy, he's all about himself, a complete 180 from you. He's flamboyant, opinionated, demanding, and an overall lover boy who loves himself most. The two of you aren't exactly two peas in a pod. So…just be careful. You actually may be getting more than you want."

Again, Janek didn't reply, at least in spoken words. His small smile to himself was an answer in itself.

* * * * *

Outside the towering hotel, an early New York Sunday morning saw little activity on the rain-soaked streets. Late night partying, or tourists oversleeping, added to the calm. In a city this big, a city with a reputation that offers something for everyone, any usual or unusual deaths that may have happened during the just-ended night were still waiting to be discovered by overworked and understaffed police. And today, being a lazy Sunday, most late-night occurrences, good, bad, or unknown, had not yet made the morning news. But in a city like this, that never sleeps, with a population as large as it is, death is never unexpected. It is a common denominator that helps maintain the balance of life. But sometimes death wears many faces.

The black town car limo patiently awaited him. Its highly tuned engine purred like a sleeping cat wanting to stretch and enjoy the day's drive ahead. With its dark midnight color, accentuated with shiny silver trim and black-tinted windows, at first glance it resembled more like a coffin on wheels. A large, empty coffin.

Waiting. Waiting for his body to enter.

It was sprinkling lightly as Janek approached the car with a young, eager bellhop trailing closely behind. Known as one of New York's most famous and stylish hotels reserved for the rich and famous, the bellhops here played a daily private game of "who's who" with all the celebrity guests and the luggage they carried. Janek was recognized by the bellhop, who may or may not have read his books. He was just another name to be added to his "guess whose luggage I carried" list. He would be counted as "somewhat important," but not as important as carrying Madonna's luggage two nights ago when she arrived with her entourage and multiple suitcases. That was one hell of a tip that day, and he anxiously awaited now to see what would cross his palms.

A middle-aged man in a black suit stepped forward from the side of the limo with a large, matching black umbrella. As if done countless times before, he quickly approached Janek and walked him to the limo's half-opened side door.

"Good morning, Mr. Janek. Everything is ready for you."

Turning away for a moment, the man handed the luggage-totting young bellhop some cash while pointing to the rear of the limo.

"Put the luggage in the back."

He then returned his attention to Janek.

"I hope the prearranged limo service for you last night was satisfactory. Sorry I wasn't available. Family thing."

Janek replied with more of a look at the morning surroundings than at the waiting questioner.

"I enjoyed a walk in the rain. The rain is always so cleansing. And you can see so much more, feel so much more, taste so much more, on the streets late at night."

"Yeah, lots of great all-night restaurants to stop at and enjoy. Something for everybody in New York."

"Yes, something for everybody." His answer may have been more for himself then to the waiting limo driver.

As the limo left the block-long, concrete-and-glass hotel, Janek looked upward at it one last time, as if saying more than just a casual goodbye. The towering structure went quite high into the morning fog-covered and cloudy, sprinkling sky, seeming to stretch forever upward, like a tired man stretching his arms above his body before succumbing to sleep or trying to stay awake. As he stared at it, it seemed to stare back at him. Not in a metaphorical manner, but in a real moment manner. As if waiting to say goodbye to him, there above, in all the many hotel room windows that adorned the towering hotel, he saw faces. Not the usual faces of the guests occupying each room and looking out at the morning daylight. No, not at all. The windows were filled with similar faces to the ones he had seen earlier in his swirling morning tea. *His* face, in each window. His face, alone.

Smiling, laughing, and sometimes staring with no expression.

Each face seemingly watched him as the black stretch limo left them all behind. Perhaps a sane person would have been disturbed by what they had just seen, or perhaps even frightened. But for Janek, sanity and madness each had a different definition. His own personal definition. And sometimes they were both one and the same.

Janek was glad to be leaving the city. He had been there for less than 24 hours. He never liked big cities, and hardly came here unless he had to. And he was here only because he had to. For the past twenty years since he came to America, he lived in a small, upstate New York community. He planned it that way. Away from the peering eyes of the nosey press and curious neighbors. Quiet and subdued so he could write whenever he wanted and without interruptions. Only his agent knew how to reach him and knew how to manage his book business-related affairs from afar. They had met very little over the past years. His agent was well-trained, well-instructed, and well-educated to know that Vladamir Janek was a complicated man, with a complicated soul. And he made sure that he would take care of business as Janek took care of writing. But he also understood that Janek, a man of his exceptional literary style and genius, would be managed differently from all the other writers he represented.

Vladamir Janek was unusual from what one would expect. Google him and there was nothing, absolutely no trace of his past before coming to America. Ask him, and he would casually smile and reply one sentence, the same sentence each time, "It was a long time ago, and I lived a very normal life." Nothing more, nothing less, but with a tinge of mysterious intrigue somewhere within those often-repeated spoken words. Maybe nothing less, maybe something more. Yet he always portrayed a stature of being polite, professional, and personable when he wanted to be, or maybe needed to be. Certainly nothing less; certainly nothing more. By all appearances, he was just another normal older person. But underneath it all, underneath his exterior persona, he alone knew, dwelled a totally different person within. A man who lived in shadows, or perhaps, was a shadow himself.

And a lot had happened in the past 24 hours.

A different limo had picked him up from his Upstate New York home the morning before and brought him directly to the New York City hospital for the scheduled procedure. He had planned in his mind to arrive and leave all in one day. But, after the lengthy medical process, and due to his age, he was told that he would need some rest rather than another long ride. His agent had made all the necessary arrangements for his overnight stay. Janek hated sleeping in large hotels. He found them cold, sterile, and filled with unfriendly, or too friendly, self-absorbed people who scurried here and there for whatever reason they had to be there. As much as he disliked staying, he made the best of it. And as mentioned to the driver, he did have a chance to walk and enjoy the late-night streets of the city. In more ways than one.

It was also better to stay here then spend more hours driving back through the night to his home upstate. Especially with the long drive planned for today.

Janek could have flown in and out of New York, but he always preferred traveling by car. He felt more comfortable and relaxed driving, or, as he was accustomed to, being driven. He never liked flying, even though statistics said it was safer than driving. Yet, statistics meant little to him, a brilliant writer with a vivid imagination, with a knack of writing about sudden and tragic death. And if statistics did factor in, it was only to be used to his advantage when plotting a story, or maybe, just maybe, plotting something else.

As for today's trip to a remote town in nearby Vermont, and his planned meeting with Lancelot Strong later, the solitude of a luxurious limo would better prepare him for the week ahead. He had formulated a pre-set of ideas of what the week would be like, and he needed his rest, especially for what he knew he had to do, and how he planned to do it. He had been thinking of these plans and of this meeting for a long time. A very long time.

Suddenly, a slight swaying of the traveling limousine on the wet highway pavement broke his personal thoughts.

"Don't worry about the rain, Mr. Janek. Just sit back and relax and we'll be there in just a few hours." The voice of the driver interrupted his solitude as it came through the limo's hidden wall speaker simultaneously as the vehicle slightly swayed again.

A few hours. Just a few more hours.

For Vladamir Janek, just a blink of the eye in a lifetime of fewer and fewer hours left ahead. A few hours more on a rainy day, filled with diminishing time, both planned and unplanned, and unexpected twists and turns. Twists and turns, both in his remaining life, and on the fog-shrouded road ahead. Twists and turns that only a master writer like himself could conjure up in a horror story that he would write or maybe even be a part of. And now, a few more hours in a long-awaited journey that only he knew was to become a real-life horror story. A horror story that involved him and someone, or rather him and "something"—something named Lancelot Strong in a "one-way" ticket to Hell.

Chapter 7

The private twin-engine Cessna was sitting on the runway waiting for his arrival, as planned and scheduled. He hated long drives, and especially the one today. Rather than sitting in a car or a limo on lonely winding roads, he preferred looking down from his own selected seat in the sky highway. He liked it that way, as it gave him a sense of power, like his writing—he felt like he was a "god" looking down at his fans below.

Lancelot Strong was a licensed pilot, and an excellent one at that. He learned to fly at an early age. When his childhood friends were on skateboards, he was in the air smiling down at them.

His father was a pilot for a small private company that transported executives to and from their various out-of-state meetings. He remembered how his father, a maintenance aircraft crew chief and a pilot himself, would take him to the airport on weekends and, as a young boy, he would watch him check out the small fleet of company-owned airplanes. Lancelot recalled how sometimes he would sit in the pilot seat and pretend he was flying—flying high above the many clouds and soaring through the sky like a fighter pilot chasing his hated enemy over made-up planets in faraway star-filled galaxies. His father always commented on his son's vivid and unusual imagination. Maybe it was the first inklings of what his life would become, a world of imaginary characters and monsters come to life on the written pages of his many books. But when he sat in the planes his father attended to, his imagination wasn't just about characters he created, it was about him being in control. Control of the plane and control of the fantasy world he flew in. Control, which to him meant power.

As Lancelot became a teenager, the fantasy of flight became a reality of life. Over the years, his father had taught him all about the various cockpit controls while he took him to the sky above on practice flights. And then, one day, out of the clear blue sky itself, his father gave him control of the plane. Just like that. In the middle of the endless sky, adorned with smiling cloud-like faces, he was handed the controls. And he flew. And he never stopped. Through all the years since, he continued to fly, especially now that he owned his own plane.

He could fly whenever he needed to clear his mind, or whenever he wanted to just be an imagined "god" and look down at all the ant-like people below. Lancelot Strong loved to fly, and today he would do just that as he prepared to meet Vladamir Janek at the place they were to share for a week. By flying, he could be there in two-plus hours, not eight hours in a claustrophobic car. His destination was a small, mostly grassy airfield, just a 20-minute car ride away from their meeting place.

And he would be in control of the trip, just like he was in control of his life.

"Good afternoon, Mr. Strong." A voice from behind him in the cabin interrupted his thoughts as he went through the plane's instrumentation before departure.

It was Harvey Sims, one of the airfield's head mechanics who was personally assigned to oversee Lancelot's private plane. At 50-ish, Sims was a flight jockey who loved the maintenance of the various airport planes he called his own. His interest in planes also began as a young boy, when he was given his first model airplane kit to assemble and paint. At the age of 13, he had a room full of them, and a dream to be a pilot. But an unfortunate sporting accident while playing high school baseball left him with a permanently injured eye and now limited vision. It kept him from his dream of being a commercial pilot but didn't prevent him from being a top mechanic at a place like this.

"Afternoon, Harvey. Are we good to go?" Lancelot asked in a friendly voice to the long-time acquaintance.

"Plane checked out; got your flight plan both on paper and electronically in your cockpit computer. Everything should be fine, but..." Sims hesitated for a moment.

"But?"

"But there's a possible change in weather. The storm we had here last night is sitting offshore and might take a turn back inland. The control tower has been watching that for hours. Weird weather this time of the year with all the southern hurricanes," Sims replied with a bit of concern.

"Take-off still planned for an hour from now at 3?" Lancelot replied while disregarding Sims' comment.

Sims nodded his head in agreement. He knew that whatever he told his friend, it wouldn't matter. They had known each other for over ten years and had come to like and respect each other. But Lancelot Strong only listened to one person, himself. He never seemed to have any fears, or disregard for any possible dangerous situation whether with feet on the ground or a seat in the sky. Not that he was a tough guy— maybe he was—but he displayed a single-minded strong character. Maybe that was an inherent part of his last name, Strong.

"Will there be a car and driver waiting for me at the airfield I'll land at?" Lancelot asked as a follow-up.

"Yeah, and they're instructed to take you to the town where you will be staying."

"So, there's a town?"

"Well, from what he said, a single-pump gas station, a grocery store, and a barbershop. Pretty much it. The house you're staying at is about another 15-minute drive from the town, kinda secluded from what the driver said. Also, kinda..."

His voice drifted off, hesitant to continue.

"Kinda?" Lancelot paused while waiting for the answer.

"Well, let's just say that it has a history."

"Yes, a haunted history." Lancelot broke a smile, as he already knew the answer.

Sims didn't quite know how to react to the smile, and finally let out a long, deep breath while shrugging his shoulders. Stumbling in thought for the right words, he continued, "Yeah, well, I mean, I heard it's a real haunted house. Like 'real.' You ever been to a haunted house?"

Lancelot smiled again, enjoying playing the question game. It was part of his writing style. Have the characters banter back and forth with questions until they found their own answer.

"You?"

"Well, when I was a kid, we had a boarded-up, old, abandoned house in the town I grew up in. Rumors were it was haunted by a ghost. As kids we would sneak into it and party and look for the ghosts," Sims answered in a serious tone.

"Did you ever find the ghosts?" Lancelot replied with a tinge of playful seriousness.

"No, not really, just some empty cans of beer and used condoms," Sims replied, disappointed.

"Well, even ghosts must like to drink and have sex." Lancelot chuckled at his own comment.

"Do you think so?" Sims replied seriously, as if he needed reassurance from his experienced writing friend. "I mean, you're a horror writer, and maybe you know something about ghosts and their existence."

Lancelot paused before replying. The question game had played itself out.

"All I know is that they're made-up stories and ghosts don't exist."

"Oh." Sims reply held a deep disappointment as if a little boy finding out that Santa didn't really exist.

Like a parent wanting their child to recapture the broken dream and make it right again, Lancelot stepped forward and put one hand on Sims' closest shoulder.

"But if they do, and if I see one, or meet one, I'll let you be the first to know."

They both shared a smile.

Sims' cell phone in his pocket rang and interrupted the moment. There was a short text message he scrolled through quickly.

"The weather report says the storm is shifting inwards. Maybe you'd better hold the flight until later."

"No, I'll beat the storm. Besides, I've flown in bad weather before," Lancelot replied nonchalantly, his mind already made up.

"Yeah, but..." Sims tried to get his concerned point across but was met with another of Lancelot's "winning-the-point" smiles.

"Don't worry, Harv, I'm a very qualified flyer. You know that; I know that; and it's not my turn to die. A lot of life ahead of me, a lot...but, if I did die, I'll make it a point to come back as a ghost to haunt you."

"Yeah." A sudden chill seemed to go through Sims. He forced a half smile. "Just get there safe. The only ghost I ever want to see is Casper, the friendly ghost."

* * * * *

The colors of the late afternoon sky were morphing from an overcast aqua blue to a dark, ominous black. Through the cockpit window, Lancelot could see the encroaching large storm clouds rapidly moving his way, as the wind from the angry ocean pushed them back inwards. He had been in the air for about an hour and had skirted the storm so far, flying in and out of a few patches of rain. Dusk was also approaching, and it looked like it would all come together sooner than he thought. The planes windshield wipers were activated, and he held steady on the steering mechanism as the wind started to shift. The plane moved up and down slightly in the turbulence. It was like the beginning of an amusement park roller-coaster ride, but without the steel tracks to guide it.

A familiar voice came over his headphones.

"Niner-one-nine, this is Harvey Sims. We see the storm on our radar getting bigger, winds increasing. Advise to reroute and head further inland away from the storm."

"And away from my destination? Not tonight. Have dinner plans with a fellow I'm dying to meet." Lancelot made a slight joke of his response.

"Lance, not kidding. Dinner can wait and you can have leftovers tomorrow when the storm blows through," Sims replied in a very serious and worried voice.

"Never been a leftovers kinda guy, Harvey, except when it came to women."

Another response from Sims started on the plane's radio but was garbled and began to fade.

The plane started to buck from the increased turbulence of the fast-moving storm that he was flying into.

His confident smile slowly started to fade into a frown, as a blinding rain suddenly struck the plane's cockpit windows like pounding fists. Again, the plane bucked slightly upward like a wild stallion trying to unsaddle its rider.

"I'll call you when I've landed." Lancelot signed off, not knowing if his voice was heard or was lost in the storm he now entered.

The twin-engine Cessna continued to lurch up and down in sudden gusts of wind. Lancelot's hands tightly gripped the plane's yoke. His instrument control panel blinked on and off, and then back on again. Something was wrong. Maybe a brief malfunction from the lightning that lit up the sky, pointing his way deeper into the black clouds. Or something mechanical or even electrical. But it didn't matter to him. He was an experienced flyer and had flown in storms before. After all, he was Lancelot Strong. A man without fear. And a writer who knew death inside and out. A man always in control. Always.

The plane straightened out for a moment as the storm's fierce winds held him tightly, then suddenly bucked again.

"Whoa, baby," he whispered to himself and to the silent encompassing cockpit. Like a kid on his favorite amusement park ride, he settled back into his seat and prepared for the exciting air thrills ahead.

Another bolt of lightning. Another roar of thunder. Another gust of wind. Another burst of rain. Over and over again.

His frown from a moment ago changed into a smile. Not a troubled smile. A calming smile. And then he suddenly started to laugh. A small laugh that became a longer laugh. A long, loud laugh that overshadowed the surrounding sound of the intensifying storm that beat against his flying metal steed. Like a knight of the round table, "Sir Lancelot" Strong became immersed into his own fantasy world in the middle of the storm of his life. The bolts of lightning became flames from a roaring dragon. The sounds of thunder were the cannons that fired from a nearby castle. His tousled plane was his imaginary warrior horse rearing its front legs as if charging through the surrounding enemy. All hell had broken loose outside in the storm, which wanted to get inside. But there was already a storm inside. Inside his mind. And throughout the cockpit, the only sound was laughter. It was a daring laugh, a death-defying laugh. A laugh so loud, and so strange, that if the outside world had heard it, they would have stopped and shivered. A laugh that echoed repeatedly inside his plane and throughout his soul and body.

A sudden nearby bolt of lightning briefly illuminated the darkened cockpit of the plane and his shadowed face. A face that had seemed to change somewhere in the storm, and no longer belonged to him. Not the face of someone, but "something." The face of a man gone mad; the face of a monster.

The storm intensified; so did his laugh.

Like a small speck of white swirling in a pool of thick, black blood, the dark ominous storm filled the entire sky, engulfing his small plane. One moment it was there, dancing in the storm; the next moment it wasn't, disappearing into darkness.

Chapter 8

The cloud-like mist rolled across the roadway in slow-moving waves, as soft, milky-like colors swirled in the autumn wind. The rain had changed from slow and steady to fast and frantic, sometimes with patches of nothing in between. Dusk was approaching early with the changing season, and there was little, if any, light left on the black roadway which zigzagged and cut its way through the surrounding tree-covered Vermont mountains. The limo ride had been steady and somewhat relaxing since leaving the concrete-and-steel skyscrapers of New York behind some seven hours ago. The intended destination wasn't much farther in actual miles, but sometimes destinations take longer depending on unexpected weather changes.

Vladamir Janek stared out the tinted limousine's window. He had been awake the entire ride. Throughout his life, he hardly slept, and of late he hadn't slept at all. Perhaps it was his troubled mind. Lost in thought—thoughts of life's passing pleasures, or maybe the now and seemingly worsening constant pain, or maybe something more—Janek sat silently in the limo's interior shadows, and within the shadows of himself. Lots of conflicting thoughts, all waiting to be emptied in a world he was growing tired of. Waiting to finally put his mind and maybe his soul to rest.

The fading landscape that passed before his tired eyes reminded him of Romania, his former homeland where he spent a good part of his life. Filled with mountains, dense forests, small towns and hamlets tucked or hidden in between, it was a small Eastern European country where legends and folklore of men and monsters still lived today. *"Men and monsters,"* he mused to himself. As a writer, he knew sometimes there was no difference between the two. All men are monsters in one way or another.

It started to rain again, very hard. He heard it loudly as it seemed to dance on the limousine's rooftop. He felt it as the car swayed even more on the rain soaked, leaf-covered road. It didn't bother him; it didn't concern him. Few things in his long life did. Sitting alone, surrounded by the dim interior lighting, he slowly, methodically, tapped his fingers across his knee, not in any usual manner. Nor in any unusual manner. It wasn't even a habit. He just did. Over and over again, and then again. Waiting, anticipating, thinking of what was to become. Or maybe thinking of what once was. A life filled with a lot of "what once was."

Janek's thoughts drifted backwards to a moment a long time ago. A very long time ago. Romania was once war torn, and as a young boy, he came to understand death sooner than most as he lived within the ugly horrors of war. He wasn't afraid of death; he had grown to expect it. And maybe appreciate it. He had seen a lot of it over the years. Especially in his childhood.

He remembered the night the occupying soldiers came to their family farmhouse as they sat eating supper. He remembered how he was instructed by his mother to quickly hide with his five-month-old baby sister in the small larder where food was stored. He was seven years old. He was young; he didn't understand, but he could feel the tension and sensed that bad things were about to happen. And they did.

He could still recall all the vivid sounds and images of the loud screaming struggles as his father was brutally beaten by the soldiers. Painful family screams lingered in his memory as his father was taken away from his life, and most likely placed in a concentration camp where he was put to death. He recalled his mother crying, pleading for his father's life and also for her older daughters' life, his thirteen-year-old sister. More than just a family member, but his best friend, too.

He watched as his mother was raped repeatedly, savagely, as he peered through a small crack in the pantry door frame while holding his baby sister and trying to keep her quiet. And then, as though it were a game and nothing more, with no care nor feelings for one's pleas for life, after all the soldiers had taken their turns raping his mother, they then each took turns and shot her in the head. Not once, not twice, but four times. Four soldiers loudly laughing as her dead body twitched on the kitchen floor with the impact of each new bullet. Dead from the first bullet; the remaining shots were like target practice in her sexually assaulted, lifeless body.

No tears, no emotion came from him as he silently remained hidden, watching it all unfold, huddled quietly with his one hand covering his younger sister's mouth tightly as she struggled to cry from the loud gun shots. His hand covered her face, but a muffled cry came through his tight, dirty, shaking fingers across her mouth. A cry that suddenly caught one of the soldier's attention enough to make him pause. To make him turn and look. To make him walk towards the small pantry where Vladamir hid himself and his little sister, now holding his hand even tighter across the little baby's struggling lips.

Through a crack in the door frame, he stood frozen as he watched the soldier stop and lean his face closer towards the pantry door. The soldier's one hand holding a gun and the other reaching for the knob. It was a face he would never forget, a face with a long scar that went from beneath his one eye to the tip of his unshaven pointed chin. A scar that seemed to point directly to his eyes filled with impending evil.

He remembered how he held his breath and closed his eyes to shut out the man's image, but the image remained burned in his mind, forever, as he remembered it today, as if it were yesterday. And when he reopened his eyes, the soldier was gone. But he never really left. His face would haunt him a lifetime. Not as the face of a man he hated, but as the face of a ghost who reminded him of his past.

His older sister was then raped, also repeatedly, but for her, there would be no wasted bullets. Being a young, budding woman, she was deemed a prize for them, and maybe for other waiting soldiers, too, who would use her to fill their sexual war-crazed lust. He watched, as her limp, ravaged, half-naked body was dragged away from their home, screaming and crying. Her screams and cries then blended into a sickening pleading sound, until it faded, and he heard no more. He never saw her again.

The last to leave, the soldier with the scar on his face paused and looked back once more at the closed pantry door. Looked back and smiled.

It was just another in all the unforgettable images he held in his head from that horrific night. All the images that made him the person he was today.

Men and monsters. Monsters and men.

And when Vladamir thought it was safe to come out of their kitchen pantry hiding place, long after the soldiers left, he finally did. Some horrors had ended; some horrors were about to begin.

He remembered how he sat silently by his mother's dead body, holding his little baby sister while still keeping his hand over her mouth. He didn't cry; neither did she. Neither would, ever again. They sat huddled together in a pool of their mother's blood for a day, maybe two, not moving, just staring. Staring silently, staring endlessly, until finally a neighboring family found them. And when they took the limp baby from his arms, they already knew. The baby was dead from his still tightly held hand over her tiny shut mouth. Dead. Suffocating her cries, suffocating her breaths, suffocating her to death. When he was taken from his home, he never spoke a word to them, nor spoke of what he saw—why should he? It was an unforgettable, never-ending horror, burnt into his childhood memory like a horrible tattoo etched into his heart.

He recalled how he was placed in an orphanage for homeless children of the war. He lived there for years, never talking to anyone. Living in his own personal silent world, he began to create stories, fantasies, to keep himself safe and sane. If ever there was such a thing. To him, then, now, and forever, his family was dead, as was a part of him. Vladamir Janek had witnessed death; he was now a part of death. And from that moment on, death had become more of a "life experience" than a "something" to be afraid of. It stayed with him through all the years, lurking in the shadows, always there. It had even become a friend to him in his books and in his life—his only friend, if death could be called by such a name.

But that was then, and this was now.

The long limo swayed slightly as the rain started again—heavier now, as it splashed across the rooftop, with an accompanying howling wind, sounding like an out-of-pitch song that struggled for a voice. Awakened from his past, Janek's timeless thoughts faded as his mind slowly cleared. His gaze returned to the outside world, a world he had long wished to leave behind, intently watching as a nearby bolt of lightning illuminated the immediate area. For the briefest of moments, century-old trees became blended blurs and surrounded the wet pitch-black roadway like the entrance to an ancient giant tomb. The rolling thunder seemed like distorted laughter aimed directly at him. And, in that moment, he reburied his painful memory of that time long ago. Of men and monsters, and monsters who were men.

The limo swayed again, and then again, as rain rolled across a long winding curve in the road. Vladamir Janek broke a smile to himself, and also to his remaining inner thoughts. He had spoken little, if any, for hours to the driver. He sat quietly, staring outside, focused on his thoughts, and lost in his silence. The driver knew him well enough to leave him alone and to only speak through the limousine's intercom when it was important.

"Sorry about that, Mr. Janek. Wind in the mountains can come up suddenly on these steep, winding roads. My GPS indicates a big storm approaching, so it may delay us slightly." The driver's voice tried to reassure Janek, and himself, as the wind and rain quickly became more intense.

Janek didn't answer. And the limo driver didn't expect him to.

While ascending the steep mountain road, there was no other sound inside the limo other than the rain. Just the increasing pounding sound of the rain, hitting the metal car as if angry fists were trying to get in, trying to get him. Janek could have put the interior music channel on to silence the sounds of the storm, but he preferred his personal silence in both the car, and now his mind. To him, the silence he created held all the sounds he needed to hear. He was safe inside, both in the car and in his tormented mind. Safe, if ever there was such a thing to him. Even so, he had no fear of the outside. The outside world, especially the thick mountainous forests on this journey, was like a second home to him. He always enjoyed the freedom of the forests. It reminded him of his once far-away home, its lush landscapes with so many places to run free and...

The limo swayed again. His thin, tall body slid slightly again across the leather bench seat. He corrected himself, as the limo corrected itself.

During the entire ride, the interior of the long limo was mostly dark except for the tube lighting placed across the ceiling and sporadically on the sides. Without warning, like closing and opening one's eyes, the interior lighting of the limo blinked. Just briefly. Maybe the rain and its wetness, or dampness, or something else combined, was affecting some of the car's electronic controls. Maybe. Or maybe it was just a sign, a message, a premonition meant only for him. Maybe. Something a writer's imagination would conjure up in a moment like this. Maybe. But most likely not.

The intercom voice of the driver interrupted again. This time it was slightly garbled.

"Minor fluctuation in the electronic panel controls. Happened before, nothing to worry about. Plan to have it rechecked after I drop you off and before I return for you next week."

The lights blinked again and then returned to its natural dimly lit appearance. Janek preferred it that way. He enjoyed the feeling of darkness with just a bit of light to reveal only what he wanted to see. And, when he wanted to see it ,Just like how he held his true emotions inside his emotionless persona. Janek was an enigma. Known as a "man of mystery"—never attending book signings, never attending publicity tours, never giving interviews. People only knew him by his writing and his picture on the back cover of each book. It was always the same picture. It never changed; neither did he. He seemed ageless, of sorts, but that, too, was another secret. A secret he kept in his silence.

No real friends, no real family, no known lovers, no known haters, except for maybe one. The one he was about to meet.

Janek knew more about him than maybe Lancelot Strong knew about himself. He prided himself on knowing more about the other person, without letting the person know more about him. Like a game of Cat and Mouse. Being in control, toying with the one who amused him, until the final moment. It had worked for years, and now would work once again. He knew Lancelot Strong's secrets. His personal and private secrets. Secrets that had remained buried alive for many years. More years than one can imagine. Discovering those secrets were the underlying reason why he agreed to this writing assignment. Those secrets matched his, and together, those secrets were a serious problem. A problem he had to confront and take care of now with the limited time he had left. To both of them, life was a real-live horror show with all sorts of monsters. Imagined and real. Men and Monsters. Monsters and Men. Vladamir Janek knew who he was, but what a surprise to have found out who Lancelot Strong really was!

The limo suddenly swerved slightly sideways. Janek slid partially across the leather seat, putting his one hand against the leather back to steady himself.

"Sorry, Mr. Janek. We're at the top of a good-sized Vermont mountain, and we now have to descend to the town below. A lot of winding curves ahead, raining steadily, and a pretty-dense fog. Expect some sharp turns. Not much longer now to your destination."

"Not much longer now," Janek thought to himself. *"Not much longer. After all these years. All these many long years filled with Ghosts of memories past. Men and Monsters. Lancelot Strong and me. Finally."*

And now, secrets were to be revealed. And revelations were to become secrets. Yes, Vladamir Janek knew who he was. And, also who Lancelot Strong was.

Monsters and Men.

And he knew who the real monster was.

And that was what he dwelled on as he stared out the limo windows at the surrounding forests in a stormy autumn twilight. Trees reaching higher and higher into the dark sky with finger-like branches, gnarled and barren of life, swaying back and forth in the howling wind outside while pointing the way to a would-be heaven. But tonight, for Vladamir Janek, and eventually Lancelot Strong, there would be no stop at heaven; only a detour to someplace else. Or maybe, someplace *worse.*

"My final destination." His thoughts repeated those three words with more than just a meaning—more of an obsession. *"And how fitting. A haunted house. With Ghosts, and Spirits of the Dead."* That was the plan, or at least part of the plan, he had privately prepared for Lancelot Strong.

As he looked out into the all-encompassing darkness, he half-smiled to himself. He would have laughed if he could have, but this was not a moment of humor, more a moment of madness. Hiding in his own world of darkness, like a spider weaving a web and waiting for its next victim, Vladamir Janek was setting a trap.

But little did he know, so was Lancelot Strong.

As the rain intensified, and the roadway grew wetter and steeper, the long, black limo silently began its descent down the long, curved-filled mountain road. One moment it was there; the next moment it disappeared into the fog. A deep, dark, foreboding fog.

Chapter 9

The lightning bolt illuminated the large house briefly. Sitting atop a sloped hill with well-worn cement steps leading to it, the house was century-old-plus, yet still majestic in its Victorian appearance. From what could be seen in that moment, it was more than just a house—much greater, a mansion, maybe a castle, steeped in darkness. A blend of gray stone and large brown brick, combined with wooden framework, it reached three stories into the night sky as if it never really ended. And perhaps it didn't. The dwelling was surrounded by several acres of dense woods and a knee-high, crumbling stone wall. Dark shadows from the giant, old oak trees swayed across the structure with the wind and rain. The entire place wore a gloomy, forbidden look. The fear that lurked in the outside world held no meaning here. Not here in this storied place that had witnessed Hell and spawned death and, yet, one can see no evil in its somber silent shroud.

With each new gust of howling wind, the property's towering trees forcibly bent and hunched over, moving back and forth, almost touching the house, perhaps trying to protect it. Wet leaves fell sporadically, like teardrops, indicating the end of a season or maybe the end of something more. The only light in the house came from the first-floor windows. Large, thick, leaded glass, held tightly by ornately carved and sculptured wooden frames, let the interior yellowish glow filter out as though long, thin fingers were inviting the way in.

Another flash of lightning illuminated an unrecognizable figure moving slowly through the storm and across the grounds. Whoever it was, moved silently between the rain-filled blackness of night and periodic quick bursts of lightning as it approached the majestic old house. Hunched over, but walking upright, with a larger-than-normal body frame, it was a strange shape. It wasn't a man; it wasn't a beast. It was someone, maybe something in between. As suddenly as it "was," it suddenly "wasn't," disappearing in the surrounding darkness of the storm.

With a growling rumble of thunder, the wind picked up in its intensity and whipped the newly fallen leaves into a spinning circle, a mini cyclone that rose and fell, keeping the moving stranger from being totally seen. Whoever it was, whatever it was, it was slowly, almost purposely, approaching the huge wooden front-entrance door of the house. And there in shadows, it stopped—hesitantly, as to whether or not go inside and reveal itself or perhaps to think about what it knew it would find inside.

Another smaller, distant flash of lightning, revealed a very large hairy hand as it slowly reached out, touching and resting on the door's tarnished metal doorknob. Five-fingered with unsightly long and sharp fingernails, it was a hand not of a man, nor of a beast, but the hand of something else. Something strange and unearthly. It remained there, patiently. Waiting. Waiting until it was ready. And when it was, the claw-like hand slowly turned the door's worn knob, allowing the massive nine-foot, unlocked front door to open inward with a creaking, yawning-like sound.

Vladamir Janek sat silently alone in the large dimly lit parlor. He sat motionless, almost lifeless, staring at the tall dancing flames within the bright burning fireplace before him. Yellow and red in color, they stretched upwards, disappearing into the long, dark chimney flue, but not before the embers of dried burning wood made distinct crackling sounds—strange sounds, almost like a laughing man licking his lips. Like Janek.

The room was spacious and paneled in mahogany. A small, ornate, rose-colored antique lamp made of carnival glass sat on a nearby round wooden table. The glowing light from the burning fire, along with the lone antique lamp, revealed that most of the room's furniture was covered in large white sheets—sheets that purposely hid the many haunting secrets of this very strange house. Strange and forbidden secrets, soon to be revealed. Sheets that were lifeless, yet, if placed over one's standing body, they could be used to pretend one were a ghost. But in this house, there was no need to pretend.

The room grew suddenly silent as if all the air had disappeared in the surrounding shadows. Janek's voice finally broke the silence.

"I've been expecting you."

Janek spoke aloud without turning from facing the fire. He either spoke to no one or spoke to someone he felt was there.

"As I've been waiting to meet you." Lancelot's voice was accompanied by way of his approaching footsteps on the house's old wooden floor as he entered the parlor through the grand hallway's entrance.

A three-tiered glass chandelier swayed high above in the hall as the wind from the opening and closing of the front door brought a cold chill with him.

Without turning to see Lancelot's entrance, Janek continued.

"Do you know why we're here?"

Passing Janek in his chair without a look, Lancelot approached the huge stone fireplace and rubbed his hands together, starting to feel the welcome heat across his partially wet clothing. He stood for a long moment with his back to Janek, then turned smiling smugly and finally answered.

"To write a story."

"Or maybe *be* that story," Janek replied without emotion, without feeling. Just five simple words that held more meaning than either one could imagine.

A distant roll of thunder and a faraway flash of lightning interrupted the moment. The storm was dying, perhaps an ominous punctuation to what was just said, and, to their encounter. Lancelot looked to the outside window and then back to Janek.

"Quite the storm. I had planned on arriving here before you. But here we are, finally."

"Yes, finally," Janek responded with a strange feeling of anticipation in his voice. After a short pause, he continued, "Although we have never met before, we are now connected together, just as this house is connected to us. We are connected to write a story about life and death. And, of course, the 'ghosts' that live between."

Lancelot paused in a troubled thought before replying.

"Yes. The ghosts that live between us and their final resting place."

He paused again, turning back to the fire while rubbing his hands together, closer, almost into the fire itself. Satisfied with his body's new-found warmth, he slowly turned back and looked fully into Janek's face.

"Do *you* believe?" he asked sternly.

It was the first time they both really saw each other's full faces in the parlor's subdued room light. And it was the first time they looked directly at each other's eyes, and into them—boring deep within each other's eyes, in a test of wills. In that moment, it was the first time they both saw what they were looking for, but it wouldn't be the last.

"I believe in what I see. Not what I don't," Janek replied in a soft-spoken tone, as if already knowing the answer to the question.

Lancelot took a small step back into the room's shadows.

"But what if what you don't see actually sees you?"

Janek smiled as he answered, "The Spirits of the dead?"

"Or maybe the Spirits of the living," Lancelot added coyly.

The large room again fell silent except for the occasional crackling sound of the fireplace's few remaining and dying embers.

Lancelot stepped back out of the shadows, his smug look gone, replaced by a more serious, inquisitive look.

"What do you feel when you write, besides the words that come to mind? Does something hidden stir your imagination? Or awaken your soul?"

"Souls are intangible; words are reality. One defines a man's soul not by his actions but by the words he uses," Janek replied with conviction. "And, by the way he uses them."

Lancelot took a step closer to the chair in which Janek remained seated. Pausing, he studied the older man. Having looked into his eyes, he now searched for a way to see into his soul.

"You don't believe?"

"In fairy tales, no." Janek's response was more conversational in manner than aggressive in response.

"In the afterworld?" Lancelot quickly added to his former question, still searching the older man's presence, studying his outward expressions while assimilating his words.

"The afterworld? A life after death? A place where angels and devils, demons and ghosts live? No. I don't believe. It's all in one's mind." Janek's reply was simple and straight forward, finally giving Strong a glimpse of his true soul.

Lancelot casually sat into a similar lounge chair across from him. He leaned forward as he continued his questioning.

"What if everything, here and now, yesterday and tomorrow, all existed in one's mind?"

It was Janek's turn to lean forward in his chair, the first body movement he had made in their entire conversation. A movement likened to a master chess player moving a "piece," in this case "a sentence," in a game of words.

"Ask that to a scientist, a theologian, a philosopher. Or better yet, ask a person who sits on death row waiting his fate. Ask any of them if what they feel is real or not. There are things that can and can't be explained. Reality exists in each of our own minds. The way we see it and the way it sees us. One has to go beyond their senses to find the truth."

"Well played," Lancelot mulled to himself, as he sat back into the plush leather chair, briefly feeling the cold texture with one hand. The outside rain that beat upon the windows and house was now the only sound between them.

"Do you know why we're here?"

"Of course. To meet our ghosts," Janek replied. "You do believe in ghosts, don't you?"

"Haven't seen one." Lancelot wryly smiled to make his point.

"Do you really need to 'see' in order to believe?" Janek's eyes narrowed, making his point.

"Seeing is believing." Lancelot sat forward and moved one open hand into the space around him, pointing out the answer.

"Or maybe believing is not actually seeing, but just knowing," Janek concluded.

Lancelot sat back in his chair and took a long moment before answering.

"No, I don't believe in ghosts, Janek, nor know of any such things. Ghosts, or shall I, or we, call them the paranormal, or supernatural, are just apparitions made up to scare people, or intrigue people, or amuse people. Ghost stories sell books, movies, and other superstitious trinkets. Ghosts are part of one's imagination, and sometimes that imagination plays tricks on us."

"So, you don't believe." Janek's eyes seemed to twinkle in delight, as though he knew something that his adversary didn't.

Lancelot chuckled. "In foolish folktales made up by writers such as us? No. I don't believe."

"Then what about the ghost behind you?" Janek asked in an all too serious tone.

Lancelot broke a small smile while keeping his eyes directly on Janek.

"So, you're testing me to see if I will turn to look back. Nice try. Yet, actually, there may be some truth in your question." Lancelot again leaned forward in his chair. "What about the ghost I see behind *you*?"

It was Janek's turn to break a small smile—a small, evil-looking smile.

"Oh, I've already seen it."

"Really?"

"Really."

"Who is it?" Lancelot mused.

"It's you," Janek whispered.

Janek's reply seemed to hang in the air for another long moment. And in that moment, they both sat staring silently at each other. Their word game had reached a conclusion, for now.

It was Lancelot who broke the paused silence, first, with a deep breath. As if the room had suddenly chilled, his breath was visible.

"Yes, this is going to be an interesting week. A very interesting week. And within our first moments of meeting, we actually have the plot to our collaboration. Two writers telling ghost stories to scare each other and see who blinks first."

"You don't have to blink to be scared, you don't have to tell stories to be scared, you just have to believe," Janek replied.

Lancelot remained silent as Janek slowly got up from his chair without another word.

Standing alone, Janek faced the fireplace taking in the last vestiges of the dying fire. It was the first time Lancelot saw the entire man in the sparse room light.

He was tall, well dressed in a dark sweater and slacks, and from what he saw, an old, frail man. Thinner than he had originally imagined. A face of deep wrinkles, or perhaps of great wisdom. But also, a man filled with sadness, and sickness, for sure.

Lancelot watched as Janek quietly stepped away from the fire and towards the open staircase, where he paused and slowly turned back.

"And, so, I believe it's time to say goodnight. It has been a long day getting here, as I'm sure it was for you, too. And, as you said, 'It will be an interesting week ahead.' Most interesting."

Janek paused to make this a point for them both to reflect on, then continued.

"The instructions I received said the room at the top of the stairs on the right is mine, as yours is indicated to be on the left. The instructions also say we have enough food and beverages for both of us in the refrigerator and pantries in the kitchen. Apparently, our agents collaborated on what we like to eat, and what we need to exist for a week together. I do not sleep late, and I will be available to begin our collaboration in the early morning. I will be here in the parlor waiting for you. Goodnight, Mr. Strong."

As Janek started up the stairs, he suddenly stopped and looked back.

"Oh, and one more instruction. I prefer not to be disturbed in my rest unless it is important—if you see a ghost, perhaps."

Not waiting for a reply, Janek turned and continued up the stairs.

From behind him he heard Lancelot's voice. "Or maybe...I will see something else."

Janek stopped midway on the staircase and slowly turned back at him. His wrinkled and tired face had a haunting look on it.

"Perhaps a monster?"

Lancelot did not reply. It was apparent that the words just spoken held a hidden meaning.

"Men and monsters. Monsters and men. Imagination plays so many different games with us when it wants, Mr. Strong."

"Yes, So many different games, Mr. Janek. So does life."

"Yes. So does life. And so does death," Janek concluded.

Turning away, not waiting for a response, nor expecting one, he resumed his walk up the stairs, disappearing into the shadowed hallway above.

Alone, standing in front of the dying fire, Lancelot's right hand began to make the shape of a balled fist— a tight-balled fist that he opened and squeezed several times as he contemplated Janek's spoken words and the answers he knew would be revealed in the coming days. He squeezed his fist tighter, digging his fingernails into the skin of his palm. A small trace of blood trickled down his hand.

The room was silent, very silent.

A bolt of lightning briefly illuminated the outside. There, in the window behind him, was a face.

Chapter 10

Outside the house, lightning flashed with an accompanying boom of thunder. But inside, the thunder had weird distant, distorted echoes.

It was almost midnight when Lancelot Strong finally entered his bedroom. As he passed by Janek's room, he saw a whisper of light coming from beneath his closed door. It had been several hours since Janek had said he was tired and had left him alone in the parlor. During those hours, time seemed to stand still for him. Maybe for both of them. But during that time, he was fixated on what was said, what was meant, and what would occur. For him, or maybe for both, it was just a matter of time.

His room was spacious and had a large Victorian canopy bed with thick, rounded wooden posts, along with several pieces of antique furniture reflecting years gone by. Outdated flocked wallpaper hung on two of the four walls, peeling at the uppermost edges. A mosaic-patterned carpet was centered in the room over the old wooden floor. Worn, but still vibrant in its orangish colors, it, too, reflected another time gone by. An unused fireplace stood at one corner of the room waiting to come to life. But not tonight. Lancelot had other things to do tonight, other things to accomplish.

His suitcase had arrived earlier in the day and sat unopened on the bed. It had a small tumbler lock on it that he immediately adjusted to a memorized combination to open. Reaching into the suitcase, atop of folded shirts was a plastic prescription bottle. Easily twisting off the cap, Lancelot shook two small yellow pills into his hand and then immediately popped them into his mouth. Small enough to swallow without water, but strong enough to…

Capping the bottle, he placed it back into the suitcase and began to put his hands beneath the clothing, looking for something else. Tucked between some of his neatly packed clothing was an old wooden box about eight inches long and four inches deep, made from mahogany. Etched across the top of the box was an ornate carving of a religious cross. The box had a metal clip latch on it which he easily opened. Peering into the open box, he saw what he was looking for. He stared at the contents for a long thought-filled and satisfying moment. No emotion crossed his face but, from within, his eyes narrowed with a series of very wicked thoughts. Closing the box, he walked across the room and opened the top drawer of a dresser. Inside a mostly empty drawer were a few assorted bed linens, slightly yellow from lack of use. He carefully placed the box into the drawer under the linens and closed it.

Connected to the top of the dresser was a large oval mirror framed in red oak. The glass had heavy dust on it from not being cleaned for many years. With one finger, he made a circle in the dust surrounding the reflection of his head. Once done, he paused and looked at his image. His face reflected more than what one would easily say was a handsome thirty-year-old man. The reflection also showed a man of mystery. And within that mystery, something strange lurked beneath his appearance. Something that only he knew and understood. Something that made him smile at his reflection. But the reflection did not smile back.

Reaching underneath the edge of the dresser top, he ran both hands in opposite directions feeling for something he knew was there. And it was. A key. Attached to the underside with tape, the key was easily pulled off. Discarding the tape, Lancelot held the key between his fingers, looking at it. It was some type of latch key. His agent told him all about the intricacies of the house and had placed this special key for him to find. It, too, matched the rest of the room; it was old, and the metal was somewhat tarnished. But it held a mysterious importance.

Walking to the closed closet door, he opened it and entered. It was empty and rather spacious, matching everything that was equally spacious in the house. Other than the bedroom's light that filtered in behind him, there was no light inside the closet. It didn't matter. He knew what he was looking for. On the back wall of the closet was an empty, long, wooden shelf. He easily pulled the shelf away from the wooden brackets it sat on, and there on the wall was a keyhole. A small, metal keyhole, once hidden by the shelf, but now revealed to the man that held the latch key in his hand.

The key fit into the hole and, when turned and pushed inwards, opened the back wall to what appeared to be a dark corridor. Before entering, Lancelot reached into his pants pocket for a small pen flashlight and turned it on. Using the beam, he surveyed the corridor. It was a hidden passageway, narrow enough, but wide enough, to have a man his size move through it comfortably. A smell of dust and aged wood hung in the air. Cobwebs crisscrossed the top areas of the passageway, but he effortlessly pushed them aside as he entered.

After a short walk, the passageway took a sharp turn, then continued. It was apparent, or maybe even known to Lancelot, that the passageway led to other rooms, specifically, from his room to Janek's room and beyond. Although the floorboards gave a small creaking sound with some footsteps, he carefully adjusted his pace to keep his presence quiet. After another turn in the passageway, he stopped in an area of the corridor where he found a knob on the wall. When he looked at it carefully with his limited lighting, he could see the outline of a hidden door. Assuming it led into Janek's room, he moved a few feet past it, and after feeling the surrounding dark wall with his hand, he found what he was looking for—a round piece of attached wood, the size of a small single eyeglass that he knew would cover a peephole. He swiveled it to the side and placed one eye onto the revealed hole.

Through the peephole he could see that he had found Janek's room. The light from a table lamp next to the bed was on and he could immediately see that this room was as spacious as his. From the angle the peephole gave him, Lancelot could see most of the room, if not all of it. The large canopy bed, similar to his, lay untouched. The fireplace had a single log in it, burning lightly. The rest of the furniture looked similar to his, except for one thing that immediately struck him as different. The large dresser mirror was covered with bed linens. It was apparent that these were the same type of linens as he had in his drawer. The covering certainly prevented any image from being seen or reflected. But why? Lancelot stared at it for a long moment contemplating the reason Janek would have done this. It really didn't matter that much to him as he already had an idea for his answer. This covering just helped him confirm his suspicions.

Moving his position against the peephole, he continued to view the room. Other than the few crackling sounds emanating from the fireplace, there was no other sound. And, there was no Vladamir Janek.

Closing the wooden window to the peephole, he immediately turned to look back from the direction he came. A very faint trace of his room's light seemed to follow through the turns in the passageway. Satisfied with what he saw, and curious as to what he saw, Lancelot turned back to the darkness ahead of him and continued further into the passageway.

After a few more turns in the corridor, which he assumed passed other areas of the upstairs, he came upon a small narrow stairway that led to the floor below. Carefully going down the small wooden steps, he came to a landing that then led to a new corridor in either direction. Apparently, when the house was built, this secret passageway was used either for someone to spy on their guests, or to hide. Choosing to go to the right, he came across another protruding wooden cover for another peephole. Swiveling it aside, he could see the dim lighting of the parlor where he first met Janek. The table lamp was still on. From his viewpoint looking into the room, he recalled that a painted family portrait was on the same wall that he now stood behind.

"I must be looking through the eye of one of the family members," Strong thought to himself before breaking a smile. *"Just like in the movies—a peephole in the portrait."* As he viewed the room again, there was still no sign of Janek. *"Odd. Where could he be? And what is he doing?"*

Closing the small wooden peephole cover, he continued down the passageway. Another protruding wooden cover gave way to another peephole, this time to a darkened library filled with floor-to-ceiling bookshelves. This room, too, was empty. From another peephole further down, he observed the kitchen area. It was also dark with no sign of any life.

Continuing his journey in the secret passageway, he came to another set of steps, also leading downwards. Pausing, he turned the small penlight he used into the darkness below to see where it led. The light was not strong enough to reveal anything but more steps.

"*A basement?*" he thought to himself before proceeding.

And then he heard a noise. Something from below, not close, but somewhere at a distance, a shuffling noise, like something being dragged. Dragged across a stone basement floor.

"*What the hell?*" grabbed at his thoughts. "*Dragging sounds? From somewhere beneath?*"

And then the sounds stopped.

Silence held the darkness. Complete silence.

But the silence didn't last long. Suddenly, he heard the faint, far-off sound of laughter from somewhere in the dark. A child's laugh. Definitely a young child. But who? It echoed off the stone walls and floor, hauntingly, almost like a broken record. Without a pause, the laughter slowly turned to sobbing cries.

A child crying.

Carefully holding one hand on the corridor wall, he slowly descended the steps, making certain to keep his presence a secret.

Surrounded by more darkness, and a smell of damp, stale air in a stone-walled basement, he turned his light to determine the area he now stood in. From what he could see in the dim light, the cellar was empty.

The child's crying grew distant and then faded altogether.

There was some water on the floor, perhaps from rain seeping through the gray walls, and a lot of cobwebs trapezing across the wooden ceiling beams above him, but nothing else. Darkness, shadows, crumbling old stone walls, empty. But then he saw another passageway, further in the cellar at one end. It seemed to beckon him. It seemed to have been waiting for him. He approached it and could see in the faint light that it was a burrowed stone-and-dirt tunnel that continued from one end of the cellar wall to...

"Where?" he said aloud.

Stepping into and across some of the water puddles, he entered the tunnel. It smelled of wet dirt and something that was familiar to his senses. Something that he knew all too well. Something intriguing, yet something concerning.

He smelled death.

The tunnel continued for a distance that was hard to determine. Whether he was still under the house, or being led somewhere, he had no feeling of direction. But the smell remained. And it was becoming stronger with each step he took.

A few more twists and turns in the tunnel and suddenly he could see a bright light ahead. No sound; just a light.

Cautiously, he continued. The silence gave way to a faint sound of water dripping and something else. With his acute senses, he recognized the flickering sound of a flame. It was the flame of a torch; maybe one, or maybe more.

And then the tunnel ended abruptly into a large, shadowed room that was twenty feet tall with four equally sized walls of gray masonry, sandwiched together by crumbling cement. A room with dense and damp air that hung in the stillness of the moment. An undisturbed room. A crypt.

With a somber, dispassionate eye from where he stood at the entrance of the room, he quickly surveyed it. Each of the walls had a look of stained, blotch-like dampness to them, perhaps from the many years of water seepage, continually permeating and degrading the cement. The air was cold and numb, and with every breath he took, a chilly, misty vapor followed. The crypt may have been as old as the house, maybe older.

Lancelot recalled being told by his agent that there was a small family cemetery close to the house. For all he knew now, this could certainly be a part of it. To his far left, a narrow, broken brick, thirteen-step stairway led upwards to a closed, gated metal door. Probably to the outside? At first glance to the ceiling above, there were no hanging cobwebs. For a place as old as this, it seemed unusual, but not as unusual or mysterious as the two lit, glowing wooden torches attached in metal brackets on either side of the room. They emitted all the light he needed. Who lit them and when were they lit were questions that troubled his mind. But even more troubling was what was in the room. The room was totally empty except for two very large items that rested on a concrete slab dais in the center. Two identical items. Two brand-new coffins.

"Damn!" Lancelot spoke aloud in an exhaled whisper of complete and unexpected surprise.

After absorbing the initial shock of this unusual discovery, Lancelot slowly circled the room while staring at the two coffins. His circle grew smaller with a full rotation and then he stepped forward, standing mere inches from the coffins. They were both closed. He touched the one nearest him. It felt as cold as ice. He moved his fingers downward and put both hands underneath the coffin's metal lid. He knew what he was doing and what he had to do now. Without hesitation, he slowly opened it and looked inside. It was empty. He carefully ran his fingers across the inside silk bedding to see if there may have been something more, something hidden beneath it. There wasn't. Slowly closing the coffin lid back down to its original position, he paused a long moment, staring at the second closed coffin, thinking about what he might find in it. Taking a step or two to the next coffin, he stopped with a hesitation, not a fear, but perhaps a trepidation. The smell of death was stronger now.

A sudden deeper chill seemed to fill the room as the two torch flames begin to flicker from an unseen wind.

Touching the closed metal lid, he slowly ran his fingers across the curved coffin's top. Smooth and cold, shiny and foreboding. Seemingly waiting for him to open it—waiting for him to see what was or wasn't inside. Letting out a deep cold, misty breath, which seemed to hang forever in the damp air around him, Lancelot moved his hands and fingers to the narrow ridge underneath the lid. Slowly he started to lift the top open. Slowly. Very slowly.

And then he saw it.

His body.

Himself.

Laying in the coffin with arms folded across his chest. Dead.

As he stood silently in a state of shock staring at himself, his eyes in the body in the coffin suddenly opened and stared back at him.

And then, the room went dark.

Chapter 11

Amber Stone loved to party. Actually, she was known as the "life of the party." Being an attractive twenty-year-old single socialite in the growing, sprawling city of New York in the mid-1920s, she had the reputation of partying all night and sleeping all day. But the reputation didn't end there. She never slept alone. The long list of men she bedded was hardly a secret. And the list kept growing, night after night, party after party, until that one fateful night of the "biggest party of the year" when she finally met him. And it was "love" at first sight. Expectedly, and conditionally.

He was tall, dark, and handsome—the definition of every unmarried woman's dream, but with the extra caveat of being rich. Remarkedly rich. With money and looks, he was the man for every woman's fantasy. And although it was easy for people to say that she fell in love with his looks, the truth is, she actually fell more in love with his money. He had lots and lots of money. For Amber Stone that was important. Very important. Hidden truth be told, Amber Stone was poor, very, very poor, living beyond her means, pretending to be someone she wasn't, playing a nightly game of looking for the "right man" to have what she needed, what she wanted: to be wealthy, and to be a real socialite; to be the real life of the party, in the small, closed circle of real rich people.

And so, it was the winning combination of both his "looks and loot" that made her say "I do" when he asked her to marry him after a whirlwind romance. And what a wedding it was! A fairytale-like affair with everyone who was "someone" attending. Every major important player in New York and all the way to California. They all came to the biggest wedding celebration imaginable. Politicians, businesspeople, socialite celebrities, family and friends. Hundreds of guests in the biggest, most opulent wedding party of the year. Everyone was there. Everyone except "anyone" from Amber Stone's side of the invitation list. A list that was empty. Amber had no real friends to speak of. If they were friends, they were jealous of her and wouldn't have come anyway. And her family? There was none. None, that were known.

Amber Stone was said to be an orphan. She told stories of how she was left at the doorstep of a Massachusetts orphanage as a baby, brought up by Catholic nuns, attended an all-girls boarding school, and remained unadopted through all her years. But in those years, she had a private plan, and she plotted it. At the age of 18, the story goes that Amber left the orphanage in the middle of a stormy night and came to the big-city nightlights of New York. Without a dime, or a nickel, or any money at all. She came to find fame and a fortune. This was a very calculated move on her part—sleeping her way into the all-night parties gave her a status of being someone she wasn't, and she used that to her advantage. All along she had a hidden agenda that drove her every moment. Like a seasoned hunter in a big concrete jungle, she was there for a reason. And one reason only. A reason only she knew and harbored as she played by her own special rules in her own special game of life. A reason that she didn't share with anyone. A reason that she never doubted would really happen. And when it did, then she knew. She knew for sure. For Amber, she got what she wanted, what she knew would happen, to meet and be with him. But as fairy tales sometimes go, it was not what she bargained for.

Jonathon Hellmark was rich, very rich, handsome, and more than just handsome, he was also very, very controlling. Beneath it all, he was also a man of deep mystery. With all the money and power built through early investments in oil and maybe a few other deals that were part of his secret life, at the age of 33, he was on top of the world of business. All he needed now was that crowning jewel, a trophy wife, a woman of beauty and charm to match his lifestyle and elevate his business status. A perfect match for a "perfect" man. And he found her. Marrying Amber, he got what he wanted, what he thought would make his life truly perfect, but it, too, was not what he bargained for.

Amber Stone had a secret. Not that of being a fictitious socialite. He actually knew that the day he met her. He also knew all about her false pretenses, all about her made-up stories of a poor orphan upbringing, all about the partying she liked to do and why she did it—all of it, and maybe more. But it didn't matter to him. None of it. For years, Jonathon Hellmark, just like Amber, also had a private plan, and he plotted it. A plan that involved Amber Stone.

With his vast wealth, he knew all about Amber from the research he had conducted. He was like her in many conniving ways. Like her, he was also a seasoned hunter in a big concrete jungle. And in his hunt, he even planned the party and made the arrangements to finally meet her. It was all for a reason, and one reason only. Jonathon Hellmark also had a secret. One might say it was business that drove him to meet her, yet actually, it was madness.

Jonathon Hellmark had known for a long time that there was something special about Amber. Something that attracted him to her. Not just in the way she moved, or the way she smiled, or the way she carried herself, or even the way she loved. After all, she was quite the experienced lover. And yes, she portrayed that she was the ideal woman for every man's fantasy, and yes, she was the ideal "trophy" wife. All of that mattered, but really didn't matter. There was something more. There was something very unusual about her, and something very secret. And it was that "secret" he discovered, and it was because of that secret he searched for her. It was that "dark secret" only she, and now, only he knew. Amber Stone was a witch.

Spewed from the depths of a witching coven in the late 1800s in Salem, Massachusetts, Amber grew up as part of a traveling gypsy family until the state laws and legislations caught up to them and chased them away. There was no orphanage, there was no boarding school, there was only false pretense; a cover-up of who she was, what she was; a cover-up that had to remain hidden from the real world that would not understand her. Throughout history anyone thought to be a witch was immediately and without question considered an embodiment of evil. Witchcraft was deemed the work of the devil. Churches made it a mission to purge those who practiced it. Those accused of witchcraft were stoned to death, burned on a pyre, or drowned in water.

Amber kept her secret hidden; she escaped those who would have sought her out, persecuted her, and killed her. With her abilities, or witching power, she knew when and where they were coming for her, and she was always one step ahead of anyone finding her out. And so, at the age of 18, the story goes that Amber left her gypsy family in the middle of a stormy night and came to the big-city nightlights of New York. Without a dime, or a nickel, or any money at all. She came to New York not to find fame and fortune. She fled alone to New York, as she had a plan, and the plan involved a very rich man named Jonathon Hellmark.

In her youth, Amber had an inkling of who she was to become. Her so-called family of "gypsies" had a long history of being practitioners of witchcraft. And as a witch, Amber Stone inherited an ingrained special gift. She had an open door to the beyond. A place which some say exists only in one's mind. A place which others say exists only in one's belief. For her, it was a combination of both. A place that not only existed, and that she believed in, but a place she had visited more than once. Her gift endowed her with the necessary link to unlock the unknown darkness of the future and return with its known answers. An unmistakable gift, one that each time lasted only seconds, but its effects were a traumatic jolt to her emotional, physical, and even spiritual human structure. She could see the future. She could touch the future, and she could become the future. And, in stepping inside the unknown, she saw things that would affect her and others and that would alter her lifetime. An insight brought to vivid sharpness in a momentary flash. Perhaps a hallucination, perhaps an imagined dream, but no matter what it really was, the impression was always clear, always real. And in seeing, she knew, and in knowing, she understood. With her great power, she could feel life as no one else could ever imagine. By just touching another person's hand, her premonitions came to life. Amber Stone was a witch that could see, and know, everyone's future— everyone's but her own.

But with all great power, sometimes comes great tragedy. The future, the great unknown we all would like a peek at, the tapestry that covers the minutes before us, whatever it is, sometimes, maybe all times, should be left alone. And that was her hidden wish, to leave it alone. And that was what she wanted in marrying Jonathon Hellmark, to leave her secret life alone, behind, forgotten, and to start a new life, with wealth and no worry.

Jonathon Hellmark had a hidden wish, too. He wanted to, he had to, and was obsessed to find a way to acquire her power. He wanted to use her gift—he actually needed to use her gift because his business ventures were failing, and his investments were in trouble as the New York stock market of 1929 began to crash. He was going broke. But with her gift of seeing the future, he could make all his investments whole again and regain all of his wealth. For in that "peek" inside the next moment, or moments to come, he could claim untold power. Power to control destiny, and power to acquire even greater wealth. Power that would make one a "god." And that is what Jonathon Hellmark wanted most—to be a god.

After an amazing and romantic honeymoon through the grand capitals of Europe, Jonathon brought Amber home, to his "home," an inherited family mansion in the secluded and relaxing mountains of Vermont. It was a huge Victorian mansion built just years prior by Jonathon's father and mother. An amazing mansion that some would say reminded them of a European-style castle. Unfortunately, for all its grandiose and magnificent appearance, his parents never spent a single night in it. Not a single night, so the story goes. But sometimes there is more to the story, something that is left untold, or maybe only whispered in rumors. What is known is that his parents died tragically together as they journeyed to the finished home. Murdered as they reached their property by a traveling group of gypsies who had secretly stayed there. Murdered not for their money, but for their souls.

Jonathon buried his parents in a small cemetery that was adjacent to their new house. He felt it was appropriate for them to be there, as they had intended once in life, but now forever in death. But even though they never physically lived there, local town's people claim that they had seen them there. Or had seen their ghosts there.

When Jonathon took possession of the house, he lived alone with a maid or butler to frequently come and clean or cook or take care of the place when he travelled. The house allowed him to escape his big-city business and his lengthy journeys. Located far from the madding big-city crowds, there was only a small town and some scattered farms nearby. A large forest surrounded the entire home and offered him perfect solitude.

It wasn't long after Jonathon's and Amber's move into the house that things began to change. Two things. Two very important life-changing things. First, romance changed to inquisition. Jonathon revealed to Amber that he knew all about her past, of her being a witch, and that he would only love and protect her at this house if she shared the secrets of the future with him. Jonathon also told her of his financial problems. She hesitantly agreed to help him reclaim his lost wealth by stepping through the portals that led to the future to learn where investments should be made. Secondly, Amber told Jonathon she was pregnant, carrying his child. It was a stalemate. He would protect her and their child, but she still needed to share secrets; he still needed her gateway to the future. And, she would help him regain all his lost wealth, and more, and teach him the art of witchcraft. It was apparent neither really loved each other, but only "used" each other.

Both got what they bargained for. Riches returned, she lived in the seclusion of the mansion where she was financially protected in her secret, and a baby boy was born to them—delivered at the stroke of midnight on a stormy autumn night after a long and complicated pregnancy. Born in the upstairs master bedroom of the mansion by a midwife, paid and brought there from the nearby town. It was an exhausting and harrowing delivery. Amber lost a lot of blood, almost too much, but survived.

Following the pain of birth, and the expected joy of a newborn, the happy midnight hour quickly changed into something else. The baby was born without a heartbeat, appearing cold and dead. Then, within the silence of the room, the baby suddenly began to breathe. A deep, long breath, as though sucking in the life from the future and beginning a new life that day as a testament to a mother with strange powers. He cried and cried, as babies should, with his tiny crying voice echoing throughout the mansion. When Jonathon excitedly held his son for the first time, he stood shocked at what he saw as he looked upon his son's little face. Shocked to see that, even with the baby's cry, there would be no tears. Now nor ever. The baby was born without eyes. Their celebration of life became a celebration of horror.

No eyes, just two dark sockets, which stared blankly as if he could really see. Two dark sockets that maybe, and possibly, and probably, led to an unknown world other than the one he could not see in. But he would. Their son was born with the gift of his mother. He would see the future; he would step through the portals that led beyond, and he would one day become an important part of all he would touch and see. He was named Jonathon Stone Hellmark as a part of both of them, but actually a part of neither of them. Perhaps he was the devil in disguise.

Jonathon wanted to keep their baby a secret, ashamed of its defect, not knowing its gift. The midwife was sworn to secrecy and Jonathon forbade his wife to leave the house with the baby. Their marriage fell further apart, and Jonathon began to travel more on business with the "foretold" information his wife had given him regarding future investments.

While he was gone, Amber cared for their son in a loving way. The child was an extension of herself. She knew it, she felt it, she saw it. In her mind and heart, she believed that her baby would possess her "special gift," and maybe more. Her son was her number-one priority. She would do everything and anything necessary to protect him.

Almost a full year passed, and, although being an attentive mother, Amber was also becoming bored being alone. She longed for the days of the all-night partying. She missed fun and socializing. It was a big house to be alone in, day after day, night after night. The emptiness in her marriage affected her heart and mind, and it began to take a toll on her appearance. Her complexion grew paler from the lack of being a part of the outside world and its sun-filled days. She never left the house. He had forbidden her to. It became a cage to her. Each day she stood holding her child and staring through the large, ornate, glass windows at a world that was becoming more distant with each passing moment. She became restless, remembering her past, partying and fantasizing about other men and other women. Her fantasies began to distort her sense of reality. Her life was changing, and not in the best way imaginable.

Amber found solace late at night in reciting her witching chants to herself as her son slept. Strange chants that came from a strange book she kept hidden from Jonathon even after they married. Throughout the nighttime, which became more of daytime to her, she wandered the house, trancelike, mumbling words and unrecognizable sounds, which seemed to come from a foreign language, a language not of this earth. She hardly slept, maybe never. Time no longer existed to her. Hours, days, weeks blended, all the same in her state of loneliness. It was just her and the baby. Her beautiful, eyeless baby. To her, it had eyes. To her, it looked back as she looked at it. To Amber, reality was becoming more imagined than real.

But the most telling sign of her change was in the painted portrait of her which hung over the parlor fireplace. A portrait that was commissioned as a gift from Jonathon to her when they moved into the house. A portrait that began to resemble someone other than her worldly self. Her once youthful beauty seemingly disappeared more each day. Her appearance began to change from happiness to hatred. She was a prisoner in her own prison, both inside the mansion and inside her mind. There was no longer an outside to escape to.

Until...

When suddenly, and out of nowhere, *he* came into her life.

It was the beginning of another autumn, and her baby was nearly a year old, when a younger man came upon the Hellmark property and stood in the gentle wind for a long time, studying the huge Victorian house. Walking around it, always at a distance, not too close, nor not too far, he finally sat in the backyard tall grass in the adjacent overgrown cemetery. He sat staring at the house. Staring, thinking. He was an aspiring college artist traveling the country, with an eye for color and composition. It was by happenstance that he wandered through the area looking for landscapes and architecture to draw and paint. He became infatuated with the look of the house, its magnificent and unusual architecture, its colorful flowers and shrub-lined surrounding grounds and, of course, the mysterious woman in the upstairs window who secretly peered out and watched him. Everything was intriguing, and for an artist, everything had to be captured forever.

Over several hours Amber watched as the young man sat in the swaying grasses as they bent to and fro in the warm autumn wind while he drew a picture of the house. And of the unknown woman in the window.

Through the entire time he did this, Amber continued to study him privately from her bedroom window. Peeking through the sheer window curtain curiously and lustfully. Peeking, in a way to not be seen, but also to be seen. From her viewpoint, she could see that he was very handsome, in his early twenties, with long, flowing, shoulder-length brown hair and a slim and toned body, revealed in the mostly unbuttoned shirt he wore. His manly and partially exposed youthful, tanned chest captured her eye. His appearance teased her and made her fantasize if he would be attracted to an older wanting woman such as herself. Her sexual passions had been suppressed and hidden for too long. She was determined to find out, although she already knew.

When evening approached, the young artist seemed to complete his work. As he started to pack his drawing utensils and paint brushes, he heard an approaching sound from behind him. The sound of soft, bare footsteps on fallen dying leaves. It was her first time outside the house in a long time and she looked more like an attractive twenty-year-old woman of the past than an aging woman of the present. Her hair was freshly washed and styled, and her skin was covered with enough makeup to enhance her eyes and give her face a youthful glow. She wore a long white, flowing, full-length nightgown, low-cut from her neck to her midriff revealing her large, firm, bare breasts, and open enough beneath her waist to show her long lovely legs. She was beauty personified. The remaining daylight cast a heavenly sunbeam around her, like a golden halo heralding the coming of an angel. With each step she took, her hair moved softly in the gentle evening breeze, as if hidden fingers caressed her. When they were close enough to almost touch, she smiled; he smiled. There was no doubt that he was immediately captivated by her. She planned it this way. She thought about if for hours as she watched him. She purposely wore the same enticing nightgown that she wore on her wedding night.

A brief conversation between both set the tone. When she touched his hand, she knew their future. They would become lovers, immediately and forever, and they were, night after night as Jonathon travelled. Night after night they embraced in the bed of the master bedroom, which was now empty of a hating husband and bored wife, but now filled with a sex-driven stranger and his wanting mistress. In their nightly passions, he rekindled her womanly desires that had been lost in her loveless marriage. He was the best lover she ever had, and the last lover she would ever have.

It was a rainy, stormy, late autumn night, a week or so after they met when Jonathon came home unexpectedly from a shortened business trip. Finding a dying fire in the downstairs parlor and two empty wine glasses on an antique end table nearby, he quietly climbed the large staircase to the second floor.

He could hear their sounds of passion, loud and echoing. They could not hear his footsteps, silent and foreboding. They were in the throes of intense sexual excitement and a deep, loving embrace when he swung the metal fireplace poker. The young artist died instantly atop her, perhaps in the greatest climax of his quickly ended young life. She screamed a long echoing scream that went from room to room throughout the huge house and it reminded him of their son's first cries of life. But that was then, and this was now, and these were cries of death. In his jealous, murderous rage, he stifled her scream believing himself to be a good father so that it wouldn't wake their sleeping son. He held one hand over her mouth with his other hand tightly squeezing her neck. He held it long and hard until her futile struggles stopped. Until her body twitched no more. Perhaps she, too, climaxed in death like her lover did. It didn't matter to Jonathon. All that mattered was the realization of what he had done, and what he had to do now, as his raging madness returned to some sense of normalcy.

It didn't take long to decide. He knew exactly what he had to do. Maybe he had fantasized about this moment during his travels. Maybe he thought about it as his love for her diminished. Maybe he wanted this exact outcome so he could be finally rid of her. Maybe. And then he picked up her naked body and carried it down the stairs.

As the nighttime rain swelled into deep puddles on the grounds, and the storm sent shivers of thunder and bright illuminating lightning to paint the scene, Jonathon dug a large, deep hole in the back cemetery. The ground was very wet from the storm, so the digging was easy and went swiftly. First him, then her. He threw them together in one dirt- and worm-filled grave. Together on top of each other, embracing in death, so they could be one as they rotted.

He even tossed in her white nightgown, which had been discarded next to the bed. It had once enticed him, and it probably enticed her lover, but now it would be forever buried, never to entice another man again.

He left no grave marker on the mound of disturbed dirt. He left no trace of their death. He felt relieved. He would make up a story that she left him and returned to the bright lights of New York, bored in her life here, which, in essence, was true. He had all the money and power he needed from the knowledge she shared of future investments. He couldn't learn her powers; it wasn't something taught. It was something deeply embedded in her DNA. She was no further use to him. "Gypsy trash," "phony socialite," "cheating witch-whore." Gone from his life, forever. Or, so he thought.

Standing in the wind and rain, drenched and muddied, Jonathon felt like a new man. Like the man who was now the "god" that he always wanted to be. He faced the heaven above as rain splashed and danced on his face. A different face was illuminated by intermittent flashes of lightning. A twisted face filled with consuming insanity. He laughed loudly, mockingly, madly. But with all the power he had, and imagined he had, even a god has a devil to face.

There was one more detail to take care of.

In his tormented mind, there were only two words, two words he repeated over and over again. "The baby."

The freak baby that he hated, never called his son, and never looked at again after that fateful night when he held him in his arms for the first time and looked into his eyes. His "no eyes." His two deep, dark sockets where eyes should have been.

That was the first and only time he held him. With all his wealth, power, and social status, how could he even admit to the world, let alone to himself, that he created a freak. There was one thought, one enabling thought, that helped him with his constant grief. No, he didn't create the freak. His wife did, the "bitch-witch" did. And now, now it was time to set things right. With her out of his life and six feet under in a bug-filled dirt hole, it was time to take care of "it." To get rid of "it." No one would ever know, after all, "it" never left the house. So why shouldn't "it" die in the house, and then disappear like "its" recently departed, cheating mother.

Jonathon had spent the past year sleeping around the world in fancy hotels, with fancy women who came and went in his married, adulterated, traveling life. Women who were either bought and paid for, or women who just wanted to be seen with a man of his status. He may have cheated, but to know and see that his wife also cheated on him, that was an unpardonable crime she had to pay for. And she did.

With rain-soaked clothing and muddied shoes from his grave digging, Jonathon left a path of his footprints behind him on the first floor of the house and up the stairway he climbed. He went back up to the room where "it" slept. For the past year "it" had slept with her. "It" was even in the room when he found and killed them. He didn't care. "It" couldn't see the murder. "It" couldn't be a witness to the crime. "It" would be a victim itself.

He smiled as he re-entered the bedroom. The bitch-witch was gone, and now it was "its" turn.

He thought about smothering "it," or throwing "it" against the wall, or even down the stairs. But that would be too easy, and "it" wouldn't see itself suffer like it had made him suffer as a rich, powerful father with a weak, eyeless, freak son. He knew what he had to do, and it would be done in a way that he could be a part of it. Standing above the baby's crib with water dripping onto "it" from his wet rain-drenched clothes, he smiled again.

A bath to clean "its" little body. A bath to wash "its" empty eyes. A bath to drown "its" freaky soul. And all the while he could watch as he imagined the last few bubbles of breath being released from its lifeless little form. Bath night would be a fun night for Jonathon's twisted and demented mind.

While the water filled the tub inside the house, the storm outside began to rage once more. Maybe to add to the mood. After all, it had been an unexpected and somewhat delightful evening of death so far.

Jonathon knew that a few inches of bath water was enough for "it" to drown. He just wanted to make the temperature right so it wouldn't cry. He hated "its" cry. It reminded him that the little freak had no eyes to shed any tears.

It didn't take long to have the tub ready for the intended bath. It didn't take long to pick "it" up from the bedroom and bring "it" into the bathroom and place it in the water. It didn't take long for the water to cover the entire body of the freak baby as it started to kick and fuss. It didn't take long for all the little bubbles of breath to stop popping out of the water that "it" was completely submerged in. It didn't take long for "it" to die. And it didn't take long for the next moment to happen.

A sudden noise behind him, from the open doorway to the second-floor hallway, caught his attention. Startled, he turned away from the tub and looked. The darkened hallway was empty. And then he heard it again. Footsteps. Soft footsteps, not loud, hard footsteps like a man such as himself would make. No, soft footsteps. Like those of a barefooted woman. Barefooted, but leaving small puddles of dripping water with each step. Drips that made sounds like nails being pounded into a wooden coffin.

He went to the doorway and looked to the staircase. Empty. He looked down the hallway to his left. Empty. He looked down the hallway to his right. Empty.

No further footfalls on the stairs; no further sounds. Silence. A long, strange silence with only the background of the constant rain beating on the roof. Rhythmically, echoing above and now throughout. Raindrops making the sound of something else. Something that would haunt him the rest of his life. Something that would make his heart beat faster, and his body shiver with fear. Something else unexpected and impossible. A baby's cry.

Within his next breath, and before the next beat of his heart, he turned back to the bathtub from where the cries seemed to come. And they did. They came from inside the tub.

Fraught with a fear unknown to him, he slowly, cautiously, took one step, then two steps, then three towards the bathtub. Not close enough to see inside the tall, white porcelain tub, but closer to the crying sounds, which grew louder with each step.

And then it stopped.

As suddenly as the crying had begun, the crying suddenly stopped. And so did his heart for a beat or two, as from behind him he heard her voice. *Her* voice. A voice that he knew so well. Her voice that once said, "I do," and repeated the loving and cherished words "until death do us part." Her voice, calling his name. Softly, almost like in a song, long and beautiful. His name.

He wanted to turn to see her. He wanted to turn to look at her. He wanted to turn to know for sure. But he was afraid to. He was afraid of what he might see.

Was it his beautiful wife whom he had just buried, or, something else?

"Jonathon..." the voice called again softly and melodically.

His name was not said in anger for being murdered—or maybe not murdered. Just his name; his name being called gently, sweetly, softly, as if it came from the voice of beyond.

And then he turned.

Quickly and hurriedly. So fast that he almost fell on the slippery tiled bathroom floor, not only from his wet clothing, but also from the sweat in his mind.

And he saw her.

Standing there alone in the hallway, in her beautiful white nightgown. The same gown from their honeymoon, the same gown he had buried with her. She was beautiful, she was happy, she was smiling. And then she turned and was gone. Just like that. Like a momentary flash that passes in front of one's eyes. There, and gone. How this all played out in his fragile mind cannot be explained. Some things have no explanation, nor should they. Some things are meant to be left alone. But "some things" lead to a spiral of complete madness. An all-consuming madness.

The baby's crying started again.

It was the very next morning that a hired carpenter came to the Hellmark home for a job that was contracted and scheduled to start that day. It was a beautiful morning. The sun was shining, the overnight storm long gone—a bright crisp autumn day.

The mansion's large front door had been left open. A path of muddied footsteps remained, now frozen in time, caked into dried dirt memories across the wooden floor. The carpenter stood in the large open doorway and called out the house owner's name. It echoed throughout without a response. He merely thought that the owner may have stepped away and purposely left the door open for him to start his work.

Entering the house, he looked at the empty downstairs, waiting one more long moment before he would realize he was certainly alone, and he should probably start his work. As he stood amid the silence of the house, he unexpectedly felt a drop of something wet, perhaps cold water, fall across the top of his neck. Then a second, and a third. Each one sent a strange shiver through his body. The storm may have left a leak in the roof, so he casually looked up. The storm had left something much more.

A dead man.

Jonathon Hellmark.

Hanging from a bedsheet, attached to a beautiful, ornate chandelier that filled the space above, was a dead man with blood dripping from his mouth. His eyes wide open. His face turned blue. Whether it was from the wind that came from the open door, or something else, the chandelier was moving slowly in a circular motion as if it were a fun carousel ride in an amusement park. And it was, if one would call a ride to the depths of hell "fun."

And that is how he was found. Alone. Hanging from the giant chandelier—an expensive, majestic glass-

and-gold chandelier that was a crowning piece to the house as one entered the grand hallway and started up the grand staircase.

But that was not all.

Also heard was the faint, far-away sound of a crying baby.

Within days, the house was closed up, and left abandoned.

The body of Jonathon Hellmark was buried in the back cemetery next to his parents' graves and close to another secret grave that remained undiscovered.

In his will, there was a trust set up for his wife Amber. But she was never found. There was no mention of the baby boy, his son, their son, as he was never seen, or known to exist other than by the midwife. Some months later the midwife was seen in the nearby town caring for a young baby boy, a blind boy, born with an eye defect—born with no eyes. She claimed that the baby was hers and her husband's, the town's carpenter—the same carpenter who had entered the Hellmark house and discovered the hanging man. They called the boy Jonathon.

With no known heirs to his fortune, Hellmark House was placed in a special trust. There was plenty of maintenance money for the many expected years of support to keep it "alive." And it was. For year after year, the house stood alone, remaining as a memory, as a living monument, a living tomb to a man who would be a "god" in his own mind.

As years passed, rumors and stories started to whisper and live within the small town which harbored and watched over the vacant house. Or maybe the house watched them.

Some said the house was haunted. Some called it the "Hell House" after that shocking, and gruesome discovery of Jonathon Hellmark's mysterious hanging, and the brutal deaths of his father and mother. Rumors and strange stories grew and even became part of the area's lore or would-be legend. From time to time, and generation to generation, kids would pay no heed to the "Private Property Keep Out" signs and would come and stare in the house's dusty front windows. They would come looking for a glimpse of the chandelier, where once a dead man had hung. Some even tried to break into the locked house on different dares. But none ever did. There was always the same sound to scare them away. The sound of a baby crying.

It was even said that on the yearly autumn anniversary night of Jonathon Hellmark's tragic death, a mysterious unknown woman in white could be seen looking out of the upstairs bedroom window, peeking from behind the still-remaining window curtains. And, as the season changed and the approaching stormy winter wind howled, strange nightly sounds lingered around the house. Sounds that seemingly came from within the house. As if someone lived in the house. Some said they heard laughter, some said they heard crying, and some said they even heard screams coming from the house. Unearthly sounds to haunt one's dreams and make one's nightmares come to life.

It was now a house without a soul. It was a house of Ghosts.

Chapter 12

When Lancelot woke up abruptly in his bedroom, he thought that he had heard the sound of knocking on glass. At first, he thought it was from the large bedroom window which showed the early morning traces of daylight. But there was nothing to be seen.

Then he heard it again.

This time it came from inside the dresser mirror.

Initially to him, it seemed like another nightmare. His whole life had been a long, constant nightmare. But not this time, not this moment. This was real. Or as real as a nightmare can be.

Sitting up in bed, he could see that he was still fully dressed from last night. The mirror attached to the dresser was directly across the room from him. Staring at it, he had no immediate answer for what he saw. Nor did he have any answer as to how he had returned to his bedroom from his lingering memory of seeing himself in a casket. But the question of the mirror took immediate precedence as another series of loud knocks from within the glass mirror filled his room.

Whether it took a moment, or an eternity, time appeared to stand still as Lancelot approached the mirror with caution. Or, maybe, a hidden fear. There was no reflection from the mirror. It was all dark. And the further he looked into it, the darker it got. But in that darkness, something moved. Something that wasn't seen, but something that triggered his mind. Something that was looking at him, as he looked for it.

Putting his hand slowly to the surface of the mirror, the glass felt cold, very cold. Unusually cold, as the temperature in the room was somewhat comfortable. Not too warm; not too cold; just right. Just like in the *Three Bears* story he remembered hearing in his childhood, a silly story that once made him laugh. "Not too warm; not too cold; just right." A reference he even used in one of his classic horror novels when describing a dead body. But at this moment, right now, there would be no laughter. The mirror wasn't right. It was all wrong. Just another wrong to everything he felt from first stepping into this house.

Moving his hand across the mirror from side to side, then top to bottom, the degree of coldness from within seemed to change. It was coldest in the center, the exact center where his reflection would have been. Instead, there was still no image, just reflected darkness. But darkness holds no reflection, and sometimes it shows the real truth.

Turning his head to the left and then to the right, his hand on the mirror's surface felt the cold which followed his unseen movement. He stepped back, thinking, reflecting on what he had just seen, or didn't see, and then the darkness in the mirror slowly changed. Changed into an image which slowly came into view.

Inside the mirror he now saw a little boy, maybe eight years old, his mid-length hair neatly in place, expressionless, with closed eyelids. His face was there, his shoulders were there, nothing else; the darkness remained behind him. When Lancelot moved his head forward to look closer, the boy's head mirrored his movement and followed, as if looking back at him. But the little boy's eyes remained closed. *"How could he see and mimic what I'm doing?"* Lancelot thought to himself. *"Is this some illusion, some mind trick that Janek set up?"* He pondered even more while trying to find reason in what appeared to be a non-existing reality.

Without hesitation, Lancelot held his left hand up above his head. So did the little boy in the mirror. Again, with closed eyelids. The boy did the same motion as Lancelot when he brought his arm back down. *"This is just my subconscious, nothing more,"* Lancelot mused to himself. Finally, Lancelot closed his eyes as if to make the image go away and make everything right. He closed his eyes to hide in the dark lonely corners of his mind as he had so many times before. But this darkness had no corners to hide in, and when he finally, slowly, opened his eyelids, the boy in the mirror did, too. But the image from within did not reflect the image from without. The boy in the mirror had no eyes, just two dark sockets where eyes should have been.

How long Lancelot stood staring at the young boy in the mirror didn't matter. What mattered was what happened next. Lancelot's hand reached out to the image, and the image reached back to him. Their fingers touched and seemed to dance together, as Lancelot and the eyeless boy moved their fingers across, and up and down the mirror, slowly, quickly, connected. In doing so, Lancelot felt a twinge of something odd, like something being unhinged or unlocked in his mind. Now, even in that moment, he wondered if this was the devil himself who had come to look upon him, to mock him, to claim him, like something he would write in one of his own horror stories. But he wasn't writing a story; he was living a story. So was the thing in the mirror.

Stepping back away from the mirror for the first time since the boy's image appeared, the boy did not reflect Lancelot's same movement. Instead, the eyeless boy smiled. A strange smile, filled with irony, or maybe something more, like he knew something more, something more which would remain a secret. As the boy's smile widened, his image slowly began to fade away, reminding Lancelot of another of his childhood recollections—the Cheshire cat's smile in *Alice in Wonderland.* For a moment he felt like the character of Alice, lost in a world he also wanted no part of, but curious to know more.

The young boy's image faded not back into the darkness of the black mirror from which it had come, but into the real image of what the room and Lancelot looked like when standing staring into it. Lingering inside the mirror as everything changed, the silence in the room was replaced with the faint sound of a baby crying. Very faint, and growing distant, from inside the mirror, and then finally ending.

Lancelot stood quietly staring at the mirror for a long time. A silence that felt even more terrifying as it became a silence of a long-lost memory he held within. A memory about his childhood terrors, how as a little boy he would awaken in the vast, dark lonely night alone—listening—looking—trembling—because something in the darkness was making sounds. Alone again, his image stared back, and finally asked him a question, "How do you bury a shadow?" And he slowly smiled back. He already knew the answer.

* * * * *

When Lancelot came downstairs, he assumed he'd find Janek either in the main parlor or the kitchen area. He had passed his bedroom door and it was open and the bed was completely made, or maybe never slept in. There was no answer when he called out his name. However, once downstairs, he found the house empty. The fire in the parlor fireplace where they had met the night before had long died out. There was a strange coldness to the room. He even saw his breath as he exhaled. It reminded him of the coldness he felt when he touched the dresser mirror, or when he was in the mysterious crypt with the two caskets. From what he could see, there were no open windows or areas from which a draft might blow. The room was just oddly cold. Colder than the rest of the house he had walked through.

In the kitchen, there was no trace of Janek having eaten breakfast. Nor was there an empty or partially filled coffee cup to show that he had once been here. Then again, maybe he didn't drink coffee. Lancelot hardly knew anything about his personal habits. From what he read, there wasn't much known about him except that Janek was a critically acclaimed author, and he was not. That ate at him, not only as it had in the past before this prearranged little writing pow-wow was agreed to, but more so now as he was about to begin work with the man he hated.

While making his coffee, which he needed most mornings after his many repeated nights of accustomed drinking and his other passions of debauchery, he heard the front door of the house creak open.

"How appropriate," he chuckled to himself. "A creaking door. Adds to the rest of this place."

From his viewpoint in the kitchen, he saw Janek slowly walk through the entrance hallway and towards the parlor with the use of a shiny, ornate, silver cane. There was something about the cane that caught his attention. Something unique and unusual. Yet something familiar. He watched as Janek put the cane next to his armchair where he sat comfortably.

Deciding it was time to start the writing journey that had brought them there, and the private journey he had planned to do after the writing, Lancelot quietly entered the parlor.

"Good morning, Janek. I take it you were enjoying a nice morning walk? Or, perhaps returning from a long midnight stroll." Lancelot greeted him without any emotion, but with the intent of getting close enough to see Janek's silver cane. It was topped with a strange looking metal die-cast image of a wolf's head. A wolf's head with a half-opened mouth as if it were baring its fangs. And on the tip of the metal fangs, there was a trace of something wet, something dark red.

Janek's eyes locked on Lancelot's eyes as he purposely moved his cane from one side of his chair to the other. He remained silent, emotionless, for a long moment before replying.

"I hope you had a good night's sleep. A restful sleep so we can begin our work. Waking from a nightmare is never a good way to start the day, wouldn't you agree?"

"Depends on the nightmare. Sometimes they can be exciting and mysterious," Lancelot replied politely and assuredly.

"And sometimes they can be foreboding and chilling." Janek punctuated his comment with a sardonic tone.

Silence remained between them as Lancelot sat across from him, same as the night before. The distance was mere feet apart, but measured in animosity, more miles than one could imagine.

Janek let out a deep, contemplating breath. There was no indication of the chill in the air as when

Lancelot let out a breath moments before, or even as it continued now around him.

"*How strange,*" he thought to himself and merely shrugged it off as another oddity of the house.

Janek closed his eyes momentarily, then continued.

"Did you ever wonder where nightmares come from? Those frightening dreams that pounce on us out of darkness when we are in a dream state ever so vulnerable, ever so close to the edge of our own death in it?"

"Actually, I relish nightmares. I use them in my writing, don't you?" Lancelot answered smugly.

"Or maybe they use you?" Janek quietly added.

Lancelot again let out a visible breath to which Janek paid no attention, or if he did, paid no care.

"Do we dare follow our nightmares to their source, where evil lurks and awaits us? Should we risk our very life and search for the truth that nightmares hide? Are we afraid of our nightmares or do we look forward to them?" Janek continued as if a sermon from someone who once experienced every word he spoke and now directed his speech directly at his congregation of one.

"Nightmares don't bother me," Lancelot quickly replied with an air of self-righteousness. "They are just that. A dream we harbor for unknown reasons. They have been blamed on meals, too much stress, subconscious anxiety, or a thousand and one other excuses. As I said, I am not afraid of my nightmares. Are you?"

Janek slowly leaned forward in his chair lessening the void between them and whispered his response, "The real question is, are you afraid of the dark?"

Lancelot slapped his arms together as if to indicate the chill of the room without acknowledging the reference Janek had made. This question bothered him, especially after the strange occurrence in the mirror. He could feel how the words the older man spoke were definitely an attempt to affect the fragile balance of an already cold relationship between them.

"Would you like to begin our writing here? Or would you prefer the surroundings of the study? Perhaps the warmth of the study would be better for your blood, I mean, your circulation," Lancelot said as a quip with intent, and inflection on the word "blood," as he watched a drop of the wet, red liquid fall gradually from the wolf's open mouth atop the silver cane.

Janek knowingly covered the cane's image with both hands as he brought it in front of himself.

"How kind of you to ask. I never concern myself as to the comfort of where to write, but more to the matter of what to write. Is that how you approach your work?"

"Actually, I work better when I'm comfortable. Sometimes after a glass of wine, preferably red wine." He paused and laughed to himself with the reference of "red" wine as he watched the red blood drop from the cane finally land silently on the floor. "Sometimes after an entertaining evening. An evening of unknown adventures that I can use and apply to my work. The unknown always makes me feel better inside and out. Let's just say it soothes my body. Unfortunately, I haven't warmed up to this place yet."

"Perhaps it hasn't warmed up to you."

"Perhaps," Lancelot said complacently. "But I'm sure it's just a matter of time. Everything is a matter of time. Isn't it? His lips curled in an expression of contempt. He had a writer's device of peppering his conversations with rhetorical questions, and then observing the person he was talking to for any telling reaction—a smile, a frown, a shifting of the eyes.

Janek offered none, nor did he reply. He quietly placed his cane to the side of his chair.

Lancelot finally continued.

"Being such a critically acclaimed author as I've heard you are, I'm fascinated by your imagination, Janek. Is that what makes your stories come to life?"

"Imagination is for children. I write from the soul."

Lancelot grinned. "Nice to know you have one, or, make that, 'believe' in one. As a fellow writer, I'm sure you must know that it's been written many times that a soul defines the man who wears it. Or...drives a man who doesn't have one."

There was no reply from Janek. He knew how word games were played, and how they sometimes played out. It was a style that some writers use when seeking an underlying truth or hiding an obvious fear.

After another seemingly unbearable pause, he deliberately reached for his silver cane again, and tightly wrapped both his hands around the wolf's head handle. Janek calmly leaned forward with his eyes locked on Lancelot's and asked, "What makes your books come to life?"

"Me." Lancelot punctuated his answer with a slight grin.

Again, there was no reply to his remark. Nor would there be. Just another moment of growing cold silence.

Unusual as it was, as conceited as it might be, Janek knew there was an ominous truth buried deep inside that one simple word.

Using both his hands to rub the room's coldness from his upper body, Lancelot broke the continued silence. "I suggest we go to the study; it might be a better place to begin." With those words, Lancelot got up from his chair and waited for Janek's answer.

"Of course, but...we have already begun, haven't we?" Janek replied cynically.

Walking to the study, Lancelot followed closely behind. He wasn't thinking of the writing to be done, but rather of the cane that Janek used. His mind was preoccupied with not so much where he got the cane, but how?

Large, painted portraits of, first, a serious-looking man of middle age and then, a smiling woman—a beautiful, young woman in a white wedding gown, similar to the painting above the parlor fireplace— adorned the otherwise stark wood-paneled hallway walls.

No names or dates were attached underneath the paintings, but from the look of the old, dusty canvas, and the style of their clothing and hair, they were from a long time past. Lancelot considered that they were probably former occupants of this old grand house, maybe the original owners. Janek paid no interest to these paintings, but something drew Lancelot's attention to both, especially the woman's portrait. Her eyes almost seemed to follow him as he passed by, as if she were alive. *"Of course,"* he mused to himself. *"Just another oddity of this already strange house."*

Three walls of the study had floor-to-ceiling, built-in wooden bookcases, each filled from top to bottom. Dust covered them as it was quite apparent no one had recently read a book there, let alone picked out a book in many years. From Lancelot's first glance, there appeared to be a lot of first editions, or books at least 100 years old. But he wasn't there to read a book or savor a book. He hardly ever did. He never even read his own books once they were written. The stories and characters he created were all buried within them like miniature caskets which he preferred to leave unopened. He contemplated whether Janek did the same when he completed his books. It didn't matter. What they were going to write together would be the last book he would ever do.

The remaining wall in the large room had a near floor-to-ceiling-sized multi-pained window, artistically carved in place. It let in the mid-morning daylight, which seemed to emit a golden glow in a long-angled ray of sun while allowing the room's dusty air to float around them. The overall feeling of the room was much warmer than the cold Lancelot had felt in the parlor. There was no visible breath of his in this room's air, only an inner coldness that permeated through his blood as he studied the older man.

Janek stood by the window staring outward, perhaps into another world other than the one that touched the house. With eyes locked on him, Lancelot decided to sit. His youthful body sat perfectly in an old wooden swivel chair next to a large, flat-topped mahogany table in the middle of the room. There were some pens, some paper, an old carnival-glass-shaded wooden lamp, and a large black typewriter neatly placed on it. Across from him, on the other side of the table was another chair, one that didn't swivel like his. Resembling a master chess player waiting for the match to begin, Lancelot claimed his position, settled in, and now waited for Janek to be seated. He wondered if Janek remained quiet purposely to assert himself as being the one in control. Lancelot knew differently. He was in control, as his plan began to unfold.

Lancelot broke the stillness of the room and spoke first.

"So, without the internet at our disposal, and being in such a remote place, I've been told we have to use an old typewriter for our work." Lancelot chuckled. "How archaic is that? I have a hand-recorder to use for notes or discussions, but an old typewriter?"

Janek turned from the window and stood in quiet response. The lighting from the window seemed to give him an ethereal glow. "It will do. Actually, it's all I use."

"No computer, laptop, or any state-of-the-art electronic devices?"

Janek left the sunlight and sat in the chair across from him as if in an interrogation setting. Accused against an interrogator. An interrogator against the accused.

"Fascinating tools for children to play with, but not part of my life. I only need paper and a pen to write words. But since it is here, a typewriter will do."

"Well, that settles that. You can do the typing," Lancelot declared.

"I already have," Janek replied dryly.

"Excuse me?" Lancelot said with a surprised look.

"From last night's conversation, I took the story we discussed and started to put it together early this morning before my walk."

"The story?" Lancelot reacted as if caught off guard and off his game plan.

Janek leaned back in his chair, still holding his cane in one hand. He moved it slightly to and fro while answering.

"Yes, the story we spoke about—how two writers who are forced to work together in an old house, a haunted house, have the task of writing the greatest horror story ever. Isn't that what we agreed on?"

"Hmm." Lancelot paused to think of how he should reply, but already knew his response. "Yes, a clever idea. Especially since that is exactly what we are here to do."

"Then it should be easy to write," Janek confirmed.

"Yes, because the story is about us."

"About us..." Janek replied, looking directly at Lancelot with a cold stare, lingering before continuing, "...and what we plan to do to each other."

"Or, perhaps what this house plans to do to us," Lancelot added while leaning forward and placing one hand on the table while tapping his fingers. Staring back at Janek, his nails, sharply manicured as if he just stepped out of a spa, tapped rhythmically, repeatedly, resonating an echoing sound in the overall silence between them.

"Yes, of course, this house. It will certainly play a major part in our story. Its history probably holds a lot of forbidden secrets, wouldn't you agree?"

"And our story will reveal those secrets. A good horror story always begins with a secret. As a writer, 'hidden secrets' are always a good beginning, a pathway to take our reader on a journey of discovery."

"Or a discovery of horror," Janek commented.

"Plenty of horror," Lancelot added.

"Yes. Plenty of horror," Janek stated as he again stared directly into the eyes of the younger writer.

Like a game of chess, both their expressions indicated an unspoken word simultaneously. "Checkmate."

Lancelot smiled in agreement. Janek remained expressionless.

"So, with this storyline we agreed on, and a beginning with a secret, perhaps sharing one of our own personal secrets, do you have any ending in mind?" Lancelot asked not as just a question, but more of wanting to know what Janek really intended.

"Somewhat," Janek paused before revealing more. "The story begins and ends...with us."

Lancelot was not amused with the answer but didn't show his feelings. As a writer, he knew how to disguise such feelings in a choice of words. Since the moment they met and shared their first conversation, the words and answers they each used were seemingly both a paradox and a puzzle.

"Interesting... I also have an ending in mind," Lancelot finally replied.

"Then we should discuss both our endings and then pick the one where perhaps someone lives, and perhaps someone dies. That is always a good way to end a horror story, and once agreed on the ending, we should write the final ending together," Janek countered, and then continued, "especially...when the time is appropriate."

"As we write it?" Lancelot asked ominously.

Janek finally changed his expression from the same serious face he had portrayed throughout the entire conversation to a singularly cold little smile. A momentary smile, resembling childlike wonder while masking a pent-up hatred.

"Perhaps...or...maybe, as we live it."

Chapter 13

Her first words were spoken half with a smile, half with a serious tone.

"You're not afraid, are you?"

His reply held no smile, just a look of concern.

"No...but...okay, so I am a bit. Okay."

"Really?"

"Yeah, well, now that we're almost there, I didn't want to say that, but, yeah, I'm not feeling right about this. So yeah, I'm sort of afraid."

"Sort of? Oh, come on. Don't be. We'll have fun."

"Fun? People have said they heard things, saw things."

"Oooohhh. Like spooky things that go bump in the night?"

"Stop it! You're freaking me out. You're kinda scaring me."

"Uhh, yeah, that's what tonight is all about, sissy boy, to see if we really get scared. And besides, you're supposed to be the big, brave boy, my hero, my protector. Aren't you?"

"Yeah, well...maybe we shouldn't be doing this."

"Stop acting like you didn't want to come with me. We've planned this. You promised me. And you know what I promised we'd do in there for coming with me. So, don't go and freak out and pretend you're already scared. We're almost there. Besides..." She paused and gave him a sexy look.

"Hey...I just have...have a bad feeling about this. Okay. I know why we planned this...but...I'm having second thoughts. I don't know if we really should be doing it there."

"Uhh...hello! Of course we should, because you're just as curious as me."

"Yeah, but. But breaking into a house?"

"A haunted house."

"Right, yeah, a haunted house. We've all heard the stories."

"The legends. The folktales. The whispers in the night."

"Uh huh, all those. Can't we just say we did, but don't."

"And not see the ghosts?"

The word "ghosts" seemed to drift silently in the air between the two of them as they stood looking at the huge old house and then back to each other. They stood close enough to kiss, and they did. A short peck on the lips initiated by her, and then she playfully pushed him back, slightly away from her. The type of fun, joking "push" teenagers do to each other. After all, they were teenagers, and teenagers do daring things.

Her one hand pushed the long blonde windblown hair back off the one side of her face. Her brown eyes seemed to glisten from the early moonlight. Letting out a half laugh, she shook her head slightly while showing a playful smile.

"Well, I kinda thought you might be afraid of a big, bad wolf or maybe the three little piggies. Oink, oink. But afraid of see-through ghosts?"

He was embarrassed, and it began to show in his flushed, red face. Even though he had an athletic built from being one of the top high school jocks, his toned body still gave a slight shiver, whether from the damp evening air, or the thoughts of what they might be getting themselves into.

"Come on, Kim, enough's enough. There are no such things. Let's just find another place to do it."

"Going to chicken out? You can if you want to, Billy, but I'm going inside," Kim replied, now with a bit of pent-up frustration and anger mixed together. Her decision was made; it was now his decision to make.

Looking into her eyes in the final fading sunlight, Billy felt a new fear added to the old one. She was obsessed with doing this. Ever since they started dating a year ago, she constantly talked about ghost stories. It was her obsession; she was fascinated with ghosts. Always reading ghost books, watching ghost movies, and now, here they were, finally, as if a dream-come-true to her, and a possible nightmare to him, which he wanted to stop right then and there. Breaking and entering a haunted house and looking for ghosts was one thing. But it was her 18th birthday, and he had made a promise. That's why they were here. And he didn't know how to back out of his promise, especially with her promise.

The sunlight was almost gone now.

"Okay, so...uh, how about, maybe, we come back tomorrow and do this in the daylight?"

He bit his lip and waited for a response that "she agreed" to his compromise and would make all his queasiness go away. That response never came. Instead, she gently leaned forward and kissed him seductively on the lips, eyes looking into his eyes, while taking his hand in hers.

"Come on, Billy. We're here now. Let's do it now!"

Standing in the overgrown grassy yard that connected with the field they had just walked through, they paused momentarily, thinking it over, each taking a deep breath while looking up at the old mansion. Her smile told him, and all the world, how excited she was to be there. To him, the excitement was all hers. Even though the house seemed far more sinister now in the early darkness, her smile seemed to melt his fear away. She knew his answer. He knew it, too.

The sun finally disappeared from the horizon. The first full moon of the autumn month ominously took its place in the night sky above. They were in the mansion's family graveyard, approaching the large house from one side. The smell of fall decay and old, damp, dirt-filled ageless graves seemed to saturate the air. A chilly breeze suddenly sprang up, although the day had been mildly hot and airless for late autumn. The breeze seemed to draw a long-sustained moan from the surrounding gravestones. It raised the hair on the back of Billy's neck; it made Kim smile even more.

"This is so cool! We're really going in a haunted house! A real, freakin' haunted house!" Kim grew more excited by the moment.

Seeing her happy smile tugged at his heartstrings and helped him overcome his last apprehensions. He was "head-over-heels" in love with her and would do just about anything to please her. Of course, this moment of her joy, for all its eerie feelings, was all that was needed to seal the deal for him.

"Okay. Okay. You win." Billy nodded his head with the last vestige of his hesitation. "Let's go find your ghosts."

With a halfhearted, but fully sincere smile, he put his arm around her as they moved cautiously forward through the grassy backyard towards the looming house. The evening shadows and patches of darkness kept them somewhat hidden as they walked. Coming through the surrounding woods and arriving there had been almost too easy. There was really nothing to be scared of—it was just an old, empty house. And, of course, he wouldn't want to chicken out now after all her anticipation, and his, too, especially when she had promised him an evening to remember.

Unexpectedly, something at the house suddenly caught their attention and made them stop.

A light.

A single white light was suddenly turned on inside the house, on the second floor.

They stopped in their tracks and he squeezed her hand tightly. Both their gazes remained on the upstairs light in the house. Nothing seemed to move in that room. There was just a stark white illumination from within.

"Uhh, isn't this place supposed to be empty? It's an abandoned house, right?" Billy cautiously asked the question to both Kim and himself.

Puzzled for a moment, it was Kim who found an answer...so she thought.

"It must be one of those lights set on a timer. They go on and off automatically. We have one in our home. My mom is always changing the timer as the day gets darker earlier. It pisses her off when she forgets."

Billy nodded tentatively to her comment.

"Yeah, of course." Kim continued to assure him, and maybe herself. "With all the 'No Trespassing' signs and the house being abandoned, there must be some automatic security lights that go on and off to scare people away."

"Yeah, well, what if there's a security alarm system, too?" he added in a last-minute attempt to make Kim give up on their "plan," turn around and leave.

As they stood staring at the second-floor window, Kim contemplated his comment. Unsure of what the real answer was, she was not going to let an unexpected "possibility" spoil her night.

"Hmm. I don't think so. The place is too old, probably wouldn't have the high-tech wiring for a security system. I've seen movies where fake security signs and cameras are set up to scare people away. I betcha there's no security system," she replied confidently.

Billy still looked for an out. Sure, her promise of romantic fun once inside the house brought him here, but now...?

"Yeah, but, if there is, and alarms go off..."

"We run," Kim quickly blurted out before he could say anymore. "We just run away. There's no police for miles, and it would take them forever to drive out here. We won't get caught. No one even knows we're here."

Batting her pretty brown eyes to complement her naughty teen smile, she squeezed his hand assuredly. "Come on, Billy, we're close to meeting some ghosts."

Although Kim seemed convinced of everything she said, Billy still wavered and wasn't totally satisfied with her explanation. His mind wasn't on ghosts. He didn't even believe in them, ever, or even now. His mind was on just one thing. Sex. He came here with her promise of having sex. Going inside the would-be haunted house and deflowering her in front of the imaginary ghosts that she hoped to see was fine by him. And if there were really ghosts in there, hey, they could watch as he planned to put on quite a show. Just like in a horror movie, the young, beautiful virgin is held captive by monsters until he, the hero in his fantasy, rescues her and gets rewarded with a hot romp in a king-sized bed, or bare, wooden floor. End movie. That's all he thought about for several days since she came up with this idea. Role playing of her being held captive and having sex in a haunted house.

It was actually her idea to finally go "all the way" after a year of only allowing him doing the typical teenage ritual of "first base, second base, you're out!" Now, with sex consuming his thoughts, his concerns of breaking and entering a storied property such as this that had so many "No Trespassing" signs and now a lone light in an upstairs window, began to fade away. *"But, hey,"* he thought to finally convince himself, *"if we got caught, it would just make me a big-time hero to my small-town jealous guy friends."*

He nodded his head to himself.

"I'm going to peek through the first-floor windows to see if the coast is clear." Kim broke the silence and laid out the next steps in the plan for both of them. "You stay here and keep an eye on the light in the upstairs window to see if anyone is really there."

"Uhh, maybe I should go with you. I don't think it's safe to split up. I mean..." Billy half-heartedly protested.

"Really, jeez, now what are you afraid of? The dark? We're under a full moon tonight. Look around. You have enough light to read a book," she replied defiantly.

"Yeah, that's perfect. Just what I want to do. Read a book." He rolled his eyes in anxious disbelief of what he was saying and maybe to bring a moment of levity to the immediate thought of being left alone.

"Get a grip!" he thought to himself. *"She's right."* There was enough moonlight to keep him protected from the darkness of the forest and the strange shadows that seemed to move from the wind in the

surrounding nearly bare tree branches. All that bogeyman stuff was just make-believe and for scary movies. He laughed at himself for admitting and showing that he was afraid. Conflicted maybe. But scared?

It had been almost an hour since Billy and Kim left their nearby town and drove there with plenty of planned time before dark. They had both grown up in, lived in, and would probably die in their small local town. Just another typical rural town which was a homemade prison for generations of people who had no ambitions. Just nice folks who grew up, had families, and watched them eventually take their place.

Their ride there was 15 miles of winding mountain roads filled with desolate-looking forests shedding their final leaves in a season-ending emptiness. On the drive there, he had to fight hard to contain his smile. Tonight's date was better, much better, than paying for an overpriced birthday gift dinner in the town's only restaurant, a not-so-classy bar and grill. After all, he hardly made enough money each week as a part-time stock boy in the small town's lone mini mart. So why not a date to a haunted house? The evening would cost him nothing but the couple of bucks of gas to get there and back. And, he did sneak a small screw-capped bottle of wine out of the store, tucking it safely in his backpack right next to the box of condoms he bought and waited to use for longer than he could remember.

They had spent several evenings planning out this entire secret adventure. She knew of an old, abandoned road close to the house where they had intended to leave his car hidden and unnoticed. It was a hardly used dirt road that led to an old barn on a neighboring, empty property. From there, it would just be a short walk through the surrounding woods. Their planned approach to the old house was perfect to keep their arrival quiet and private.

After parking in a large, dense-covered bushy area, and before beginning their walk to the house, the birthday girl showed her excitement and previewed her intentions to him immediately, suddenly kissing him quite deeply while rubbing her hand firmly across the crotch of his pants. He had wanted more right then and there, but she was just teasing his sexual hunger and signaling hers. Kim had been doing that for a year now. But tonight, tonight was finally the night! He, too, was a virgin, and although hesitant at first to come to the house, he relished her plan to lose their virginity together, as the perfect, unbelievable, ultimate birthday gift idea for her, and of course, an extra present for him. His insatiable teenage desires overcame any rational reasons as why not to.

Billy suddenly snapped awake from his fantasy.

He had a strange feeling and was sure that "something" was watching him. His gaze slipped around the boundaries of the small backyard cemetery and into the dense lifeless woods bordering it. But there was nothing. Nothing but silence and the intermittent soft wind that stroked his face.

Letting out a deep breath to slow his sudden racing heart and return to some state of normal, drops of perspiration started to roll downwards across his youthful face. He tried to calm himself by saying he was just imagining things; he was hyped up on the excitement that he would be soon having sex. He already had felt the "on and off" feelings from his waiting manhood.

Feeling safe from his imagination, his mind again found other things to think about while he waited for Kim's return. He recalled how they had approached their final destination from the woods and through the overgrown field to the far left. No one had seen them because no one lived within miles. And when they eventually would leave, no one would know that they had disturbed the grounds.

Kim brought her cell phone to get a picture if they saw a ghost but cursed herself for not charging it more as its battery life was limited, plus there was no Wi-Fi service in this remote part of the area. All she needed, wanted, and had to have was just one picture. Her and a ghost. It would be the icing on her birthday date, adding to her "becoming a woman" with her first taste of all the sex bases covered with her first sexual partner. And if there were no ghosts, or spooky spirits, or supernatural happenings, maybe this visit, once and for all, would change her young curious mind into seeing the phoniness of it all. Billy relished the "cherry" on her proverbial birthday cake, her cherry, and his, as, in reality, he planned to have a lot of sweet "cake" that night.

An unknown sound disturbed his daydreaming.

Was it a footstep on an old dead tree branch on the ground, or something that scraped against one of the old gravestones that stood close by? He rolled his eyes and smirked to himself. Most likely it was just Kim returning from her reconnaissance around the house.

Billy's quick look went around the edges of the tilted gravestones, not expecting to see ghosts, which he knew would not be there. Actually, he didn't know what to expect. He saw nothing at first and then suddenly took a short jump backward almost knocking himself over. The fierce tiny red eyes of a scavenger field mouse, or maybe a hungry rat scampered by his feet. He let out a brief, sarcastic chuckle.

And then he saw him.

In the upstairs window, the one filled with light, there now stood a man. With the light coming from inside the room and behind him, and the distance between them, Billy couldn't see his face. He was just a silhouette. Standing rigid, not moving. Just standing, staring out at him.

Billy's mind raced with a dozen different scenarios. It couldn't be a real person could it? It was just his overworked imagination; it was a mannequin, or a life-sized blow-up doll put there to scare people away. It was just a shadow from something else. Something else. Yet, it had to be a man; what else could it be?

Billy's eyes turned from the upstairs window to see where Kim was. But he could not find her in a quick turn towards either side of the house. He then looked to the shadows hugging the back of the house. Again, no Kim.

"Shit!" he muttered out loud to himself and to the haunting cold night while he shook his head trying to figure out what to do.

She was nowhere to be seen.

She must have still been at the front of the house. He wanted to run to her to tell her what he had seen, but he didn't want to leave his position. He wasn't sure if the man in the window could actually see him. And he didn't want to chance a movement and give himself away. He held his breath and stood still. He didn't move at all. Neither did the mysterious man in the window.

Billy's mind raced with both thoughts of Kim and what to do next. He cursed his situation again.

Out of his sight, Kim was cautiously looking through the front windows of the old house. It was dark inside, totally dark except for the moonlight that let some light in through the large windows. All she could see was rooms of furniture, some covered in sheets, untouched. Others uncovered. Just lots of furniture and shadows and darkness. Nothing else. It appeared empty of any life.

Through another window she saw a room which appeared to be some sort of library. Lots of books, from ceiling to floor. Standing calmly by herself, her young mind didn't have any trepidation of being caught, it merely wondered if, once inside the house, there were some old books with ghost stories that maybe she could sort of borrow, permanently. Her eyes marveled at all the old books. With make-believe images of candy canes and sugar plums dancing excitedly in her head as she stared at all the wonderful books, she did not see the typewriter on the table in the middle of the room, the stack of paper, or the empty cup of coffee next to an empty wine glass.

Moving quietly across the long, slightly rotted, wooden front porch that wrapped part way around the old house, she approached the tall, front-entrance wooden door. She stood silently for a long moment before gradually reaching for the metal door handle. If it triggered an alarm, she was prepared to run and find Billy in the back of the house and then run some more. If it opened, she'd go back and get Billy and they'd be able to go inside without breaking a window, as they had previously discussed.

It was locked. And there was no alarm that went off when she tried to push it open.

"Damn." Her whispered voice was simultaneously drowned out in the growing wind as she tried it again.

"Would have been too easy," she thought to herself. *"Looks like Plan B, breaking a window."*

Thinking her investigation of "look, see, and didn't see" satisfied her concern if there was an alarm system to contend with, or maybe seeing someone else surprisingly in the house at this late hour, she casually came down the crumbling front concrete steps to return to the back of the house and check out any other possible entrance, and report back to Billy.

Along with the increasing wind, making low whistling sounds across the house and overgrown property grounds, a few dried leaves left untouched from the previous night's storm made dying, crunching sounds with each of her steps. Kim's mind raced with her anxious thoughts of how it wouldn't be much longer before they'd be in the house, looking for her ghosts and losing her virginity. A happy smile spread across her face; it was all coming together as she imagined.

Then she saw it.

Before returning to the backyard where she left Billy, she suddenly saw it. Whatever it was, she didn't know.

Approaching her rapidly in odd animal-like leaps was a large, shadow-like creature. Very large. The size of a lion, or maybe bigger. But, of course, this was not a lion, this was something horribly unrecognizable, something coming right at her with a low rumbling growl. Whatever it was, leapt upon her quickly before her voice could let out a scream. The thing's glowing red eyes contemplated the pleasures yet to come as it sunk its slobbering fangs deep into her terrified face.

In the darkness where Billy still stood, he thought he had seen Kim standing at the back edge of the house. And in the deafening silence from where he stood, with only the damp wind protecting him, he also thought he saw something big and husky move between the shadows of the trees and gravestones towards her. Something hunched over so that it could hide and maybe mock him and his fear. He shut his eyes, refusing to believe it. His eyes were playing tricks on him. When he forced them open again, Kim was gone. Gone! He didn't see her anymore. And so was whatever-else he thought he saw. He let out a deep, long breath.

"What the...?" he muttered into the increasing wind.

Maybe it wasn't her, maybe it was just his imagination, his mind tried to convince him.

But it didn't.

He quickly did a 360 turn to look for her.

Nothing.

He stood alone. Alone under the spell of a full moon in the presence of a haunted house.

All he could do was call out her name.

"Kim."

No answer. Just silence.

And then he called it again, "Kim."

Again, there was no answer. More silence. An alarming suspicion began to form within his fear-filled mind. *"Where was she?"*

He called her name one more time, louder. He didn't care if the mysterious man in the window heard him or not.

Again, as before, no answer.

"Where the fuck is she?" His mind raced in turmoil. She had to be playing a game. She loved to play games. She loved to scare people, and right now, she was scaring him. Maybe that was her intention all night, just to bring him here, scare him and leave him on the metaphorical teenage third base without sex.

"Damn her," his mind wanted to yell out loud. He had enough of all of this. Promised sex or no sex. More

cold perspiration rolled across his face. His hands became clammy. His body took on a strange chill like he never felt before.

The wind stopped. Everything seemed to stop.

There was only an eerie silence.

Then, silence no more.

Suddenly, something touched his shoulder and he cried in fear and jumped forward.

There was a sound now—a low growl, the heavy, measured inhale and exhale of a mammoth pair of lungs, breathing down on his bare neck. Frozen in place, Billy felt the breath as not being warm as if from Kim, or any other earthly person who could be doing this. No, the breath was ice cold.

As suddenly as it had started, it suddenly stopped. Whatever it was, whatever it could be, it was apparently gone. A cold unknowing chill made his body tremble.

Letting out a long deep breath, Billy gradually turned to look behind him. But it wasn't gone. It was still there. Still there waiting for him. From his own height of nearly six feet tall, Billy had to look upward at it. The thing that stood before him was taller than any man he had ever seen. Its head was bent as if placed on a misshapen twisted neck. It wore torn and tattered clothes, as if it had just ripped out of them and now the remnants hung loosely on its huge frame. Its entire body and face were covered with a mat of damp furry hair. Its shoulders, more than a yard across, rippled with muscles.

A long foul-smelling drool came from its sneering mouth. It had a face that was almost human, half man, half animal, all monster.

Billy felt his one lone scream choke in his throat, unable to exit his open mouth. Blood red eyes stared directly at him as he stared at the folds of flesh that was the thing's face. It deliberately opened its mouth and closed it, as if it were laughing at him, enjoying a sudden unexpected joke that only they shared. Huge, pointed animal fangs revealed themselves as if savoring its cornered prey. It turned its head back and forth ever so slightly, ever so slowly as if to smell him, twisting its grotesque face closer and closer to him. From its huge hairy body emerged the smell of freshly turned earth and rotted flesh. Billy could not believe what he faced. His traumatized mind turned upside down as his only words stayed stuck in his head and reverberated with the thoughts this could not be, such things could not exist. No, this could not be, but it certainly was. This was a werewolf—a real live werewolf.

There would be no sound, no scream from him, as Billy was scared frozen from the watchful gaze of those terrible bright red eyes.

He saw nothing again, nor heard anything ever again, as a mighty sweep of the monster's powerful right claw quickly slashed across his face, tearing it half apart.

As suddenly as it began, it suddenly ended.

As the monster dragged away Billy's lifeless body, it abruptly paused and turned back to look at the old dark house. It knew where it had to look as its head turned and tilted directly upward. Its eyes locked on the eyes of the still-standing shadowed figure in the only lighted second-floor window.

A long, low snarl came from its blood-filled mouth. Inside its crazed mind, the monster's menacing sound turned into actual human thoughts and formed the words, "Midnight snack."

Chapter 14

It felt like someone drove a stake through his heart.
But it really was more like stabbing in his head over
and over and…

The pain was growing worse. He expected it to; he
was told it would; and it was.

Janek stared at the swirling images in his special
daily morning tea, which had always helped to take
the pain away. Today there would be no help. Nor
would there be any relief from the medicine he was
prescribed after the MRI. To him, these so-called
painkillers were nothing more than worthless white
chalk tablets that contained all the special "cure-all"
medical ingredients known to mankind. Janek knew
about these last-resort hopes. That's what they were,
just hopes. But hope was fading as Janek had come
to terms—he was going to die. Finally. After all these
years of wanting to die, finally he would. There would
be no more pain. Neither from the unexplained
disease in his brain nor the emptiness in his long, long
life. He was the last. And it was time. Death was
overdue. Now that he had a one-way ticket to his final
destination, there was just one more stopping point
on that journey. There was still an important problem

to solve or, as he thought about it, a solution to the problems he endured. And that's why he was here.

"Another early morning, Janek?" The now-familiar voice of Lancelot came from behind as he entered the spacious kitchen area. The surrounding wooden cabinetry appeared as new as it had when it was built over 100 years ago. With a marble-inlay tile floor, an oriental rug underneath the table, and a ray of sunlight coming through the lone window, the kitchen was quite relaxing for a morning rendezvous.

"Whatever it is you're drinking smells interesting." Lancelot sniffed the air, long, deep, savoring sniffs, more animal-like than human. "Hmm. Peculiar aroma. I'd say it had a little bit of this, and a little bit of that, and with something special in between. A homemade brew?"

Janek responded expressionlessly.

"My morning tea."

As he sat at the kitchen table, he slowly turned to Lancelot and continued, "Passed down through generations. Quite satisfying, quite warming, quite inviting. Would you like some?"

Lancelot took a seat across from him at the mid-sized wooden kitchen table. It, like everything else here, looked like it came with the house, belonged to the house—a dark, well-crafted table from a century passed. An antique, like Janek was to him.

Smiling, he took a long look at the older man's face. He could tell that he was hiding something. Something that resembled an inner personal pain. He could see that in his eyes. It was a familiar look to him. Lancelot knew pain. He had seen and experienced pain as it had always played an important part of his life. To him, pain was his hidden pleasure. Lancelot broke the stare, as if it were never there, and replaced it with another of his many different smiles.

"Actually, I'd prefer a morning shot of grenadier in a nice mixture of imported rum. Or maybe some champagne. I take it you don't drink much, do you? Maybe some wine?"

"A little wine, yes," Janek answered with a polite smile. The first real smile he exhibited since meeting Lancelot.

"Of course," Lancelot replied cynically. "Wine. Red wine, I assume. A nice cold glass of merlot, perhaps? A deep, satisfying taste of dark red liquid. They say it's good for the body and the blood."

Janek sipped at his tea.

"I prefer my wine warm, body temperature."

"Hmm. I'm sure you do; easier to blend in with your blood."

There was no response, other than another brief smile from Janek.

"So, did you have a good night sleep?" Janek finally spoke.

"I slept well, and you?"

"I did also, mostly, but I was awakened by a sound before midnight. It almost sounded like an animal, and then a scream. Did you hear anything?"

Before answering, Lancelot poured himself a morning glass of wine.

"The darkness of the night holds many interesting sounds. Sometimes the wind can stir the imagination to make us think of things that may not exist."

"Like the sound of a strange, large, howling animal?"

Lancelot sipped at the wine. Furrowing his eyebrows, he answered half laughingly, "I can only imagine that in these mountains there must be some wild animals seeking prey at night."

"Of course, a wild animal, perhaps a wolf? In these mountains and these surrounding woods, there must be a wolf out there hunting in the shadows."

"Yes, hunting. Hunting for a midnight snack."

"Yes, a midnight snack." Janek stared at him, their eyes locked together like two bulls locking horns in a battle for supremacy. But this was a different battle. A clash of underlying words filled with writers' metaphors.

Lancelot broke the stare and stretched his arms over his head to get rid of the last vestiges of his body's sleepiness. "Thinking of that makes me hungry." He paused and let out a fake sleepy yawn. "Time for breakfast. Did you eat yet?"

"I'm still quite full from last night's meal. Aren't you?"

"Yes. But I can always eat more," Lancelot replied smugly.

"Eating late at night can sometimes cause bad dreams," Janek responded hinting at more than what he said.

Lancelot leaned forward in his chair with both hands on the table and spoke slowly as if sharing a secret.

"And sometimes...quench the appetite."

They both stared at each other. It was becoming a testament to their willpower to hold their real feelings at check while they danced with words with hidden meanings. Meanings, as writers, they both understood.

Lancelot leaned back into the comfort of his chair.

"Well, I'm up for a hearty breakfast. Nothing better than some eggs and bacon. Although I prefer sausage. I've always been partial to some type of tasty meat with each meal."

There would be no reply, no revealing expression. Janek merely stood up and started to turn away, then turned back.

"I'll be in the study, looking at our notes. Please join me...when you are finished eating."

Using his cane for balance, he left the kitchen, leaving his half-empty teacup behind.

Lancelot watched him carefully with his eyes trained on his every step. He was old and frail. He was sickly, and he was hiding that, Lancelot knew, for sure. Not by just by the way he looked or walked, but by the way he smelled.

Picking up the half-empty teacup left behind, Lancelot walked to the porcelain kitchen sink holding it in his hand. The tea, like Janek, had a strange smell. A smell pretending to be life, but concealing death.

Looking outside the kitchen window above the sink, he could see the early morning light casting interesting shadows across the adjacent graveyard. It looked oo peaceful, so calming, so untouched.

He smiled to himself as he poured Janek's remaining tea into the sink. He watched its dark chocolate liquid color swirl quickly into the sink drain, disappearing into the depths beneath without a sound.

No, actually, he wasn't quite ready to eat now. He, too, was full from last night's meal. But he knew he would be hungry later. He would be very hungry to eat again.

* * * * *

The day passed quickly. Their progress moved slowly. The air in the study where they worked again was a mixture of cold and hot, not temperature, but attitude. Maybe a time to reflect, or maybe a time to think of what was next. Not in the story, but in *their* story.

For the first hour, Lancelot stood at the large window looking out in the surrounding morning glow, seemingly lost in a distant writer's world of his own. Janek picked out a book from the countless many on the giant bookshelves that filled the room and sat at the table, reading. It was a history book of sorts, its leather-grain binding showed little wear and the pages were pristine white. These books and the stories contained in them were like the house itself, relics that lived in the past. Janek could relate to that. He was becoming more comfortable here, almost as if he belonged, knowing that his private life existed exclusively in the shadows of the past, like a part of the history he read. The past was his playground of memories that he held onto and relished; it had seemed forever, and it was. But the book he held, the story they would write, and his life here and now in this strange old house would all have an ending.

Janek looked up for a moment at Lancelot who still stood silently staring outside. He knew that his adversary, his collaborator, this person who he was thrust together with to write the greatest horror story of all time would also have an ending here, too. A perfect ending just like in his books.

Without a word, Lancelot sat down across from him. Same as yesterday. As if nothing had changed in between. He looked at Janek without a hint of emotion and finally spoke.

"In my stories, the payoff comes from a twist ending and a moment of dramatic irony. Is that how you see our story ending?"

"A happy ending? Or an act of shocking violence?" Janek replied.

"Humph. Perhaps a touch of both." Lancelot smirked as if he knew something Janek didn't.

"A psychology of grief. Yes. I have found that there is nothing more powerful than the frightening results of blending happiness with horror," Janek stated thoughtfully while touching the silver wolf's head on his cane which remained by his side.

Lancelot's eyes watched as Janek's hand stroked the cast-metal wolf. No words were spoken during the long moment. Finally, his eyes left the cane's wolf's head and looked back to Janek.

"We have our beginning from yesterday's work. We can start from there and let it lead us to the middle of our story, wouldn't you agree?"

"The middle has a lot yet to reveal." Janek closed his opened book as if the ending of one story was the beginning of another.

"Then let that reveal bring us to the end," Lancelot dared him with a smugness in his tone.

"The ending must wait till the right moment," Janek casually replied.

"Or happen unexpectedly." Lancelot smiled with his response.

"Or...expectedly," Janek concluded as if winning the first morning battle of words between two writers who had more than writing in mind.

The cold air in the small room suddenly grew colder.

"You know, Janek, you never smile. Are you always this serious?"

"I have my moments."

Lancelot leaned slightly across the table while his eyes studied Janek's face. "Hmm. You seem bothered, as if quietly grieving, almost saddened as to what may eventually come. I have felt it from the moment we met. It is written in your eyes."

"My emotions are in my books, not in my expressions." Janek stared back impassively.

Neither blinked as the uneasy moment held as though waiting for more to come.

"Emotions, expressions, whatever they may be, whatever you may call them, in my books I write about the present and of people and places I know. In your stories, you always write about the past, of people and places that once were. Why do you choose that? Are you afraid of the present?" Lancelot asked coyly.

Janek's fingers left his cane's handle and came together with his other hand, crossing them comfortably but firmly, in front of himself on the table.

"The past defines us. It defines my characters. The period I set my stories in holds so much history. It is a pathway back to a time of great adventure, romance, a time of living each day with great expectations of what can come next. I find the present boring. Everywhere you look, everyone you meet, has so little feeling, compassion, or caring. People today are more self-centered, interested in mostly themselves and their playthings, their worldly possessions and devices that they embrace as necessary social technology. And that technology has changed the way people write and read books; it affects our life and turns us into different writers."

"Perhaps better writers," Lancelot replied while repeating Janek's previous hand movement, now crossing his fingers together in front of himself while leaning slightly forward, closer towards the older man who sat across from him.

Coldly, Janek responded.

"If you think today is a better place than yesterday, then you must think tomorrow will be a better place than today. I don't. I've been at this game for a long, long, time, I don't know if I remember a time before it. I remember images, people's faces, different places, fleeting feelings, bits and pieces of the past I walked through, and I use all of that in my writing. You avoid the past, seemingly you hide from it. Your stories dwell on the here and now. Your world hides all that came before. It is a tormented world echoing a tormented mind. That is the difference between you and me."

Lancelot loosened his hands and sat back in his chair.

"Our differences, whether past or present, share one common denominator, death. We both write about it."

"But we both tell it differently." Janek's words held his first sign of real emotion.

"Yet we both seem to enjoy it," Lancelot smirked with a bit of arrogance.

There was a long moment of deep silence between them before Janek responded.

"Death has been my life since I've come of age. And yes, I've embraced every moment of it. I'm not afraid of death, nor do my characters in my stories run away from death. Like the characters I create, I know what I've become. Death has defined me. I know what role in life I'm meant to play. It's not just a satisfaction, death is more of a wanting, or a needing, and I use the elements of death in my writing as an underlying pathway of the unknown to come. To me, death glorifies life."

"Oh, please," Lancelot began sarcastically and continued with a growing self-righteousness. "Don't you want to break free of who you are beneath the words? Death is just a symbol; how it comes is the reality. And we both know death comes in so many different ways. We both know it, and we each say the same words and maybe even wonder if they were written in one of our books long ago. As writers, we use death as our own private graveyard. We manipulate and worship our moments of death as we each equally hide the real truth behind our stories. Truth we secretly covet and really want to say, words beneath our personal pain that conceal who we really are for all the world to never see."

Janek took another long moment before replying, not trying to find the right response, but knowing what the right response was.

"I know who I am. And I know who you are." He let the words hang in the cold air between them, resonating with something more than just the truth.

Lancelot's underlying temper seemed to grow as he began his reply both carefully and caustically.

"What makes you so sure? Most people agree the truth, or what we call the unseen truth of who we really are will never be discovered. It is something we carry within us and keep to ourselves for reasons of our own. Do you think that if everyone pulled back the curtain on the so-called Wizard of Oz they'd finally see the real person behind it? No, because he, like you and I, lives behind many different curtains. We play God in our writings and have become that man behind the curtain. Everything we write is an illusion. The only reality for us is that our books live on forever; they are the real "ghosts" we leave behind. They come back to life repeatedly every time someone picks up one of our books and reads it. In their imagination these stories and characters are alive. Alive. Ha! They only live in a make-believe world, the ones we create. You and I, Janek, like our creations, are different from the real world. We both live in our own outside worlds looking in. The truth behind who we really are is buried forever in our stories."

"And sometimes it's unburied for all to see," Janek replied firmly.

There was a moment of uneasy reflection between them. Each seeing the other as part of themselves.

Janek continued, "Your writing seems to speak to your readers as something unwholesome and unthinkable. Something that hungers for the souls of others. You write about monsters; I write about men."

"Men who are monsters...one hiding within the other." Lancelot slowly leaned forward to the table again, his eyes locking on Janek's eyes before continuing. "What difference is there really between us? We are both one and the same on the inside, aren't we?"

Whether a second, whether a minute, whether an hour, their eyes remained locked together. There was no measured amount of time between them, only a cold, unmeasurable silence.

Lancelot got up quietly from the table and turned away toward the large window. He didn't want Janek to see the full anger and hatred in his face. That would come later, in due time. Both of their outside worlds were now revealed, similar to the inside worlds they both existed in.

He took a moment or two to compose himself, to put his emotion in check. Satisfied, he turned back to Janek putting both of his hands on top of the chair back and began anew as if nothing was just said.

"So, it is apparent you have read my work?" Lancelot asked with a newfound calmness.

"Your work speaks for itself," Janek casually replied, leaning back in his chair while folding his arms and waiting to see where the conversation would go next.

"Yes, it does." Lancelot seemed delighted to focus on his work, on himself, not on what the old man believed in or thought he believed in. "I think of my stories as having a kind of music to it. You know the expression: music soothes the savage beast. For me, my music is my words. And my words, my stories, bring my beast to life."

Lancelot returned to his chair and continued.

"You say you know who you are, so do I. You may have gotten all the critics to kiss your ass with favorable press, but I sell millions of books to my fans. I don't need to work with you. You need me more than I need you. I know a lot about your secrets, Janek, more than you can imagine. And I know why we're really here together, and it's not just to write a book."

"No, the book is just a part of our story. How our story ends is the real book that we write," Janek added.

"No, it is the book we live," Lancelot concluded with a sarcastic sigh.

Lancelot paused, studying Janek's face once again, looking for something else, something he knew was still hidden. "What good is a writer unless he is read by all the world? Don't you sometimes feel trapped in your words, in your thinking? Or do you pretend to know how to keep in harmony with all the craziness that you imagine and seek comfort with yourself through your stories? Don't you ever ask yourself how much of what we have written before was a planned part of this grand design called life? Part of what brought us here to this would-be house of ghosts to find and add to that eventual ending?"

"Perhaps we're here to write about ghosts of our past," Janek replied with a hint of a smile.

"Or ghosts of our present," Lancelot added darkly.

"Or maybe...both." Janek's final words were colder than the cold in the room.

No other words were spoken for the rest of the day. The only sound that was heard was the occasional pounding of a single metal typewriter key, adding its carbon ink to the white paper in the roller. Sporadic at best. The rest of the time was filled with silence.

At the end of the day, they each left alone, without a word, the same way they started. Each got up and walked out of the study, similar to finishing a long day's working shift. Each took a cue from the time spent and the thoughts that remained in the room, leaving behind a stack of empty paper on one side of the typewriter and a single typed page on the other.

Chapter 15

Janek hadn't touched much of the food that remained on his plate. His appetite was diminishing as his limited strength and waning willpower fought the growing sickness that was taking over his body. He used to enjoy food. He had his favorites. His agent knew them all too well, and the prepared meals that were left for him for the week were all neatly packaged and marked in the kitchen refrigerator. It never crossed his mind that Lancelot would use his food in place of his own, nor at this point in his life did he care. He knew he had other nourishment in his room that awaited him after his planned walk. Morning and night. He had the same routine for years upon years. Morning and night. Stretch the body, awaken the mind, walk in the outside world and seek the solace he needed for both his writing and planned quest. Especially with the time he now had left.

Like a praying mantis planning a trap, he knew who his prey was, and how the trap had been set.

After Janek left the long, formal dining table without a word for his evening walk, Lancelot sat alone and watched the frail older man use his cane to steady himself with each hobbled step. There was no hiding the fact, it was quite apparent that Janek was growing weaker, much weaker day by day. And for Lancelot that was a good sign, not a bad sign. Lancelot smiled to himself.

"Finished eating?" Lancelot thought to himself caustically, a question he had pretended to ask but which would have fallen on deaf ears as Janek left through the front door. And then he smiled some more.

They hadn't spoken a word throughout their dinner. A chilled silence and twelve long feet separated them as they sat at opposite ends of the ornate, wooden dining table. They hadn't spoken since their time in the study. But "time" didn't mean the same to either of them. One knew that time was on his side; the other knew time was not.

When the front door closed behind Janek as he left the house, Lancelot stretched back in his chair with his arms behind his head and put both feet casually on the table's top.

"Maids, clean it up," he spoke aloud to no one but himself. And then, he started to laugh. A strange laugh. A dark laugh. Somewhat lightly at first but growing in volume until it was so loud that it echoed through the entire empty house. An ominous, almost mocking echo. Disturbing and evil.

As quickly as it began, it ended.

He sat alone, knowing what he had to do next.

* * * * *

Dying trees with branches, long and spindly, moved slowly in the slight evening breeze. An overcast sky with fading daylight showed the remnants of the midafternoon autumn storm that had passed while they were in the study and now signs of another storm approaching. Several broken tree limbs of assorted sizes and shapes crisscrossed the mansion's grounds. The quiet evening air was disturbed by Janek's footsteps on twigs and leaves and the splashing in the small puddles of leftover storm water. Spending the day writing with Lancelot had been unfulfilling for him and a chore, but it was just part of the process, part of the endgame that was yet to be completed, not only in book form, but in the necessary steps leading to the eventual conclusion. He knew what it would be. He pondered the facts and wondered if Lancelot knew, too.

Vladamir Janek walked slowly away from the house following an old, overgrown cobbled path which led to the small nearby family cemetery. He had seen this cemetery from his bedroom window last night. Tucked in one corner of the house's property, the graveyard was illuminated by the last vestiges of twilight, almost beckoning him to come and see it, to come and feel it, to come and be part of it.

He had avoided this area on his morning walk as he, instead, chose the long, winding mountain trail which stretched across the property boundaries and led to and from the front of the house. That walk was quiet and undisturbed as nature awoke to another dying day of changing seasons. As long as he could remember, his morning and evening walks were exactly the same time and distance every day: 33 minutes, one mile. The same every day. It was a routine, but tonight he needed it more to rid himself of the long and physical mind game of wrestling words he had with his collaborator. Holding a pencil or typing on a keyboard was by no means exhausting. It was the motion behind their emotion and the effort to unlock the mind and bare the soul that punished his body the most.

Tonight, as earlier that morning, he thought of why it had taken them so many years to finally cross paths, to meet and to attempt to work together. So far, they both carefully danced the dance of words and kept a cautionary distance between one another in their own free time. Janek knew that his task was the same as yesterday, same as today, same as tomorrow, finish the book first, then...

Wet brown leaves littered the path to the gated cemetery entrance. Too damp to blow in tonight's on-and-off autumn breeze, they lay still on the ground, smelling of fresh evening dew and leftover moisture, waiting for another day's sunlight to dry up the entire area, giving them a few more moments of living color before they faded and rotted like the others. A single lone oak tree stood by the cemetery, its branches swaying softly in the gentle, yet sudden gusts of wind. One storm had passed; another storm was on the horizon—both outside the house and inside the house.

Janek pushed the iron cemetery gate open. Its rusty hinges creaked in response to having been awakened from a long, long sleep. Inside the gated area, thirteen weathered and worn headstones of different sizes and tilted at different angles created a macabre atmosphere. Overgrown, unmanaged, long forgotten, this resting home of the dead felt as though it had lost its will to survive and waited to crumble and be buried with the once-living bodies below.

The surrounding forest that touched the gated boundaries of the cemetery was deep and dark. There were no nearby houses, nor nearby neighbors. It was a perfect fortress of solitude for them to do their collaboration and a perfect setting to play out the plan and add to the waiting graveyard.

Janek stood solemnly looking at the old and crumbling headstones, looking for something. Something he expected to be there, or maybe wanted to be there. As his squinting eyes read each name on the individual headstones, there, he finally found it, waiting silently for him, as if anticipating its discovery. A name. A name he knew, and another piece to the puzzle in his would-be game of life and death.

Standing silently while resting on his cane, faint whispers seemed to be carried on the chilly air and touched his senses. Faint, sometimes human-like, sometimes not. He was pleased that his acute senses were still sharp through all the passing years. Although his body was failing, his senses had remained strong. They were an asset to his being, to his survival. And now he could hear and smell something strange approaching. Something very strange, and something quite different.

A low growl came unexpectedly from somewhere behind him, and then from somewhere in front of him. Between the fading daylight and another night of a full moon, he peered into the diminishing twilight and looked for whatever it was that had interrupted him. Whatever it was, it could be heard moving slowly and tentatively closer, seemingly slobbering and drooling, as if tasting its own taste and wanting to taste something else. Whatever it was, it seemed to intensify his acute senses as it came closer, and then it stopped. Stopped as if it never existed.

A cold silence touched his cheeks.

"I know who you are. Why don't you come out of hiding and show your true self?" Janek stated confidently as his wrinkled fingers tightly clutched the walking cane's cast wolf's head.

He squeezed the cane's silver handle firmly as he slowly lifted its one end from the damp ground and brought it upwards to a parallel position in front of himself. His other bony hand ran the length of it and clasped it at the end, waiting to be used, to be swung in self-defense at anything and everything that approached. His head turned from side to side as his eyes tried to follow the invisible thing before him which lurked in the encompassing shadows. Whatever it was, its growling began again, growing louder as it somehow crossed the distance between where it was first heard, and where it was now coming from. Then it stopped.

So did the wind.

So did the world.

Everything halted in a moment of frozen time as whatever-it-was suddenly leapt high out of the shadowy darkness and into the chilled air towards him. Janek felt its hot, hungry breath drawing closer and closer to his exposed throat as he stood his ground and raised his cane. He was prepared. He knew this would happen. He had planned for this moment.

Janek swung his cane with the force of a once Mighty Casey at bat. He swung it hard, fast, powerfully. It sliced through the air, once, twice, three times. And each time it cut into nothing. Seemingly, he missed the mark, if even there was one. Collapsing to his knees in exhaustion and out of breath, he knew there was nothing there. Whatever it was, it was gone. But whatever it was, it still hid somewhere deep in his tormented mind. In his sudden emotional strikeout, he slowly turned his fear to a slight but growing laughter, and his laughter turned to one, then many tears. Whatever-it-was was just a part of him, nothing more, nothing less, just a memory of something long ago. But that "nothing" he faced revealed that "something" he hid. He was going mad. Or maybe, as he wiped away the beginning raindrops that had recently fallen on his face and disguised his tears, just maybe, he had been this way for a long, long time.

Kneeling on the wet ground, as his trembling hand still held his ornate wolf's-head cane tightly, he felt something more in the nothingness that surrounded his frail body. He turned his head sideways, back towards the house. Back towards what had become his part-time sanctuary and part-time horror show as he wrestled with his personal demons and the one called Lancelot Strong. He turned back and gradually looked upwards towards the second floor. He knew where to look and he knew what he'd see. There, in a window in one of the old house's upstairs bedrooms, he saw an unknown figure, illuminated as a shadow from the light within. A figure who stood silently watching him as he looked at it. It was his bedroom, and his old, tired eyes slowly made out who it really was.

Himself.

Somewhere between the standing figure in the window and the kneeling figure on the wet graveyard ground, a low, evil growl rode the haunting wind. From where it came, only the graveyard knew.

Chapter 16

When Lancelot entered his room, his face wore a mask of pain. He held his one shoulder as he pushed the door closed quickly with his body. Fresh perspiration rolled down his face and his shirt was dirty and torn. He went directly into the small bathroom and immediately spit out a mouthful of saliva mixed with blood.

"Damn him," he muttered beneath his whispered breath.

A shaky hand turned the old sink faucet handle. A hint of rusty water from years of non-use chugged from the faucet, swirling around the metal drain. He let the water run long enough to have a fresh, clean flow into the small white porcelain basin.

While splashing a handful of water once, twice, on his face, he looked at his angry image in the old, discolored wall mirror above the sink. He noticed the bruise across his face. A fresh bruise, reddish and starting to swell. A bruise as if something had struck him.

He cursed aloud again.

Turning the faucet off, Lancelot leaned with both hands on the sink's outer edges and took a long look at himself. His swollen face seemed to expand then contract, almost as if it were massaging itself from within. And then it returned to normal, and the swelling was gone. But a trace of the fresh bruise remained.

"Damn him to hell," Lancelot muttered as his image stared back at him. And then it began to change again. This time in the mirror, not in the room.

An older man's face appeared, wrinkled and hairy. An unkempt bearded face seemed to make a grimacing look and sniff at him while it twisted its head slowly back and forth. Its deep-pocketed eyes were bloodshot and troubled. It was a face that looked like himself but didn't. Perhaps a glimpse of his future fifty-plus years from now, or perhaps a glimpse of him today hiding the face of a half man, half something else, trying to escape the mirror.

Without any effort, he turned away and wiped his face in the white hand towel next to the sink. The whiteness turned muddy brown from the cloaks of dirt that remained from his washing. Staring at the towel, he could see an outline of his face, almost as if he had wiped off what was there and now had something new to see. Slowly, he looked back in the mirror.

A young boy's face looked back.

A smiling young boy. A happy young boy. Lancelot at nine, maybe ten years old. The exact age didn't matter. What mattered was the memory.

The face of the young Lancelot Strong now reflected in a window as he stared out into an evening landscape. Everything he saw was blurred, moving past as quickly as his eyes could identify what he saw.

Blurred trees, unshapely shrubs, open land, a mountain, more trees, close and far. And then everything shifted slightly like a bump in the road, but he wasn't observing from the road. It was a...

"Quite a view, Son, the train gives quite a different look at our country's landscape. Quite beautiful."

The voice was soothing, that of a mature woman, not the boy he saw in the train window.

"Yes, Mother, everything goes by so fast, so quickly. But it is so much fun! Riding the train is so much fun!"

And with those words, Lancelot's smiling face suddenly froze as the train unexpectedly turned upside down.

The screams and sounds of twisted metal coming apart filled his head. His youthful smile changed into a look of sheer fright, engulfing him in the last moment of light from within the tumbling train car. The images of the dead and dying changed so fast, so quickly. The train ride was no longer fun, but, rather, filled with great horror.

And then everything went black.

When young Lancelot opened his eyes, he saw a sight he would always remember. A sight that would always haunt him. He was lying underneath the twisted and bloodied body of his dead mother who still held him tight. His mother had grabbed him and tried to shield him as much as she could as the train plunged from the broken tracks and turned cartwheels down a small ravine. Held him so tightly that he somehow survived.

Inside the mangled train car, the surrounding air smelled of fire and burning flesh. The air also held the sounds of constant moaning and the pleading of dying passengers. Lancelot was lucky to be alive. Lucky for the moment, but not for what was to come. For that was not "lucky" by any means; that was what would become his "curse," binding together the memory of his past and present forever.

Staggering alone from the wreckage, the young boy showed no tears, no emotion. The nightmare of this tragic moment was filled with an undeniable shock which he was unable to fully comprehend. For a boy his age, his childhood world had just ended. His world of survival and what was to come next was just beginning.

Somehow, he managed to leave the burning train wreckage. Somehow, he managed to wander through the surrounding forest following a broken path. Somehow, his minor wounds, bruises, and cuts were just there, nothing to stop him or hinder him as he went further into the shadows of the dark foreboding forest. The full moon above gave him a roadmap that twisted between large gnarly looking trees and thickets of bushes. He didn't know where he was or where he was going. Lonely and lost, it was instinct and fate that led him forward as he searched for safety and shelter. From his school learnings and the trip he and his mother were on, Lancelot knew he was in the Carpathian Mountains somewhere between the start of the journey in Budapest and now somewhere on the way to their destination in northern Romania. It was just the two of them on summer vacation. His father was too busy working to come. It was just a special trip for his mother and him. Now, it was just the forest and him. This was his world for now. And unbeknownst to him, his soon-to-become playground.

How long he wandered in the cold night air he had no idea. Nor did it figure into his mind. He just walked forward following whatever trail he could find and whatever path the light of the full moon gave him. He had hoped it would lead him to safety, security, and freedom. Instead, it was leading him to some other place and something else.

And then he heard it.

The far-off cry of an animal howling at the moon. A howl that made young Lancelot stop, listen, and shiver.

It was the cry of a wolf.

Unsure of where it came from. His left? His right? In back or from ahead? All that mattered was that the wolf's howl brought the first real fear of the night into his still numb body and mind, which continued to struggle to make sense of the train accident and his mother's death.

And then it came again.

The wolf's howl was closer.

A lot closer.

And so, he ran. Fast, faster, and even more so. He ran through the thick, prickly bushes, between the towering, spooky-looking trees, and across the winding path that was there, and not there. He ran as though he were a wolf himself being pursued, or maybe being the one leading the pursuit.

The moon went between passing clouds and the pitch darkness made him stumble and fall. When he got back to his feet and tried to catch his exhausted breath, the sound of breathing became more than what was just his. There were two breaths. His, and one from the beast, which now towered before him. A beast that was more than just a wolf you would see in a zoo, or a wolf you would look at in a schoolbook picture. This thing before him was something more. Maybe an animal, maybe a man gone mad, maybe something that was part of both. This was a six-foot-tall living spawn from hell, with glaring red eyes and long fangs that dripped of the blood of animals or other things this beast had killed earlier. And now, it was about to kill him.

Without a weapon, without a way to escape, one might likely just cower and succumb to the inevitable. Most would. But not Lancelot. Why? God only knew, that is, if one believed in an all-knowing god. At this moment, there was only a beast and a boy. A slobbering, horrible, giant beast and a lonely young boy without fear.

But there was something else.

The long, thick, broken, and sharp tree branch that he had tripped over, somehow, laid at his side and next to his open hand.

As the wolf monster sprang forward Lancelot grabbed the sharp, thick piece of dried wood and held it before him. Held it strong enough and long enough for it to pierce deep into the forward-moving creature. Deep into its belly and up into its throat and even further into its head above. Deep enough to save himself from immediate death, but not enough from the quick and painful bite the beast inflicted into his chest. Long, sharp fangs that went deep into his body and inserted the bloody saliva of the monster which now blended into his own blood.

The creature stumbled backward howling in pain, grabbing at the thick, protruding tree branch as blood gushed from its open mouth. Lancelot watched in the shadows of the intermittent moonlight as the creature staggered backwards screaming and fell to the earthen forest floor, twitching its long hairy legs and limbs in the few remaining moments of a life no more. And then to Lancelot's surprise, and a shock to his mind which had already seen so much that night, but never saw anything like this before, the monster changed. Transformed. Became something else. The monster was a man. The man was a monster. And then Lancelot passed out.

When he woke up, he found himself in a quilted blanket-covered bed inside a moving wooden wagon—the wagon of a gypsy family. A swaying lighted lantern attached above gave him enough light to see the person before him. An older gray-haired woman bandaged his wounds and gently pushed back the matted hair from his boyish face. Her gentle smile made him know he was okay. His childlike smile told her, *"Thank you,"* as he drifted back into a deep sleep. When he opened his eyes again, he was older.

Now, as a young man in soldier's clothing, he approached a small farmhouse on a winter's night with a group of other soldiers. He was the youngest, the most confident, and the most handsome of the group. The others wore faces of war and hatred. His face revealed nothing. He was smart and cunning. He seemed to know how to survive the fears of war. He had the cunning of a wolf.

Inside the farmhouse there was commotion; a farmer's family pleaded for their lives. The father struggled, was beaten, and was taken away by several of the soldiers. The wife begged for her life, but she was raped like a plaything by four of the remaining soldiers. He watched them as they finished their sex, not interested in participating, but enjoying the sight of their hunger and satisfaction. His attention quietly went to a nearby closet door. Approaching it, he sniffed the air as if smelling something hidden. With a gun in one hand, he slowly reached for the closet doorknob. His hand touched the knob and started to turn it, but he stopped when he heard the sound of a gunshot from behind, then another. He observed the four soldiers taking turns shooting the raped woman in the head. Her body twitched on the wooden floor like a ragdoll in target practice.

Kneeling and crying before the soldiers was a thirteen-year-old girl. Never having seen death before, and now witnessing the shock of her mother's trauma and death, she sobbed uncontrollably. He walked over to her and gently offered his hand. Terrified, and not knowing what else to do, she took it, and he allowed her to gradually stand. He held a finger to his lips to indicate for her to be quiet and led her out of the house. The young girl hesitated as she turned back to look at the closed closet door. He looked, too, and smiled. A set of fangs was revealed as he licked his lips and turned, taking her with him.

Later that night as the kitchen closet door remained closed, a howl of a wolf was heard in the distance. Not far from the quiet farmhouse, in the full moonlight, the young girl's lifeless body laid face upwards, staring in frozen horror, with her throat torn wide open. A pool of her fresh red blood stained the surrounding white snow.

A blizzard began and quickly covered her body.

Still looking in the bathroom mirror, the young boy's face disappeared, and Lancelot's face returned. The recollections drifted back into the hiding place of his dark soul. How many years passed between then and now was hard to fathom. Years are just numbers and numbers only hold meanings for those who are human enough to understand them, not for those who may not be human.

Letting out a deep breath and shaking his head to rid himself of those haunted memories, Lancelot reached to tear off the remnants of his tattered shirt. Perspiration from whatever happened earlier that night, along with the drops of water that he splashed on his face, still ran down his exposed chest. His toned and muscular chest heaved out a long sigh.

The scar around his heart was still visibly there. The scar of teeth marks from a monster or a man. Or maybe the devil himself. The scar of what made him what he was today.

"Damn him," he snarled again, as he angrily smashed his one fist quickly into his face in the mirror.

Shattered glass fell to the floor as his blood from his now-cut hand dripped into the sink.

Outside the room one could hear the sounds of a man crying.

Chapter 17

In the early morning sunlight, Janek sat alone in the study, stirring his tea. An open book beside him lay untouched. His mind was somewhere else. Somewhere far, far away.

The only sound in the room came from Janek slowly moving a spoon in the special brew in his porcelain cup. From outside the room, approaching footsteps could be heard on the hall's wooden floor.

Lancelot entered without a word and quietly took the seat directly opposite him. Same as yesterday, and probably the same if there ever would be a tomorrow.

Janek looked up and stared at this co-writer's face where there was an obvious bruise.

"It looks like you injured yourself," he remarked sarcastically as if he already knew the reason why.

"It's nothing. I bumped into something in the darkness of my room."

"Or maybe something bumped into you," Janek was quick to reply.

Lancelot's one hand rubbed the bruise. "One never knows what the night might hold," he answered back after letting his hand return to the table.

"Or what the day will bring," Janek added.

Lancelot leaned back in his chair and smiled. He enjoyed the bantering wordplay between them.

"Then here's to whatever comes our way! May it be a surprise we both enjoy."

Janek didn't respond this time. He politely gave a fake smile back.

"Shall we begin?" Lancelot asked as he stared directly at him.

"We already have," Janek answered, and then took a long sip of his special tea.

* * * * *

The day went quickly. The day went slowly. Time was of no importance to either of them. They discussed plot ideas; they mimicked characters' words; they agreed and disagreed. Their voices acted like swords pairing against each other for supremacy but blending together in culmination. Pages were typed. Pages were tossed. The writing was coming together while their partnering was falling further apart.

The sun had played its course and nightfall had come quickly as if waiting to play its part. They had worked longer than expected. At the end of the day, a stack of completed pages sat on one side of the old typewriter.

Lancelot let out a long breath as he leaned back in his chair and stretched his arms freely over his head. Turning his head back and forth, he rid himself of the long, uncomfortable sit in the wooden chair. Finally standing, he took a moment to survey their work.

Janek paid no attention, nor offered any conversation, as he gathered his notes into a leather notebook that he carried with him.

"It feels good, doesn't it?" Lancelot remarked.

"To find the right words that bring the story to life?"

"Or have the right characters meet their destiny," Lancelot asserted.

Outside, the wind suddenly picked up as it started to lightly rain. A roll of faraway thunder gave them each a moment to reflect and consider what to say next.

Janek stood and held his notebook in one hand and his cane in the other. He started toward the door without another word.

A faint flash of lightning illuminated the inside from the outside. A heavier rain now started, then intensified with another gust of strong wind.

"Looks like we're in for a stormy night. Guess you won't be able to have your evening walk," Lancelot pointed out with veiled sympathy.

Janek stopped and turned to reply, taking a moment, as another roll of thunder prevented his immediate response.

"Are you afraid of the storm?" Lancelot questioned him first.

"Actually, I enjoy a good storm. The sounds remind me of a story I once heard as a child."

Janek paused with another sudden rumble of thunder outside. Not far. Not close. Just there.

"The thunder is the noise made by the angels bowling in heaven. With each thunderclap, the pins are knocked down. And with every lightning flash, a match is lit by the ghosts who want to see us, and who we get to see during that brief moment."

"Sounds like something a child would believe."

Another clap of thunder, this time closer, seemed to interrupt his remark.

"Are *you* afraid of the storm?" It was now Janek's turn to question him. "Or are you afraid of this place?"

Lancelot chuckled to himself, then let out a long breath.

"Intelligent people laugh at the stories about this place. It's a made-up ghost story to scare ignorant people away," Lancelot replied with a casual self-assurance.

It was Janek's turn to chuckle.

"But, what if it's not? What if someone, or something, still exists here? A presence, a spirit, something that watches us. Waits for us. As we wait for it."

"It?"

A flash of bright lightning and a roll of thunder punctuated Lancelot's one word. The rain seemed to subside, lessening in its intensity, but remained as a backdrop to their conversation.

"Don't let your imagination fool you, Janek. Ghosts, or what some people call 'the things that go bump in the night,' are always brought up on a stormy night like this. Every scary book, every horror movie, has played that bit to death. I have no fear of storms.

I have no fear of this place. I have no fear of a childish play on words or make-believe supernatural things. I live to scare people, not to be scared by people and their foolish imaginings."

Lancelot paused and gave one of his phony smiles before continuing. "And so, it's late. And I'm starting to get hungry. And my thirst is for some refreshing red wine, not tales of haunted houses and imaginary ghosts."

Walking away, he laughed to himself under his subdued breath. He left Janek behind in the room.

Closely eyeing the departure of his co-writer into the shadows of the hallway, Janek stood alone for a long, undisturbed moment.

Another dying roll of thunder broke his train of thought. Janek's attention was drawn to the splattering of the raindrops hitting the room's large window and, using his cane for support, he made his way there to look out into the darkness.

Staring silently into the outside, Janek had a suspicion that the outside was silently staring back at him. Yet, there was nothing to see. Or, was something looking in at him?

The storm seemed to be passing and the sound of now soft rain against the glass made him contemplate and consider his conversation with Lancelot. And maybe something more.

The rain turned to a slight drizzle. In his mind, he recalled again the story his mother told him of the angels' noisy bowling game in the stormy clouds above. There was one final far-off rumble of thunder.

One last ghostly match struck. One farewell flash of lightning.

In that final flash, something caught his eye.

There, in the graveyard, stood a woman in white. Next to a freshly opened grave.

Chapter 18

Standing in front of the parlor's large fireplace, Lancelot felt the warmth of the fire as he sipped quietly from his freshly poured wine. Out of the corner of his vision, he saw Janek pass quickly through the hallway and exit through the large front door. It remained open behind as he watched him disappear into the drizzling rain.

"What the...," he mumbled to himself.

Hurrying to the open doorway, he peered outside into the cold night and watched Janek briskly walking toward the shadowed graveyard. A diminishing flash of lightning was all that was needed to illuminate the yard and allow Lancelot to see what, or whom, Janek was pursuing.

There, next to a large mound of wet dirt and an open grave, stood a woman in white.

Her dress, perhaps a wedding dress, was somewhat torn, somewhat tattered, with streaks of fresh mud across the bottom, which gently touched the earth beneath her bare feet. A soft rain fell upon her. A few billows of a thin, white fog delicately surrounded her.

Catching up to Janek was easy, as the older man needed to steady himself as he trudged carefully through the wet, overgrown grass.

"Janek! Wait up!"

Together, they stopped about twenty feet away from her. The rain had ended, and a fresh, moist evening mist rose from the ground between them and the woman. They stood staring at her. She was a vision of loveliness...the most beautiful woman either of them had ever seen. Her long blonde hair, catching the wisps of moonlight that peeked between the passing rainclouds, fell about her bare shoulders. From where they stood, she appeared to be in her early twenties. With one hand, she tightly clutched the plunging neckline of the gown, accenting the soft, flowing curves of her shapely body. Her only jewelry was a small gold cross affixed to a chain, which laid between her partially exposed breasts. She appeared wet, cold, frightened, and maybe confused. Without a word, her eyes turned and met theirs, seemingly to beckon them to approach her. Seemingly to carry a silent message that she wanted them to find her.

The distance closed between them as they cautiously moved forward. She turned her head about, as if getting rid of long, leftover sleep from her body. She remained emotionless. There were no apparent injuries to her body. It was just a puzzling question of who she was and why she was there.

Janek broke the silence with a comforting voice.

"Do you need help?"

They now stood mere feet apart.

She stared at them. There was something about her eyes, something unusual. They were mesmerizing and seemed to captivate both men.

"I was lost. I saw the light in your house. I saw you in the window." Her voice was soft, almost melodic. Almost angelic.

Lancelot looked to Janek for his reaction, then back to the girl.

"Lost? What's a girl like you doing here in this remote place?" Lancelot's question was equally caring but more to the point.

Before replying, she took a moment to study Lancelot's face.

"I'm not sure. I live in a place like this. I thought I might be home."

She dropped her eyes and smiled. Her soft lips parted slightly open, seductively as if she wanted to say more but couldn't. Or at least, wouldn't, for now.

"I guess that's what happened," she added with a look of shyness.

"You'll catch a death of cold. Let me give you something to wear," Janek offered.

"Thank you," was her only reply.

He took off his button-down sweater during the conversation and politely handed it to her. Not wanting to touch her, or scare her, he gently offered it to her.

"This ought to do," Janek added.

"It's too dark out now and too stormy for us to try to take you back to wherever your home is. You can stay here tonight, and we can take you home in the morning," Lancelot assured her.

She looked at the house, then back to the two men.

"I would like that."

"Good, then, let's get you inside. Just be careful of the fallen limbs and wet grass," Janek pointed out.

She reached over and touched Lancelot's arm, being the bigger of the two men, and most certainly the sturdier. He put his arm around her shoulders, drawing her shivering body closer to his. Her eyes looked up to his to say that she was comfortable with his support and felt safe. She also looked to Janek and smiled another thank you.

As the three of them walked together towards the house, the darkened graveyard and the open grave were left silently behind. But not for long.

Just before they reached the porch steps and returned into the house, a faint cry was softly heard from behind them. Only Janek seemed to hear it as he stopped briefly and turned back to see where it came from. But there was no further sound, only the intermittent wind making a long whistling noise through the surrounding trees. Whatever it was, was no more.

Once inside the house and after closing the door, they left the outside world behind. The after-storm wind seemed to die away and the other sound, the sound that had caught Janek's attention before, was heard again. Only this time, much louder and much more distinct.

A baby crying.

* * * * *

Inside the large parlor, the mysterious woman sat on the sofa next to the fireplace, huddled under a blanket tossed over Janek's damp sweater which she still wore. Leaning forward in the chair, she silently sipped on a hot cup of tea, while staring into the dancing flames of the fire.

Lancelot stood next to the fireplace, adding in another piece of dried wood. The fire roared as it came back to life and the crackling of the embers was the only sound in the room.

Janek came down the stairs from his bedroom, carrying a clean, dry shirt and a pair of his pants.

"These should fit you. Wasn't much of a decision between his clothing and mine."

"Mine would be more stylish." Lancelot quipped, trying to add some levity to the moment, even though they all knew his clothes would be too big for her.

"You can go upstairs to change, or in the study, wherever you would feel most comfortable."

"Thank you."

"Bring your wet clothing and we can let it dry overnight by the fire," Janek added.

He handed her his clothes, and she nodded her appreciation. Removing the blanket from her shoulders, she seemed to glide across the room as she took the dry clothing and went toward the adjoining kitchen to change. But then, she suddenly stopped as if something changed her mind, something that prevented her from going further. There was a light in the kitchen, but there was something that made her return to the fireplace.

Without a word, she turned her back to the two men and faced the fireplace. Without hesitation she removed Janek's sweater first and placed it onto the mantlepiece. She then placed her hands on the upper shoulder straps of the gown and took each side off her shoulder then let the dress slowly fall to the floor. She wore no undergarments. She took both her arms and raised them high above her head, as she arched her back, seeming to enjoy the long, uninterrupted stretch in the warmth of the fire. The flickering light of the flames revealed her flawless naked body.

Both men stood in silence watching the entire undressing. Whether she was an exhibitionist, or just a wet person wanting to stay close to a warm fire, neither knew, and neither did they ask why. Both just watched.

When she was dressed, she turned around to face them. Janek's clothing fit her nicely, too nicely...as though it had been the perfect fit for her curvaceous body.

"Well, that must feel better," Janek stated, respectfully.

"It does," she contentedly replied.

Returning to the sofa, she sat down with her legs tucked under her.

"So, who are you?" Lancelot took no time, nor pause, in asking a question.

"I was lost. I saw the light in your house. I saw you in the window."

Both men listened to what she said, as they were the identical words to what she had spoken when they first encountered her.

"You must have a name?" Lancelot pressed.

"Yes."

Silence.

"Amber. My name is Amber."

"Amber what?" Lancelot continued the questioning, looking for more of a response.

She turned her head away, thoughtfully, as if thinking, searching for the answer.

Lancelot rocked on his feet at the fireplace bothered by her lack of a reply.

"So, just Amber?" Lancelot raised his voice as he seemed to lose his patience.

Again, there was silence as if she continued to seek an answer.

Janek stepped forward and leaned on his cane, purposely interrupting Lancelot's questioning. Amber wrapped her arms around her legs on the sofa, almost curling up into a ball. He could sense that she was becoming closed in, perhaps afraid. And why wouldn't she, being alone in a strange house with two strange men? But still. She had been comfortable enough to undress in front of them.

"Amber, I'm Vladamir Janek, and this is..."

"Lancelot, Lancelot Strong."

Knowing their names seemed to make her more at ease as she loosened her curled position on the old sofa. She looked to both men, as it was her turn to ask a question.

"You live here?"

"No," Lancelot refuted.

"Actually, we're staying here." Janek's additional words gave the impression of a more calming explanation.

"Isn't that the same?"

"We're staying here for a week. We're writers. We're working together," Lancelot quickly added.

"I see." She paused, thinking this over. She turned very slightly towards him. "You're not going to hurt me?"

Both men looked at each other, somewhat taken back by her sudden question.

"Of course not," Janek assured her.

She seemed satisfied with his comment. He continued.

"The question is, are you hurt? How did you get here? Where are you from and..."

"Why?" Her one word interrupted and begged a new question.

"Okay, why?"

Amber took another long moment before answering.

"I don't know. I mean. Everything is confusing."

"Can I look at your head to see if you have an injury?" Janek asked.

She nodded an approval. Janek leaned close to do a quick visual check and found nothing.

"So, what do you remember?" Lancelot asked. "After all, it isn't a common occurrence to find an attractive woman like you standing in a graveyard."

"You find me attractive?" She looked at him with both a look of innocent curiosity and a touch of womanly infatuation.

"Yes."

Amber smiled.

"You're both nice."

"You don't know us." Lancelot laughed lightly, as if covering the truth.

"You don't know me." Amber smiled politely, as if telling the truth.

Lancelot and Janek remained silent to her comment. A few new crackles of burning wood in the fireplace filled the air between.

"Your dress? A wedding dress?" Janek finally asked.

"I...I think so." Her response was tentative, unsure, but still unpersuasive.

"So, you were at a wedding? Were you getting married? Somehow you got lost and ended up here. Won't people be looking for you?" Lancelot pushed the narrative back to finding the truth between her words and her presence there.

"I'm not sure," she answered tentatively, seemingly to avoid the obviousness of the question.

Lancelot looked to Janek, then back to her.

"Well, we have a bit of a problem. We don't have a telephone to call for any medical help, and we don't have a car to drive you anywhere. We're here a few more days until someone comes to pick us up."

"Then maybe I can stay here," she answered without reservation or concern.

"Ah. Don't you want to find a way to go home?" Lancelot quickly replied back.

"Home? Yes. I want to go home."

Realizing that this mode of questioning wasn't leading to real answers, Janek stepped between Lancelot and Amber to give them all a chance to relax and search for more answers later.

"Are you hungry?" Janek asked.

"Yes. I am. Yes," she responded politely.

"Why don't you wait here, stay warm, while I get you some food. A sandwich?"

"Sure."

Janek used his cane to steady himself and move slowly towards the kitchen.

Lancelot poked at remaining wood in the fireplace to rekindle the now smaller flames. The metal poker dug deep into the charred wood creating an immediate burst of new flames. When Janek finally left the room, he turned on cue, as if waiting for this moment for the two of them to be finally alone.

"Okay, Amber, so who are you really and is this some sort of stunt?" he asked sternly.

"Stunt?" Her answer was one of complete surprise. Or so it seemed.

"Yeah, stunt. You know you've been sent here, or you came here purposely because you already know that we're the two most well-known horror writers in the world. And you came here crashing our writing party, maybe sent here by our agents to check up on us or make us believe that there's something spooky going on to get us to write more. Maybe you're a celebrity stalker or maybe..."

"Maybe she's just a woman who needs to warm up and have a dry place to stay."

Janek harshly interrupted Lancelot as he re-entered the room with a small plate and a sandwich. Lancelot turned away, back to the fireplace, annoyed. He casually placed another log on the fire. It was enough of a break to diffuse his anger for the moment.

Amber looked at the two men, from one to the other, and calmly asked, "Do you want me to leave?"

"No." Lancelot turned back to her and this time spoke more calmly. "I just want you to tell me the truth. Who are you?"

She looked away into the fire. The new increased blaze seemed to sparkle in her beautiful eyes. Both men, although concerned as to whom she was and why she was there, were also captivated, almost spellbound by her presence.

"Maybe I'm someone who needs you to help me find out the truth about myself."

Lancelot and Janek mused over her comment. A new silence reigned for a long moment.

Janek handed her the plate with the sandwich.

As she quietly ate, both Lancelot and Janek were drawn to the life-size portrait of a young woman that hung over the fireplace. In a moment of revelation, they glanced at each other and silently agreed that the woman in the portrait had an uncanny resemblance to the woman who now sat before them.

Noting the portrait as well, Amber smiled but responded as though it held no meaning to her, but underneath her smile was something more. Something only she knew.

"Such a beautiful woman!" she stated.

Lancelot stepped forward briefly, looking intently at her. "Enchanting, at the very least. There is quite a resemblance in the portrait to you, don't you think?" Lancelot remarked inquisitively.

"How nice of you to say that!" Amber nonchalantly shrugged with her response, "Must be a coincidence."

Janek had a different reaction to her words. It was apparent to him, and perhaps to her as well, that there was more to the portrait and to her resemblance to it.

"More tea?" he offered.

"No." She smiled thankfully. "Maybe a glass of wine."

Lancelot handed her his glass. "Listen, I didn't mean to upset you. It's just that..."

"...you find it difficult to believe. Believe that a woman in a wedding dress could unexpectedly show up at your doorstep on a stormy night, lost, and not knowing who she is."

"Well..."

"Sounds like a made-up story. Or maybe a plot to a book," she concluded before casually taking a sip of the wine.

Janek lightly laughed. "All of life is just another plot to another book," he stated, whether alluding to her comment or to the way the evening had transpired.

Lancelot turned directly to him, now bothered by his apparent word riddle that added to hers.

"Yes." He pretended to agree and spoke softly with a sinister-like smile, "Everything is a book. A yet-to-be-written book of one's life."

"Or, maybe, of one's death," Amber interrupted casually before taking another sip of her wine.

The pauses and the silences between the three of them were common now. As she continued to eat her sandwich in silence, she studied the faces of both men. Whether they were tired of their own questions and lack of her answers or just sorting out what was known and what remained unknown, it seemed to be written on their expressions.

Lancelot finally let out a deep breath as he adjusted his attitude to be more friendly and less argumentative.

"So, you remember nothing, nothing further to tell us...to help us help you?

"No."

"Hmm." Lancelot's utterance seemed to answer for him.

"Well, maybe a good night's sleep will help your memory. In the meantime, you're safe here. We can try to sort it all out in the morning," Janek added his opinion to the discussion.

She nodded. Nothing more was needed to be said for the time being.

"You can use one of the bedrooms upstairs. Only two beds have been made—mine, and Lancelot's. The other bedrooms have been left untouched. We weren't expecting guests. So you can look at both and decide which one you want."

"That's kind of you. I've imposed enough already. I can stay down here. The fireplace is warm, and I feel comfortable here."

"Are you sure?" Lancelot asked.

"Yes."

"Okay. Well, if you want company, I can stay with you a while longer," Lancelot was quick to add. His question seemed less sincere and maybe something else.

"Thank you. No. I'm fine, just tired. As you said, maybe in the morning I will remember more."

"Yes, in the morning. To sort this all out," Janek stated as an agreed plan to their conversation.

"Yes. I suppose so." Amber gave another smile. Seemingly sincere. Seemingly content.

"Goodnight then. If you need anything, our rooms are the first ones on either side of the upstairs landing," Janek concluded.

She nodded her understanding while wrapping herself tightly with a blanket. Her eyes turned away and stared at the remaining fire.

Lancelot's eyes lingered on her for another moment before turning away himself and following the older man up the stairs.

At the top of the stairway, they stopped to face each other. Lancelot briefly looked back down to feel comfortable that they were far enough away so as not to be heard.

"Do you believe her?"

It was Janek's turn to look back. She was there as they left her, huddled under a blanket on the large sofa in front of the fireplace.

"Possibly."

"Possibly? Some things are hard to believe that they just possibly happen. A mysterious, hot-looking woman in a torn wedding gown on a stormy night comes suddenly out of nowhere?"

"Don't forget the open grave."

"Yeah, another nice touch. An obvious touch to this whole thing. Something we both might conjure up in a story if we were writing this."

"Maybe we are."

"You know, Janek, for being the 'supposed' critically acclaimed horror writer, your answers bore me."

Janek showed his reply with no expression, nothing at all to reveal what he thought. Instead, and unexpectedly, he reached out with one hand and put it lightly on Lancelot's closest shoulder.

"Then maybe you'll sleep better."

Lancelot was surprised at his words. Before he could say something clever back, Janek removed his hand and added, "I know I will. It has been a rather long day. We have a lot more to write tomorrow, and now we have her here. So, before I bore you anymore, I'm tired, too. Enjoy your sleep. You'll need it."

His words and look left a lasting impression on Lancelot. It was like he and the mystery woman were in on this together and he was the one they were playing for a fool. *"You'll need it?"* In his mind he pondered if that last comment was a threat or meant to be something else.

Quietly turning away, Janek's cane made a series of small thumps on the wooden floor as he entered his room and closed the door behind.

Lancelot remained, reflecting on their conversation and the events of the evening. He privately contemplated going back downstairs, maybe to question her more, or maybe to...

With a strange sardonic-like smile, instead, he turned and entered his room, leaving the door partially open.

In the morning, she was gone. So was her white dress.

Janek's clothes lay neatly folded on the sofa. As if they were never worn.

Chapter 19

Janek was the first to arrive downstairs as the filtered morning light came through the large windows. He passed the parlor without even a glance. The flames in the fireplace had died out and left the large room darker and colder than the other parts of the house where the early morning sun chased away the shadows of the night.

In the kitchen, Janek went about his usual morning routine making his special tea. The ingredients were in two metal cannisters on the kitchen counter marked with his name. The small microwave, which had been left with their food supply, made a soft humming sound as the tea went round and round on the glass carousel within. Pushing the button to open the microwave, he carefully took out his tea and savored its smell. It would be a moment before he tasted it. It needed to be the exact temperature he was accustomed to. Pushing aside the old, faded, cloth window curtain, he quietly stood looking outside. The sun was rising higher and the day appeared to be a pleasant one in the offing. Last night's storm was long gone. But today's storm was yet to come.

Noting sudden creaking sounds, he heard Lancelot's step on every stair as he came down. Somewhere between the bottom of the stairs and the entrance to the kitchen, Janek knew he must have paused. There was a lengthy, awkward silence before he entered the room. His first words were far from a pleasant morning greeting.

"So, where is she?"

"She?"

"Don't play games. Amber, or whatever her real name is. The clothes you gave her to wear last night are on the sofa, and her gown is gone. So, where is she?"

Janek looked back outside, not to avoid the question, but maybe to find the answer. Without turning back, he finally replied.

"Have you checked the graveyard?"

Without another word, Lancelot rushed out of the room.

Janek casually took a sip of his tea while continuing to look out the kitchen window. He watched as Lancelot hurried across the damp morning grass towards the fenced-in family cemetery. Putting his empty teacup on the counter, Janek gave a slight smile, reached for his cane, and left to join him.

When Janek finally met up with him, Lancelot was finishing his walk through the graves. His face wore a mask of confusion. He had stopped and was staring at one grave in particular. The early morning sun cast a bright ray of golden light on it. Visible in the gray rock face was a very worn etched name.

Amber.

"Well, it looks like we found her," Lancelot pondered.

Janek came next to him and also looked at the standing gravestone.

"We found a headstone with a name that is the same as hers," he remarked.

"And this is where the open grave was," Lancelot quickly added, unbelieving what he wanted to believe.

Janek did a quick visual survey of the small, overgrown graveyard. Whether from age, wind, or trespassers' damage, several of the standing tombstones were tilted and worn. The waist-high metal fence surrounding the cemetery was very rusty and leaning inward in several places.

There was no open grave to be seen anywhere. Nor any indication of a freshly dug, or recently covered hole in the ground. Nothing.

"You looked through the surrounding area also?" Janek asked with a genuine tone in his voice. It was as though he was also puzzled by all of this.

"Well, we're not exactly at the sprawling Forest Lawn Cemetery in Los Angeles. This is where we found her last night. There are a few family graves here. Nothing more, and..."

"Amber's," Janek solemnly stated.

Lancelot's gaze went to the surrounding woods, expecting to see movement or a glimpse of a white gown. There was nothing. He irritably turned back to Janek.

"Is this some type of joke, or are you fucking with my head, Janek?"

"Is that what you believe?" Janek calmly replied.

Lancelot let out a deep breath. It was visible in the crisp air. He, again, did a quick look to the woods to see if anyone was watching them. In that moment, satisfied that they were alone, he brought his temper back in control.

"Look, we both know we don't like each other. So, is this some type of con created by you, or your agent, to try to scare me, to get me to leave early so you can take all the credit for the writing?" Lancelot presumed, as if he already knew the answer.

"I didn't know you scared that easily."

"I don't," Lancelot stated arrogantly.

"Good. Neither do I."

They both studied each other's expression, perhaps looking for a clue as to who was telling the truth and who wasn't.

A sudden morning breeze came through the graveyard. It had a chilling effect, adding to the growing chill between them. The sun darted between a series of passing clouds, mimicking their hot-and-cold conversation.

"So?" Lancelot's one word seemed to challenge Janek.

Janek leaned downward to look closer at the name on the headstone. His wrinkled hand ran his fingers across the letters of her name. He studied it a moment before straightening back up as much as his body would permit. His age and his illness were definitely taking a toll on his stamina and posture.

"So, we have a mystery on our hands. We both saw her. We both talked with her. We both watched her change into my clothes."

"*That* I won't forget," Lancelot interjected with a sly grin.

Janek did not answer his comment. His eyes glanced at the immediate ground and then back to the rest of the small graveyard.

"And we both saw an open grave," Janek added.

"Here."

"Or at least somewhere here," Janek concluded.

"So, we both agree we saw her?" Lancelot's question held a growing feeling of annoyance.

"Or we thought we did."

"Fuck you."

Again, Lancelot's temper got the best of him.

Janek grinned at his comment.

"Maybe you scared her away."

And with those words, seemingly satisfied as to what they discovered, or what remained to be further uncovered, Janek turned and started to walk away.

Lancelot stared silently at him, still annoyed.

Feeling the younger man's cold stare, Janek stopped and turned back, briefly.

"Whatever 'ghost' there was, it can wait till later. We have a story to finish." Janek turned and continued walking back to the waiting house.

Lancelot turned his attention away and looked again at the nearby surrounding ground, still not seeing a trace or any indication that there was ever an open grave. His expression held a contained resentment. He looked back at Janek who was now entering the house. Under his breath he spoke to himself, "That's not all that remains to be finished."

Walking away from the fenced-in family cemetery, he did not see the small, shiny object which lay in the tall grass near the tombstone with Amber's name on it. The tiny item may have been dropped or recently left behind—a small gold cross attached to a thin neck chain. The same one she wore last night.

* * * * *

Back inside the study, both men put aside their differences, questions, and opinions of the past evening and the recent morning. The working mood was neither pleasant nor somber; it was just business. Being day four of their seven-day planned collaboration, they were halfway through their written story as their real story had also started to unfold. Both men had played the game as a skilled card player would, holding their cards close to their chest, or in this case, their true intentions. Both were watching and waiting for their opportunity to reveal their plans and take advantage of the other. Unfortunately, both had already made errors. Lancelot made the mistake of losing his temper and verbalizing his dislike and mistrust of Janek, and Janek had encountered something in the evening walk that reminded him too much of...

"Shall we add her into the story now?" Lancelot interrupted Janek's typing of the previous day's notes. "Since we're using this setting as a metaphor of the haunted house in the story, we could introduce her as one of the characters who helps unravel the clues that reveal the killer," Lancelot continued.

"Bringing the surprise element of an unexpected visit by a spirit from another world," Janek added.

"Or someone pretending to be a spirit," Lancelot countered, making an assumption.

"Or shall we write it as life imitating art?" Janek replied solemnly.

Lancelot momentarily reflected about his comment. Walking to the large window, he looked outside, taking a brief respite to collect his next thoughts. Finally, he returned to face Janek.

"We can use this unknown woman, this spirit, shall we call her, as a character who channels between the conscious and unconscious minds of our other characters, a pathway through which our monsters exist."

"The dark thoughts of the unconscious can give access to one's physical world. That will certainly work in the story. And certainly, within our monsters," Janek indicated.

"Yes, our monsters," Lancelot thought aloud for him to hear. He took his time returning to the table and again sat across from Janek.

"Men and monsters," he continued.

Janek moved his hands away from the typewriter and folded his arms across his chest. Without any expression he stared at Lancelot.

"Monsters and men," Janek replied.

Lancelot once again contemplated the older writer's response.

In the new silence, Janek unexpectedly started to cough. His hand held his chest to try to suppress it. It was a long, deep cough, echoing ominously throughout the tall room. His face tightened from the pain he tried not to show.

Lancelot curiously watched Janek's pained expression but offered no help. He showed neither concern nor enjoyment of the older man's discomfort. Janek's declining health was not a hidden secret; it was very apparent, especially now. After a few short moments, which seemed like an eternity between them, Janek's coughing subsided.

Once the coughing ended, and they both were seemingly satisfied that they could continue their work, Lancelot carefully leaned across the table and folded his hands together, waiting for the right moment. He looked directly at Janek.

"Ever since we started this collaboration, you seem to be hiding something. Something which seems to be affecting you. Affecting us. I'm not a doctor, nor a friend, and what becomes of your physical health I could care less. But it's your mental health that concerns me. Or, shall I be honest and say, 'fascinates' me. Don't you sometimes feel trapped in your words, in your thinking? Or do you know how to keep in harmony with all the craziness that you imagine and share with everyone in your stories? Especially what you imply."

"My stories reflect the truth."

"Or maybe hide it?"

There was an awkward pause between them, different and unlike the previous silences. Almost as though both had touched a sensitive, hidden chord within each other. Lancelot casually rubbed his chin, thinking before speaking again.

"Why are you really here?"

Janek tilted his head, turning a blind eye to the real answer. He grinned slightly, not quite a smile, nor a sneer. Just a look as if he knew something the other didn't, and it was his turn to play his cards.

"I'm here because of you."

* * * * *

Nighttime came quickly and its surrounding shadows embraced the house both outside and inside. Lancelot sat alone in the parlor in front of the warm burning fireplace. He sipped on his wine thinking of the mysterious woman who also drank from his glass the previous night. The image of her removing her clothes and revealing her beautiful body in the light of the fire pleasantly resurfaced in his memory. Taking another taste of the wine, he licked his lips slowly.

In the hallway behind him, the front door opened and closed. Lancelot paid no attention; it was Janek returning from his nightly after-dinner walk. Except this night, Janek hadn't joined him for dinner. He had been eating less and less with each meal and seemed to be drinking more of his special tea, instead. After their day of writing together, Janek had silently left the study and went directly to his room. He resurfaced later without a word and went outside on his own.

Lancelot had watched from the parlor window as Janek went to the graveyard, stood in front of the headstone with Amber's name on it and seemed to talk to someone. It was the same area where they had found her last night. He could see Janek's lips move, or so he thought. But there was no one there to talk to, at least no one he could see. Maybe he did this purposely, knowing that he was probably being watched by Lancelot. Was he putting on a show, another part of this strange scenario involving the mystery woman? Or maybe he was doing this because he was crazy. After all, Janek had shown some strange characteristics of being a bit crazy the past few days. But, so had he.

From his viewpoint at the window, Lancelot saw that Janek had suddenly stopped his imaginary conversation. He remained alone in the early evening breeze. Lancelot also watched as Janek slowly reached down to the ground and appeared to pick something up. Something small that he couldn't see from his perspective. Something Janek put into his pocket. Something he brought back into the house with him.

Lancelot heard the door close behind him. Silently passing the parlor, Janek went up the stairs to his room. Only the crackling embers of the burning wood in the fireplace drifted through the otherwise stillness of the house.

Lancelot put the half-empty glass of wine on the table next to him and left the room. It was his turn to go out into the night.

* * * * *

There would be no storm that night. That would come another night. Tonight, it was just windy and cold. Autumn had been knocking on the doorstep of each passing day and soon the trees on the property and the surrounding deep forest would be barren and hibernating. But not quite yet. Although the recent storms had brought a lot of the leaves down, a lot more remained. Enough to hide someone or something in the shadows of the woods. Hiding, it watched him. Watched and waited for him.

Lancelot went directly to the graveyard. Carrying a flashlight, he retraced his earlier steps from the morning and also retraced the recent steps he had watched Janek take tonight. It was a small flashlight which he found in a kitchen drawer, but it gave enough light to help him see in the falling darkness of the night. With his beacon of light, he carefully circled the outside cemetery perimeter before feeling comfortable enough to enter through the single hanging gate. A full moon came into view from behind the clouds that it had hid in, synchronized with Lancelot's entrance into the burial grounds.

Standing in front of the grave marked *Amber,* he contemplated what exactly Janek might have found in the overgrown grass. The flashlight was becoming dimmer and he cursed it as he hit it against his leg. Somehow it was enough of a jolt to bring it back to life temporarily. His eyes searched the ground directly in front of him. Nothing. And then…something.

A soft sounding voice from the woods called out his name.

"Lance..a…lot."

His name was pronounced like a song. A song chanted by a woman.

Again, he heard it.

"Lance…a…lot."

The one word was stretched, soothing, hypnotic. It sent a chill through his mind and also his body. And as quickly as he heard it, it ended. Only the cascading wind remained, bending the old tree limbs slightly as if fingers were pointing directly at him.

His eyes scoured the surrounding woods, looking for the woman or whatever it was that the voice had emanated from. But he saw nothing, and the light of the small flashlight was now nearly gone. Alone in the moonlight, where he would normally enjoy his nighttime secret activities, he was now shaken by the unknown. Shaken by hearing his name called out in such a strange and melodic manner, shaken by what he tried to understand was yet to come.

"Lance..a…lot."

Again the woman's soft voice beckoned him.

"Who are you? Where are you?" he shouted into the empty, dark night.

"I'm here. Find me."

The woman's voice was alluring, stirring something sexual within him. Awakening a primal animal instinct, a mating call...

"Lance...a...lot."

He gave a low growling-like sound as he spun around quickly.

"Where are you? Who are you?"

Again. "Lance...a...lot."

"Fuck!" he muttered as he turned yet again and hurried into the direction the voice had come.

"Not there. Here."

He quickly stopped, almost losing his footing. The voice now came from behind, not in front.

"Can't you see me?" the young woman's voice teased him again, this time from behind.

"Amber?"

The woman's laugh lightly caressed his ears. He spun around.

Nothing, just the wind.

"I see you."

"I can't see you," he shouted back into the black emptiness.

"Yes, you can. I'm here next to you."

But no one was there. It was like a child's game of hide and seek.

Then he suddenly felt something. He felt a touch, a playful caress, as though someone were whispering into his ear. His neck tightened from it, responding with what a child would call goosebumps, but what an adult would call *fright*.

Ever so gently, the voice whispered his name again, directly into his ear for only him to hear.

"I want you."

This time the words weren't playful. This time they were haunting.

Lancelot spun around and around again. Looking into the woods. Nothing. Looking back to the house. Nothing. Looking everywhere. Nothing.

And then he saw her.

Amber. There, fifty feet away at the edge of the deep woods in the same white wedding gown she wore the night before. There, standing between the night's darkness and the moon's brightness, a vision of unbelievable beauty. There, smiling at him. Ever so coyly, ever so lustfully.

As suddenly as she had appeared, she turned and disappeared into the woods.

How fast he ran, only he knew. Faster than he had run in many of his years. He ran towards the woods and then into the woods. There she was ahead, looking back at him, laughing as she ran almost in slow motion. She seemed to float, her bare feet never touching the wet leaf-filled ground beneath her. And yet, the faster he ran, he could never get any closer. The distance between them always seemed to remain the same. It never changed.

Chasing after her through the woods and then out of the woods, she was there and then not there. He ran after a voice that kept echoing in the air between them, a voice that kept repeating and repeating...

"Lance...a...lot."

And then the voice was gone.

And so was she.

And he was now standing in the exact place he had stood minutes ago when he held the dying flashlight in the graveyard and first heard her voice. The exact same place. As though he had never moved a single inch.

The only difference between then and now was that he was covered in sweat. A cold, clammy sweat.

Exhausted. Perplexed. Dismayed. Only his deep, panting breath from the run he had done or thought he did, filled the immediate air. He glanced one more time to the foreboding woods. Nothing.

Slowly, he returned to the waiting house. There were no further sounds to attract his attention. Only a deep and dark loneliness that seemed to accompany and embrace him.

Back inside the house, he immediately drank the rest of his wine. He poured another half glass and then drank that, too. Not sipping, as before, but downing it immediately into his mouth to erase the memory of what had just happened. The fireplace made a few small crackling sounds. It needed more wood to survive, but it didn't matter to him at this point. What mattered to him was the madness that raced through his mind.

"Lance...a...lot." This time her voice wasn't from outside. This time he heard her voice in his head.

As a man on the edge of madness, he furiously threw his empty glass into the remnants of the fire. It shattered into a thousand glowing pieces, each piece showing a sparkling image of a woman's laughing red lips. He turned and abruptly left the room behind.

"Lance...a...lot," the room softly whispered to itself as the fire died out and darkness took its place.

When Lancelot entered his bedroom, he was shocked at what he saw.

There, on his open, turned-back bedsheets, Amber lay totally naked.

The dim room light gave her an appearance of an angel, yet her strange, alluring smile revealed her more as a devil in disguise.

Without a word, Lancelot quietly closed the door behind him and stood motionless staring at her naked beauty.

She slowly opened her mouth and her tongue sensually licked her lips.

Their eyes locked together.

"I've been waiting for you."

Chapter 20

Janek sat quietly in his bedroom turning the delicate item in his hand over and over, back and forth. Lost in thought, he held it tightly, yet gently, knowing where it came from and to whom it had belonged. Yet, he pondered, could it possibly belong to someone else? The blazing fire in the room's fireplace illuminated his larger-than-life shadow on the wall from his position in the single upholstered chair. But he wasn't alone. Another shadow sat opposite him on the same wall. Together they remained as a portrait frozen in time. The fire suddenly flickered from its steady burning flames and made both of the still shadows seemingly come to life.

"So, when did it begin?"

"The pain?"

"If that's what you call it."

"It has always been with me. A part of me. I don't recall a beginning. I am just looking for an ending."

"To the pain?"

"To everything."

"So, when did it begin?"

"A long, long time ago."

"How long?"

"Longer than I can remember."

"Forever?"

"If not more."

"What do you remember most about the pain?"

"Mostly darkness. Mostly sorrow. Mostly emptiness."

"And yet you're here today. You're a survivor."

"But I'd rather be dead."

"And you know that will happen soon."

"Yes, but not soon enough."

"So, when did it begin?"

"I can tell you a story."

"I would like that. But not 'a' story, *the* story."

"Of course. The story. The story begins with my earliest recollections as a child. We were traveling from town to town. We had two horse-drawn covered wagons. We slept in them; we lived in them."

"We?"

"Our family. We were gypsies. We carried a mixture of things to sell, to trade, as we went from town to town. We never stayed in one place too long. We had to keep moving—it was important. We had to protect our secret to make sure that no one outside the family discovered what we so carefully kept hidden."

"Secrets are important. And, sometimes, should be taken to the grave."

"Yes, as I was told it should. And it will."

"What do you remember most about your family?"

"I remember my father. He was a good man, a good provider. He was always thinking of us, taking care of us."

"He was also a good father."

"Yes. I think so. I was young, and only knew him a few years before he died. But yes, from my recollections, he was a good father. I miss him."

"What else do you remember?"

"I remember my older sister; she was my best friend. She was thirteen, smart, attractive, and kind. She cared for me and my little sister."

"Tell me about your little sister."

"She always smiled."

"Did you smile too?"

"I didn't know how."

"Do you smile now?"

"Does it matter?"

"Sometimes."

"I suppose."

"Do you remember him?"

"Him? How could I not? It's because of him that I'm here."

"Finally."

"Yes, after all these years of searching for him."

"What do you remember about him?"

"How we found him. That dark starless night. I remember the howls of a dying creature from somewhere in the forest where we had camped. Ungodly sounding howls of something evil. And I remember how he stumbled into our camp shortly after. I remember how he was bleeding to death and how we saved his life. Why we did that I'll never understand."

"Maybe it was meant to be."

"Maybe we should have left him to die."

"Then everything would have been different."

"For the better."

"Or maybe the worse. What else do you remember about him?"

"After we nursed him back to health, he acted strange. Withdrawn. He never spoke to us. Whether from the shock of whatever happened to him that night, or the fear he held secretly in his soul of what he was to become. He never spoke a word. He just stared at us. And then when he healed, he disappeared."

"Perhaps he knew."

"That he was hiding a beast?"

"Or maybe he knew you were hiding a beast, too."

"He was a child like me, how could he?"

"A beast can smell; a boy can't."

"He wasn't human."

"Neither were you."

"Nor our family."

"No."

"I knew we were different from all the others. My father told us that. He told us that we were the last of a long-lost family of..."

"And you didn't know you were one of them as a child?"

"No. No, I didn't quite understand what he said. How could I? I was too young to realize the truth. I didn't come to know it till later. Until I made my first kill."

"Your first kill?"

"Yes, my first taste of blood."

"And then you knew?"

"Yes."

"You enjoyed the taste. But it wouldn't be your last?"

"No. There can never be a 'last.' If I only knew then."

"Then?"

"The night he came back."

"When he came back to the house?"

"Yes. Years later. We had settled down in a remote area at the base of the Carpathian Mountains. Not far from our ancestor's home."

"They once had a castle."

"If you believe the legend."

"I lived there as a child."

"I never knew that."

"It was not the time to tell you when you were young. And of course, it was part of protecting the secret."

"From me?"

"From the others."

"But it was no secret to him. And it was no secret that he was the one who came back."

"As a soldier?"

"Yes. A soldier."

"He was there when it happened. You watched him."

"Yes, I was still young. He was older than I was then."

"You aged differently. It was part of the secret."

"His secret, too."

"Yes. His secret, too."

"After all we did to save him when he was a young boy, I still can't understand why he came back to kill us?"

"Perhaps it was the beast within."

"Men and monsters?"

"Monsters and men."

"Yes. Monsters and men."

"If you really want to know for sure, you can ask him."

"I will."

"Before you kill him?"

"Before, during, and after."

"And that's why you're here?"

"He killed my sister. He killed my family."

"And now you know."

"Yes, I know everything."

"But are you sure it was him? That he was the one who really did all the killing?"

"I know everything through his writing."

"His writing?"

"His books. He wrote about it in his books. He told his story in his story."

"And you read it?"

"I lived it in my dreams."

"And that's what brought you here, to meet him, to meet the ghost that has haunted you?"

"And for him to meet the ghost that haunts him."

"He knows who you are?"

"Yes. I have told my story in my stories also."

"The story of how men and monsters chase each other, find each other and..."

"End the story together."

"As we will finally be. Together again."

"Yes. Together again."

There was a pause between them.

"Do you miss me?"

"Yes."

"Do you love me?"

"I always have. I always will."

"You've been a good son."

"You've been a good mother."

"It's almost time."

"I know."

"But first you have to finish the story."

"I will."

"It will end soon."

"Yes. Very soon."

"I will wait for you. I always have."

"As I have waited to be with you and the rest of our family."

"Before you go, can you hug me?"

"Yes. I miss your hugs."

"I know. I miss yours, too."

Listening to those final words, Janek exhaled a long, deep breath and slowly got up from his chair. With a cane to steady himself, he crossed the bedroom to where she sat.

Bending downwards, he lovingly put his arms around her. In the silence of their embrace, a single tear came from his eye. It was his first real emotion in a long time. A long, long time. The tear slowly rolled down his thin, wrinkled face and gently fell into her open hand. He held her for a long moment, not wanting to let go. And when he did, he gently kissed her goodbye on her cheek. He smiled a real smile for the first time in *forever*—a telling smile of an approaching happiness. They would be together, finally.

Opening his hand, he took the small item he had held throughout their entire conversation—the chain with the gold cross that he had found in the graveyard. Gently, he placed it around her neck. It belonged to her now, forever.

With his hug, with his kiss, and now with this symbol of his undying love, he knew what had to be completed so that his pain would finally be gone. And soon he would be, too. He had come to terms with himself, and now everything was coming together and, before long, it would all be finished.

Again, using his cane, Janek turned and left the room, closing the door silently behind him.

She remained quietly in her chair opposite his. Not moving. Just staring ahead into empty space and at the closed door from which he left. Maybe reflecting on the words spoken, or maybe remaining silent, content to await his promised return. Although the room lighting had remained dim, the moonlight from the window behind bathed her in a tender glow. The dress she wore was the perfect outfit for their long overdue conversation. It seemed made for her, covering her from the neck down to her exposed feet.

A combination of delicate white lace and woven golden silk. For her age, she looked stunning. She looked so alive for someone so dead. A full-bodied skeleton in a rotting dress. A skeleton, with traces of dirt and mud from the grave from which he had just dug her up. A skeleton with worms and maggots still hiding in between her brittle and broken bones. Although still lifeless beyond the years of her burial, she almost...almost looked alive once again. And perhaps she was...to a man gone mad.

She smiled.

A skeleton that once was his mother, now also shed a lone tear from the dark empty sockets that held no eyes.

Chapter 21

Somewhere far away he heard a scream. But there was nothing he could do.

Chained to a crumbling mortared cellar wall, he was alone except for the accompanying black shadows. Shadows that seemed to hold a hundred staring eyes which opened and closed like twinkling stars in his eternal night of horror. The room held a stench of rot from years of being left unattended. But at this moment, he was not alone. There was something waiting for him there in the darkness. And only he knew what it was.

He pulled at the thick chains which held him. The rusty metal links tore at his wrists and added more blood to the blood that already flowed from previous attempts. His bare feet moved frantically beneath him, erratically in the puddles of cold, dirty water that came from the dripping rusty pipes above him. Although he had no idea of how much time had passed since he was chained there, he knew time was not a friend to him. Time was an enemy, and it was quickly running out for him. There would be no escape.

Not this time.

He was naked, stripped of his worldly clothes and left like a newborn baby to await its fate. Naked and cold. All that covered him were his own beads of perspiration and dried and wet patches of blood from before and now. But unlike a baby, he could not let out a cry, a moan, or even a word-filled whimper. His mouth was sewn shut. Completely shut. He couldn't see it. He could only feel it. The sharp silver needle that held the long thick thread that weaved in and out of his bloodied lips still remained at the very end of his swollen skin. And the pain was still there—a pain that held his hurt, his fear, his despair from ever being heard again, from never being allowed to tell his side of the story and to beg forgiveness for what he had done. A physical and emotional pain that he knew was just the beginning and would grow even more painful until the eventual end.

He knew he had to keep trying to break free of his metal bonds if there was any hope at all. He knew what would happen if he didn't. He knew what waited for him in those moving shadows which seemed to grow closer with each exaggerated breath he struggled to take.

He knew everything, and yet, he knew nothing.

Whether it was the remnants of his sanity or the continuation of his insanity, his past life spun before him. And it wasn't pleasant.

The tumbling train car. The blended screams. The smell of death. Those images chased him and lived with him. They haunted him, as did all the other images that flashed before his watering eyes: The giant beast's breath on him. The sharp fangs that entered his chest and cursed his life forever. The family that found him and cared for him. The family he left, returned to, and killed. The many years of running from place to place, hiding from others and himself. He had to, because of who he was, and what he had become. A revolving door of identities to keep himself safe and to keep his secret safe. The metamorphosis of who he really was and what he became never changed. Neither did his appearance. The truth was, he could no longer age.

The chains, which rattled with his body movement, brought him back to the present. He shook his head to shake out the past. The façade of boring book tours that helped him satisfy his hunger and feast on the desires of his adoring fans. He hated them, and yet he found a sickening way to enjoy them, if "enjoy" was the right definition. And, of course, her. Her. It was all because of her. The mysterious woman in white. He loved her. He hated her. He craved her. He spurned her. They were together as one. And now she was gone again. Gone. And he was alone again. Alone.

He knew nothing, and yet, he knew everything.

He stopped struggling. Exhausted. Beaten. Angered. His body begged for sleep; his mind cried out for salvation. The darkness turned to quiet. The quiet turned to...

Drip. Drip. Drip.

The growing sound of water dripping into a nearby bucket acted as the beat of a loud drum. Drip. Drip. Drip. Thump. Thump. Thump. Although its sound was minute, its effect was deafening. It didn't stop. It wouldn't stop. It was there to torment him, as he had done to so many others. And now it was his turn to be tormented. His vision became blurry, then clear, then blurry again. He struggled to see clearly. But everything remained hazy. Was he drugged? Is that how it happened? How else could it have happened?

Drip. Drip. Drip.

The cellar shifted its angles, and his mind shifted its reality. He was trapped, and he could not escape. Nor would he escape. He was finally on the other side of all the hell he had created and left behind. If this is how his victims felt, now he knew. For this time, he was the victim. It was his turn. And it was all because of her.

If he could have laughed, he would have. If he could have cursed, he would have. If he could have screamed, he would have. But the one thing he couldn't do was beg forgiveness. He didn't know forgiveness. He didn't understand forgiveness. How could he? He was a madman gone madder, a killer waiting to be killed, a monster waiting to face another monster.

He knew. He knew it all. He knew the taste of death, and now he knew death would taste him. Finally.

Drip. Drip. Drip.

He struggled again. He *had* to. It was his body reacting, not his mind. The shackles cut deeper into his flesh, but it didn't matter how much blood he was shedding tonight. He just knew there had to be a way out. There *had* to be.

And there was. Or so he thought.

She effortlessly came out of the far cellar wall. He blinked his eyes. She actually came "through" the brick-and-mortar, water-stained wall. Not bursting through it like a make-believe superhero, but coming out of it like a real...

"Ghost!" his sewn mouth wanted to shout out.

His eyes widened in shocking disbelief. How could this possibly be? Ghosts. Spirits. Apparitions. Specters. They didn't really exist. They were just a writer's fantasy or maybe a crazed person's delusion. That's all, nothing more. But...whatever she was, human or not, she now stood before him. As real as someone made of flesh and blood.

Her full-length bridal gown was pristine, as if she just stepped out of a bridal show, not through an old concrete crumbling wall. Not a speck of dirt, dust, or mud on her. Her hair and facial features were perfect. Everything in place, like a timeless portrait of beauty. He imagined her as a store mannequin for all to see and behold. She was flawless, almost. Her bare feet were covered by the dirt and his blood that mixed with the basement floor water. She had to be real. But she came through a solid wall.

With one finger to her lips, she indicated for him to be quiet.

Silently, she stepped through the water. Or was she gliding above it? He wasn't sure. It was all happening so quickly that his mind couldn't process what he saw. Coming closer. Closer to his chained, naked self.

His struggling stopped, and his eyes followed her every movement. Expressionless, she carried a long, brownish rope in her hand. It dragged in the water, making small ripples like a snake swimming behind her. The rope had a full-head noose on one end. In the other hand, she carried a large key.

His hands were individually cuffed to two long chains attached to the wall. She easily inserted the key into the lock of each cuff, and they opened with a loud, creaking sound. Once released, his hands fell forward, weakened from all his struggles to escape. Free of his confining shackles, he sat in the puddle of dirty water beneath her. She smiled and bent forward as if she were going to kiss him. But she didn't. How could she? His lips were stitched together. Instead, her eyes locked with his. In them, he could see an image of the two of them running hand in hand in a sunny summer field of golden flowers. So many beautiful flowers! Then, her eyes suddenly turned black.

He sat there mesmerized as she put the noose around his neck and tightened it. He didn't resist. It felt like it belonged. Backing away, she stood motionless gazing at him while holding the long rope in one hand. The rope around his neck felt cold, felt good, felt like it belonged.

Slowly, he got up from his cramped position. She didn't tell him to; he just did. Too weak to run away, too weak to stand and fight, he teetered on his bare feet, finding his strength. With one finger held to her lips, she again indicated for him to be quiet, before turning the finger around, beckoning him to follow.

Like a dog on a leash, she led him out of the damp and dark cellar into the surrounding shadows and through a long, winding tunnel. He didn't know where they were going. He didn't care. He was free. Or so it seemed.

Her bare feet made no sound or ripple in the puddles. Her long blonde hair blew gracefully in the wind back towards him, except there was no wind, just a stench of dampness and an ominous cold chill which embraced his naked body.

Through the blackness and dimly lit tunnel, he felt eyes watching him, but if there were eyes, they remained hidden, as there was nothing to be seen. But what he didn't see, he could feel. Invisible tiny fingers seemed to touch his body as he walked. Touched him with each step he took. Not in a grabbing manner, but in a caressing manner. He wanted to cringe, but his mind didn't know how.

From the tunnel, they entered a large room—a room he had been in before. The chamber room with the two coffins. They were still there, both closed as before, waiting for him. He wanted to stop and look within as he had done previously, but she tugged on the rope, and it tightened uncomfortably around his neck. She was leading him somewhere else, apparently not here.

He could see traces of fresh blood starting to seep out of both caskets. The seeping turned to oozing and more blood started to pour from each of its sealed lids, flowing down the sleek metal coffin sides. Endless blood cascaded more and more, as if something or someone was bleeding from the inside. But what? Or who? The floor beneath them became permeated with the pouring blood. It quickly covered his feet as he was forced to walk through it.

Ahead, at the end of the room, at the top of the crumbling steps, the only door opened to the outside. How and by whom he did not know or could not imagine. It just did. A starry dark night awaited them as she led him up the gray concrete stairs and into the outdoors. A strange, invisible column of cold air waited for him, making him more uncomfortable in his naked state. He was prepared for the unexpected, but not for what he saw next.

The small family cemetery was completely lit by a ring of tall, standing wooden torches. A whistling wind came from the surrounding trees making the flames dance to a silent song. In the burning light, he could easily make out the few headstones and the surrounding graves. His eyes went directly to one grave in particular. The one he wanted to see and, at the same time, did not want to see. The one marked Amber. It was freshly dug open. A mound of loose dirt lay on one side of it. But there was something else. Something that made his whole body shiver. A tall man, or maybe not a man, stood next to it, completely shrouded in a black robe and wearing a full-length red cape. His face was hidden by a large hood and a deep, foreboding darkness.

He knew who it was. But could it really be?

He wanted to stop and go no further. He wanted to pull back on the lead rope and end the walk now and run away. Run as fast and as far as his legs would take him. But run where? Back into the house of horrors that he just came from, or maybe into the darkness of the surrounding forest to be never seen or heard from again? Swallowed whole into an abyss of the unknown? Yes, that's what he wanted to do. But no, that's not what he could do. He couldn't. It wasn't her strength that pulled him forward; some unknown force was drawing him into the graveyard.

His face was wet with perspiration. What concerned him most was that he wasn't sure if all of this was real or imagined. He had suffered so much already. He had felt the pain from his shackled ordeal and had seen the blood flow from his chained wrists. And his mouth. *God almighty*, it was sewn shut, and it hurt as he tried to open it. The stitching stretched and started to tear, and his lips began to bleed. This was real. All too real.

She led him through the rusty hinged gates. As they opened, the scraping noise sounded like laughter.

She brought him directly to the headstone with her name on it. Directly in front of the open grave. Leaving him there alone, directly across from the mysterious hooded person. He watched as she placed the end of the rope into the stranger's waiting hand. It had all been planned. Like a story he would write. But tonight, it was being written in the night wind.

The stranger's red cape seemed to come alive and flapped in a sudden gust.

From the dark, open grave beneath him came the same chanting sound he had heard before. His name.

"Lance-a-lot..."

Except this time, it wasn't in a woman's voice, nor an unknown person's voice.

"Lance-a-lot..."

It was his voice.

His own voice calling out his own name. His voice, his name. Coming from inside the empty grave.

His neck felt a sharp sudden pain. He was yanked forward. Suddenly, quickly, perhaps expectedly. The rope around his neck tightened as the robed person across the open grave pulled it firmly.

He was falling—falling face-first into the pit—into the encompassing darkness and perhaps into his own private hell. The fall lasted forever, but it only lasted a moment.

Six feet down into the damp murky ground, he landed on his hands and knees like a begging dog. He winced in pain. Breaking the fall with his open hands and naked knees, he was fortunate not to have broken any bones. But not fortunate to prevent what happened next.

A shovel full of cold dirt landed on his back. Then another. He looked upwards into the rectangular grave opening. Looked upwards at the stranger holding another shovel full of dirt, waiting to throw it on him. But he didn't. The hooded person stood waiting, savoring the moment. Waiting for one more revelation to add to everything that had already been revealed tonight. The final act. The final chapter.

From his position in the bottom of the dank grave, he watched as Amber floated above the open ground, her bare feet exposed inches above the dirt and grass. It was more than he could believe, but now he finally did. He finally knew.

Her white gown moved with the wind as she leered sensually at him. Smiled, as if this were a climax to their earlier lovemaking in his warm bed. A long-ago memory that seemed to taunt him, but still left a wanting, stirring sensation throughout his naked body.

The wind's intensity blew her hair wildly, covering her beautiful face in a game of forbidden hide and seek. Alluring. Haunting. She was every man's desire. Amber the angel. Amber the Devil.

She turned to the stranger and carefully lifted back the hood that covered his face. The surprise was expected. The expected was a surprise. It was Janek. But not the frail, old-looking Janek he had grown accustomed to watching this week in their moments together. No, this was a stronger-looking, straighter-looking, taller-looking, imposing figure. It was Janek, but it wasn't. How could that be? He watched in amazement as Janek's face glowed in the moonlight, laughing menacingly. And then the laughter stopped. The wind stopped. All sounds stopped. Everything stopped. Everything, including his own heartbeat. He watched this person, or "non-person," slowly open its mouth. Slowly, oh so slowly. Deliberately. So, so deliberately. Wide enough to show the long, sharp fangs that dripped with reddish, blood-stained saliva. Fangs that didn't belong to a man or a monster, but fangs that belonged to a *vampire.*

"The dead are everywhere," Janek's words echoed into the open grave.

"Everywhere!"

And in that moment, the dirt walls suddenly caved in and covered him completely.

He was buried alive.

Chapter 22

A misty rain had settled over the cemetery. Drizzle, the kind of light moisture that one's body soaks up like a sponge leaving one damp and chilled, wrapped itself around the old house and its surrounding property. Wrapped itself like a cold, wet shroud. In the nearby woods the hooting of an owl was heard. Maybe the owl was just making its typical nightly call to the other animals hiding in the dark. Or, possibly, the call was alerting that something was about to change, and not for the better, so that all the creatures could take flight, find safety, and leave the peril behind.

At first glance, it just looked like a pile of freshly dug dirt. At first glance, especially in the bright moonlight, it just looked like shadows dancing between the dark passing midnight clouds and the threat of another nightly storm. But then the ground began to gently shake. Ever so slightly. Ever so lightly. Something in the earth seemed to push and scratch, determined to release itself. The dirt at the top of the mound began to move as if something, or maybe someone was forcing at it from beneath. Pushing at it with all its might to find a way out. Pushing upward and outward in an attempt to free itself. Free itself from the depths of a freshly buried grave, its own private doorway to death.

The dirt moved more and more, as a single hand slowly arose from it—a large, hairy hand that grasped at the cold air while opening and squeezing its long, hairy fingers together in a show of unspoken triumph. It reached upwards, clutching at more of the invisible air as its wrist and then bare arm followed. Thick and muscular, the arm was covered in long dark-black hair—not the hair of a human, but that of a wild animal.

Having seen enough, and not waiting to see any more, the owl flew away across the face of the full moon. Its flapping wings and the soft pitter-patter of rain drops on the grave's dirt were the only sounds that broke the midnight silence—an ominous silence that would soon showcase the roar of an enraged beast being let out of a trap.

Another hairy hand quickly followed the first one, which continued to grab at the wet dirt and chilled night air as if climbing an imaginary ladder to freedom. The second hand also clutched at the surrounding air and ground, struggling to force itself even more upwards. And it did. It kept moving up towards the black, drizzling sky above. And with the arm's twisted movement, the dirt poured down from its disturbed mound, rolling backwards onto the overgrown and trampled grass from an earlier evening disturbance, creating new little piles.

With another unseen push from beneath the earth, more of the mysterious thing began to emerge through the loose and now mud-encrusted, wet ground. The top of its large head began to surface through the soil. Long, matted, dirt-filled hair appeared first, followed by a wrinkled, furrowed brow across the wide, creased forehead. But that was not all. Next came its eyes. Closed at first, but quickly opening for all the world to see. Eyes red as blood. Looking outwards in absolute anger. Not the eyes of a man, or an animal, but evil and frightening. The eyes of a *monster.*

Suddenly, the remaining ground restricting it burst open. Dirt, mud, and pebbles flew through the air like a volcano erupting and the thing within crawled out quickly. As swiftly as it happened, it stopped. Whatever it was, it remained motionless for a long moment. Exhausted and hunched over, its breaths came quickly, gasping for the air it so desperately needed and sucking it all in to bring it back to some form of full strength from its incredible struggle. It had clawed its way through six feet of dirt atop it. Buried in a grave to die and rot. Buried forever. But now unexpectedly free. Free to take revenge and kill.

From its crouched position, it slowly stood up. Loose dirt rolled off its massive body and wide muscular shoulders. Its hands opened and closed revealing long, thick fingers with sharp-pointed nails. A low snarling sound came deep from within its towering torso. Standing nearly 7 feet tall and weighing over 300 pounds, it was a force to be reckoned with. Turning its massive head and neck, it stretched even more. Its hairy body made snapping sounds like bones being broken or somehow growing even bigger, even longer. This was not a man. This was not a beast. This was a *werewolf*—a werewolf with the heart and mind of someone once named Lancelot. But something now without a mind or a soul.

The drizzle turned to a light rain. The water seemed to bathe the dirty fur of the monster and give it a new appearance in the peek-a-boo moonlight. It sniffed at the wet air, moving its hairy face while smelling the wind. It searched for a scent. The scent of its adversaries. The scent of a man and also the scent of a woman. Scents which emanated from the large mansion standing in the shadows.

A sudden gust of cold wind came through the cemetery's headstones and seemed to carry a siren-like voice with it.

"Lance...a...lot."

The one word stirred something in the monster's awakening thoughts. It turned its head in curiosity looking for the source of the voice. But none could be found.

The one word came again, floating between the increasing raindrops, which bounced off the surrounding headstones.

"Lance...a...lot."

It was clearer this time, more pronounced. It wasn't a woman's voice, as it once recalled. And it wasn't the voice that he faintly remembered as his own. This time, it was clearly Janek's voice.

"It's time to end the story, Lancelot. I'm waiting for you." Janek's solemn words were there, and then not there.

Enraged to the point of madness, the man-monster spun swiftly around and growled. Where was the voice coming from? Where? It was teasing him, mocking him. The raindrops continued splashing in the newly formed puddles and on its large misshapen paw-like feet. It stopped and slowly turned its hideous face to find one headstone in particular. With eyes blazing, its huge burly hands gripped either side of the chosen grayish monument. Arching its back, bending its thick, hairy legs, and forcing all of its strength into a deadly grip, the monster pulled at the large stone and slowly ripped it from the ground. He pulled it entirely out of the earth from where it had stood for only God knows how long. Raising it above his head, the beast held the stone high, with arms outstretched, as the moon illuminated the name on it. *Amber.* With a deafening exhale of all the air it needed to do the task, the monster hurled the headstone into the half-open grave that it had once marked. The engraved stone slab shattered into a hundred pieces like broken glass.

As the moonlight faded behind a long, dark, passing cloud, the cemetery filled with strange-looking shadows. The monster paused, staring at where it knew it needed to go, staring at what would become the long-awaited ending for one of them. Turning his head upwards as far back as it could go, it opened its drooling, saliva-filled mouth and let out an unearthly howl. A howl that could wake the dead. And in that howl, a new voice came floating through the wind. A voice that seemed to gurgle its words as if trying to speak sanely in a moment of raw insanity.

A voice half monster, half man.

"I'm coming, Janek. It's time."

Chapter 23

As Amber started down the grand staircase, it began to rain outside. The sound of the falling raindrops seemed to accompany each of her steps. The lingering beam of moonlight that peeked between the rainclouds and shone through the hall windows made her excited smile even more radiant. She had been looking forward to this moment when they could finally be alone. And she knew he felt the same. It was their time to be together.

Vladamir Janek sat by the fireplace in the same chair where he always sat with his ornate silver wolf's head cane leaning next to it. The fire bathed the mostly darkened room in a warm, soft, yellow glow. A comforting glow. He seemed relaxed and unconcerned as he held an open book in his hands, lost in faraway thoughts as a reader, not a writer. He sat quietly, paying no attention to her entrance.

"A favorite of yours?" she asked.

"A favorite telling of one's life," he casually replied.

"Similar to yours?"

"Similar to ours."

"I'd like to hear it."

He looked down at the open page and started to read. "The eternal wave in the ocean. We can see it; we can measure it; we watch it pass us. We know it's a wave and then it crashes on the shore and then it is gone. But the water is still there."

Her voice, as if on cue, joined together with his, continuing the reading, reciting the words aloud in her head and heart.

"The wave was just another way of the water being a part of life, then it returns to the ocean the way it should be."

He closed the book.

"Camus," she stated matter of factly. "A favorite author of mine."

"I know," he replied.

"It is a shame that great authors are being forgotten, becoming lost in today's clutter of new authors," Amber contemplated out loud.

"Replaced by people who think they are authors, but who don't understand the true meaning of what words they write," Janek added sadly.

"Or how to express."

"But mostly, how to feel," he added.

"Unlike you."

He placed the book on the end table next to his chair.

"I never critique my work. I leave it for others. I write because I must," Janek commented calmly.

"To clear your mind?"

"To cleanse my soul."

"Does *he?*" Amber asked innocently.

Janek took hold of his cane with one hand. He clutched the top of it tightly, wrapping his bony fingers totally around the silver wolf's head.

"Lancelot writes as a way to use his fan adulation to find new prey."

"And kill?"

"We all kill don't we? Whether in action or words."

"Some of us prefer to express our feelings through love," Amber tenderly countered.

Janek let go of his cane, replacing it at the side of his chair. His gaze went past her to the fireplace, watching the flames flicker while dissecting the meaning of her words.

She reached for a small log at her feet and placed it into the fire. A few sizable sparks rose high in the air with a popping sound. Turning back to him, she rubbed her hands, enjoying the renewed heat.

"You are a brilliant author. You write beautifully, Vladamir. I admire your writing," she spoke profoundly.

He smiled a reply, acknowledging her kind words. "Do you write?" he asked.

"Sometimes."

"What do you like to write about?"

"People. People like you."

Vladamir looked at her closely, studying her angelic-like features.

"Do you believe in ghosts?" she asked in a serious tone.

He thought for a long moment before answering her question.

"Does it really matter what I believe?"

She looked at him carefully, trying to find his answer to her question in his expression. In his face she saw so many different answers.

"Sometimes," she finally replied.

There was an aura of strangeness about her and her answer. It was as though she knew something he didn't. But he knew something she wanted to know. Janek enjoyed this private conversation with her. He wanted to find out more about this mysterious woman who had entered his world.

Without another word, she left her position at the fireplace and deliberately crossed the distance between them. Standing directly before him, his eyes searched hers. He saw so many different emotions in her face.

"Why are you here?" he politely asked.

"To meet you," she answered without any hesitation.

Janek sat silent, not believing her entirely.

"To meet you both," she added. "You both fascinate me." As she revealed one mystery about herself, she hid another behind it.

He let out a half-laugh.

"You remind me of someone," Janek gently spoke, as if looking at a totally different person from the one who now stood directly in front of him.

"Someone? Someone special?" she teased politely.

"Hmm. Yes. Very special," Janek added sincerely.

He closed his eyes briefly, searching for a particular lost memory.

"I'm glad if it makes you happy." Amber smiled.

"Happiness is such a fleeting moment in the overall time of one's life," Janek replied with a sad sigh.

"Who was she?"

"A woman I knew a long time ago. She had beautiful eyes.

"Like mine?"

"Aqua blue, like an untouched ocean. Her hair was like yours, too. Perhaps a bit more golden."

"As if the sun shone through it wherever she went?"

"Always."

"What else?"

"She was tall like you. Your features resemble hers."

"Or maybe she resembled me."

He looked at her again, this time in a different sense, looking at her as though he could read every thought in her head.

"And her smile would bring me much happiness whenever I was sad."

"She must have loved you."

He didn't answer.

"Where is she now?"

"Here."

"So, you think I'm her?"

He touched his heart.

"We all carry our loved ones somewhere within. It is a part of a tragic love story we all have experienced and hold throughout our life."

"Do you dream?" she questioned.

"Of her?"

"Of me. Do you remember anything about me?"

"Should I?"

"Perhaps."

He rubbed his eyes with both hands and then rubbed his hands together, whether erasing a memory or trying to bring one back. Letting out a deep breath, he looked away from her and at the fire.

"My life is like a dream—a lot of fleeting images. People's faces, places, colors, then nothing. Then it repeats again. A timeless, endless dream."

"Do you think you are dreaming now?"

"Perhaps."

"Then say goodbye to me now, before you wake up." She smiled softly.

Janek returned his look directly to her, searching deep within his memories—searching for something he wanted to ask her since the moment he saw her.

"Are you real...or are you a ghost?"

With a happy, yet sad expression, Amber deliberately reached downward and gently touched his face with the back of her hand.

"When I kiss you goodbye, see if I leave lipstick on your face."

Slowly, she leaned forward and kissed him on the cheek.

His eyes locked on hers, as they seemed to dance in the firelight.

She leaned in again, and this time, kissed him on the lips. For how long and with what amount of passion remained a timeless secret between them. She slowly pulled back and smiled, her eyes shining.

Janek closed his eyes and sat back in his chair. He took in a deep, satisfying breath. The fireplace wood crackled, and a feeling of warmth and serenity washed over his body.

When he opened his eyes again, she was gone.

He was alone. Alone again, like most of his life. But not alone for long.

The front door suddenly burst opened.

The sound and feel of a fierce wind blew into the house and all the way to the fireplace, wrapping Janek with an ominous chill. The flames jumped in response, illuminating hidden shadows that seemed to have waited for this long-awaited moment. He turned his head and stared at the sudden intrusion. In the doorway, with a storm brewing at his back, stood Lancelot.

Or something that was once Lancelot.

Chapter 24

"You're going to kill me?"

"Yes," the monstrous thing growled back in a half-human voice.

"I don't die easy," Janek stated shrewdly.

The monster's voice searched for human words. "I...know," it uttered, pronouncing each syllable slowly as it fought to balance the mind of a mature man with a mindless beast.

A faint, amused smile crinkled Janek's lips. "And I'm going to kill *you*."

The man-beast nodded and whispered back, "Yes."

It twisted its neck sniffing at the air and drooled thick saliva onto the floor. Then the werewolf's eyes locked onto Janek's. The creature spoke again, this time more discernable. "It is...the way the game...ends."

"Or the end to the story," Janek replied as if his words had been already planned, rehearsed, just waiting for the right moment of revelation.

"Our...story." The monster licked its lips in anticipation. It started to move forward slowly, its thick, long legs steadying it upright as it walked as a man, not as a beast.

"Yes. Our story." Janek unhurriedly stood up from his chair, balancing himself with his cane. He wasn't as anxious for battle as he had been in the cemetery, facing an invisible enemy. This time he stood calmly, waiting to meet the monster head-on. Waiting.

It moved so fast! It was like a blur. One moment it stood halfway through the hallway entrance; in the next moment, it had Janek's throat in its huge, furry, claw-like hands, lifting the tall, thin man off the floor and breathing its foul-smelling breath directly into his shocked face.

Janek's feet kicked in the air hopelessly, as the monster lifted him higher off the floor. His hands struggled to break free from the creature's vise-like grip.

With a tremendous burst of inhuman strength, the man-beast easily threw Janek across the room to the fireplace wall. Janek's cane became dislodged from his hand and landed directly into the fire and settled between two burning logs, with the bottom of the cane protruding outward. A sickening cracking noise came from Janek's back, as his broken body slid down the brick mantle and onto the floor into a sitting position. His hands laid at his sides, twitching from the severe and sudden damage done to his frail body. His eyes closed. He was dying.

The monster snarled its enjoyment and gradually crossed the room and stood mere feet away, stretching its huge hairy body in a moment of triumph. Savoring the moment of the expected kill that was to follow, its jaws opened wide as if laughing at the easily defeated old man. But it wasn't laughter that came from within the beast's belly. It was a hissing sound as it leaned its hunched-over frame closer to the seated, dazed victim—a horrid hissing sound as it prepared to deliver a final deathblow.

To the monster's surprise, Janek's closed eyes abruptly opened. With one hand, Janek firmly grabbed the cane and quickly pulled it out of the fire. The silver wolf's head, now a sizzling hot poker, glowed bright red. With all his remaining might, Janek thrust it directly into the monster's leaning, exposed chest. Directly into its beating heart. Directly into it, and through it.

The beast's huge body exploded in pain. Howling, thrashing, screaming! The entire house seemed to shake.

Injured from the attack, Janek used his hands to crouch forward and slowly rise to his feet. He held onto the fireplace to steady himself. The monster thrashed backward across the room, knocking over furniture while futilely pulling at the cane stuck so deeply into his chest. Whether it had burned a hole into its heart or was lodged between its chest bones, it wouldn't come out. The werewolf roared again.

Composing himself while catching his breath, Janek smiled, a slow, ominous smile. His blue eyes grew brighter like a star bursting in the cosmos. Under his clothing, his body seemed to stretch itself in anticipation of its increased deformity. His veins began to pulsate and bulge from his skin.

Something behind those eyes began to blaze with a hard and purposeful delight. A thread of reddish saliva dangled from the corner of his mouth, which continued to stretch along with his body.

His lips pulled away from his glistening teeth in a rather frightening sneer. Two front cuspids started to grow longer, pointed. His eyes now glittered yellow like the center of a fire. Janek was changing, growing stronger. Transforming into something other than himself. It was his turn to show "his" monster. It was his turn to unleash the beast within—he was no longer a frail, weak, dying old man. He was now an unholy thing spawned from a century-old family of similar things. He was a vampire.

And it was his turn to attack.

Grabbing hold of his cane's handle sticking out of the werewolf's chest, Janek shoved it forward, deeper, all the way through its thick body until it burst through the monster's hairy back. And with it came its heart, beating on the end of the ornate silver wolf's head as blood dripped from it. The creature's exposed heart was stuck at the end of the wolf's head cane like a burned piece of meat.

Janek leaned forward, his face was now mere inches away from the monster's face. Their breaths combined in a struggle of pure hatred—pure unadulterated pent-up hatred. The vampire twisted and snapped the cane breaking it in two inside the werewolf's shuddering body. Its eyes became glazed, partially closed. It had trouble breathing and gasped for air. It was dying. Without a heart, how can one live? Not a human, nor a human turned into a thing.

Exposing his fangs in the glistening room light, Janek's disturbing smile said what words could never express. He sunk his fangs deep into the werewolf's neck. There would be no escape from this ending now. Janek's fangs savored the taste of Lancelot's blood.

But again, death didn't come easy. While its blood was being sucked out, the dying beast's eyes snapped open in a moment of final strength and its paw-like hands swiftly pushed Janek away. Enraged with a reborn hatred, it reached to its own chest and slowly pulled out the protruding cane. As it held the cane, it sniffed at its own blood which dripped onto its furry hands. It smiled, if a monster could do such a thing, then licked the blood off its hands.

Without warning, it howled from the top of its lungs and thrust the sharp stake-like cane deep into Janek's heart. Deep into it and through it. Snarling, as it twisted and turned it. Roaring, as it enjoyed the moment of giving pain as much as it had received pain. Pushing, as it impaled the cane deeper into Janek's chest. The beast's hand pierced through the screaming vampire's skin, pulling at tendons and arteries exposed from the brutal penetration of the killing weapon. Plunging its hand even deeper into the screaming vampire's body, it discovered the prize it searched for. And once found, the beast slowly brought its hand back out of the vampire's body, holding its closed fist high above its snarling face to admire the prize. Opening its fist, it revealed Janek's bloody, beating heart.

Janek's eyes filled with horror. His mouth filled with blood. Gurgling sounds came from his throat as he gasped for air. It was his turn to die. Perhaps they both would die, not as men, but as monsters. They both fell to their knees clutching at each other's throats.

"Stop It!" Amber's voice yelled from behind.

The two words seemed to reverberate throughout the room, throughout the house. Rattling it from the bottom of its foundation to the top of it steepled spire. Her words held an appalling immediacy, like an invisible knife being held at their throats.

Neither moved.

Amber stood midway on the long staircase, her long blonde hair flowing across her shoulders. Dressed in the same long white gown that she wore since the night they first saw her, she stood looking curiously at them both. How long she had been there didn't matter. How long she had watched the struggle mattered most.

They both remained frozen. Bloody, exhausted, drained of their inner demonic strengths. Panting for air to revive their spent bodies and altered minds. Both loosened their bloody, deadly grips on each other's necks. Their wounds, which once bled profusely, stopped their bloodletting. They started to heal, as though their wounds were never there. And both monsters also began to transform at the same time, back from the shapes of uncaged wild beasts to the forms of normal, sane men. But this wasn't normal. This was...

"Aren't you both tired of being who you are, hating what you've become? Don't you understand what you are?" she spoke in a scolding voice.

Amber came down the final few steps and stood at the entrance to the parlor.

"Monsters and men."

There was a long terrifying moment of silence.

With those three words, their transformations were completed. There were no longer any signs of wounds. Just two tired men standing before her, being judged for what they had let themselves become, or what they always were.

"You both came here to hunt each other, and all you can do is haunt each other," she stated scornfully.

The men listlessly separated—Janek returning to his sofa chair; Lancelot leaning against the still-burning fireplace.

It was Lancelot who spoke first. His deep breathing returned to normal.

"We know who we are. What we don't know is who, or what, *you* are. You came from a grave."

"No, I live in the real world. I came to take you back to the grave," Amber somberly replied.

Lancelot laughed. "Is this some type of trick? Ever since you arrived here you have played us against each other. We're not fools to believe this isn't some sort of scheme. I knew it from the first day you showed up. How appropriate for you to arrive on a rainy night next to an open grave. Which one of our publishers is behind this?" Lancelot angrily questioned.

"No one is behind this. I came here on my own. I was drawn to the house. I was drawn to you. I had prearranged the open grave as a way to lure you out," Amber replied calmly.

"I knew it! You're just a crazed fan. You're part of this elaborate hoax," Lancelot smirked.

"No. This is no hoax," she said in a small, strong voice.

"Bullshit! That's all it is. Bullshit. And I've had enough of your theatrics," Lancelot defiantly interrupted. He turned and faced Janek. "Maybe you're both in this together. Playing a head game with me while I play games with you. I'm bored by all of this. I can end this charade and walk out of here right now if I want."

Janek did not respond to his accusation. Instead, he studied Amber's face intently, then calmly spoke up.

"Maybe we should hear her out."

"Don't tell me you're falling for this. If you're not working with her, then our agents probably set this up, like they set us up here. It's all part of the story we're supposed to write."

Both men stared at each other as the stillness of the house seemed to hold them captive. Finally, Janek turned to Amber.

"We each know our part in all of this. We each know what we want to take from each other, and we each have spent the time moving all the game pieces into their final position. What is your part?”

“To learn the truth and to tell you the truth,” Amber replied assuredly.

“The truth?” Lancelot countered with a raised voice. “Searching for the truth is a moral justification and an unending task. Truth be damned! The only truth is what we believe it to be.”

Amber took a moment before responding, carefully choosing her next words.

“Believe me that I tell you this place is evil. It has some force of power, terrible power. All I know is that it is a living, breathing thing of evil. It plays tricks on each of you. It distorts what you think is real. It controls you. This place holds you here. I don’t know why…but it does.”

“Oh, please. How naive do you think I am?” Lancelot challenged as he analyzed her with narrowed eyes. “You think this place is a real haunted house. That’s just foolish nonsense. Haunted houses only exist in one’s mind, or one’s writings. This is just an old, big house with a sordid past. It’s just a house. It might scare you, but it doesn’t scare me. Now remind me more of why I shouldn’t really leave?”

“This house won’t let you leave,” Amber spoke steadily, knowingly. “Even though the door is closed, unlocked, you are afraid to try to open it, because you know what lies on the other side of the door, the truth to everything, and you don’t want to know that.”

A cold wind unexpectedly blew through the house. Chilling all of them.

She paused and looked from one to the other.

"You feel it now, too, don't you?"

They both stared back at her in silence.

"You know it now...don't you?" she continued.

The quick burst of the wind that wrapped the room abruptly ended. Only the strange chill remained.

"It's not what you believe, it's what everyone else knows."

She paused and stared directly at both of them.

"The truth is...you're both dead."

Lancelot let out a loud laugh as he took a step forward towards her. "Lady," Lancelot stated touching his skin. "I'm flesh and bones. I'm alive, not dead."

Amber remained somber as she shook her head slightly, as the only one who really knew.

"If you're really alive, why don't you just walk through the door and leave here forever."

Lancelot looked to the front door, paused, then looked back to her.

"But you can't," Amber replied in a low whispering tone. "You can never leave. This house is your grave."

An unsettling, eerie calm held the room and its occupants in an icy grip. Neither Janek nor Lancelot moved; they both stood quietly, letting her words sink in.

"You both died years ago on that night when you came here to write a story together. But you never made it here, physically. You both died in accidents, at the same moment, at the same exact time. Lancelot's plane was lost in a storm and then disappeared into the ocean. Vladamir's car missed a turn on a slippery mountain road, plunging a thousand feet into a rocky ravine where it crashed and exploded. Neither of your remains, your earthly bodies, were ever found. An unbelievable tragedy to both your tragic life stories. The two greatest horror authors who in life plotted to kill each other died together and now metaphorically live together.

Before either could speak, Amber continued.

"This is your home. This is where you live. These are the grounds you are confined to. You can never leave, you don't know how, and you are neither alive nor truly dead. Somehow you are trapped somewhere between. You were so obsessed with each other that when you physically died, your spiritual selves appeared here to finish what you had started, what you planned. This is your legacy, your final story. This is now your house, a house you both haunt, and I've come here to find you, to uncover the reality and let the world know once and for all."

Lancelot looked at her nervously, then to Janek.

"What you say is nonsense. We're not dead. That's impossible. We see each other, we touch each other, we fight each other. Everything that happens, exists."

Amber looked at each compassionately.

"They are the stories you tell yourself. They are the stories you write. And then there's the truth."

She let out a deep sigh.

"You're both ghosts. And you exist only in your books."

She watched the startled expression of both, the unconcealed thunderstruck emotions in their eyes. A mind-shattering, numb-like dismay was written across their faces. Each thinking of all the possibilities. Unbelievable, but...the logic of her argument could not be denied. There was now no doubt to what she said after everything that had happened, everything that happened since she arrived. Everything.

They looked at each other with the first real emotion of genuine understanding. Their expressions changed to emptiness. With the finality of her pronouncement still swaying in their heads, they now finally had the answer that they had been searching for.

Their quest to kill each other had ended with them killing themselves.

"So, this is our fate. To remain here, trapped forever?" Lancelot asked grimly.

Amber did not reply.

"But we don't need to remain here forever." Janek turned to face Lancelot, no longer as an adversary, but now as a partner in a puzzling situation. "Acceptance would perhaps be the necessary solution if all were true as she stated."

"Then how do you kill someone who is already dead?" Lancelot responded impatiently.

"That's not the question. The question is how do you finally agree to death so that you can find the peace you both want," Amber interjected.

"A writer's paradox. How does one find a way out of their own death?" Janek nodded solemnly, thinking aloud.

Amber saw the growing creative realization in the minds of both men.

She interrupted their thoughts. "Sometimes there is only one way."

Wordlessly, they both turned to stare at her and listen to what she had to say. Amber faced them directly.

"To write yourself out of your story."

The vague thoughts that had already come from them, came now in a more concentrated form from each in turn. There was no further reluctance or unbridled fear in either. They each knew they had to accept their conviction of not existing as an unalterable solution. They both knew they could no longer be part of a story. It was the only way for "their story" to have a final ending.

It is written somewhere in time that some people plead for forgiveness in their final moments, some express no remorse whatsoever, and some ask for deliverance. For both Lancelot Strong and Vladamir Janek, two men, two monsters, two lost souls, they neither asked for, nor acknowledged, any of that. For them, it was all about believing who they now had become. Ghosts in a story. And in their acceptance, their final fate would no longer be denied.

The entire house seemed to take a deep breath and become strangely alive. Alive in a way it hadn't seen in so many, many years. Years that once belonged to a story of a young married couple who were first to live in the house, who gave birth to new life here, only to see themselves end in death, leaving their ghosts behind. A tragic story within a love story. A story that became this horror story. A story of ghosts.

The house groaned an unearthly sound, whether it was another burst of unseen wind or actual moans coming from the walls. The floors and the entire structure's foundations seemed to shift as if the earth beneath was unleashing something, somethings, that sought to return from a time long lost. Both Lancelot and Janek could feel and hear the same sounds the house made. Breathing and sucking noises. Shuffling of footsteps, the whispers of voices. Voices that were murmuring their names—both their names together.

Amber stepped backwards, away from them, as she, too, could sense the sudden and dramatic changes the house was making. She could hear the evil on display in the house but could not see what Janek and Lancelot experienced.

The room flashed bright white then became mysteriously absent of all light. Then it came back, this time darker and more shadowy. The fireplace roared with its flames climbing the chimney, seeking to escape at the top. The windows in the room became empty—empty from a totally dark sky outside. Something terrible was about to happen. They all knew it.

The sounds grew closer, grew louder, until they blended into an intensity that became deafening. Faces appeared from all angles of the house's many revealed shadows. Happy faces, sad faces, curious faces, worried faces, angry faces. Different faces, each with different expressions, yet each one all the same as the others. Lifeless, and all covered in dripping blood.

The faces were those of all their victims revealed. These were the ghosts of those they had killed in their writings. Ghosts that now came back to life one more time to take both writers with them, away from their stories and into this new final story. Away from this horrid, haunted house and into another place. Crossing over to a place that only existed in one's mind and beliefs, or maybe one's bestselling or critically acclaimed book. A deserved place, a place reserved especially for them. The darkness of eternal Hell.

As the cacophony of sounds reached a breaking point, all the faces screamed at once. Louder than any sound ever made on earth.

Amber forced her hands over her ears as tightly as she could to block out the maddening noise. Her body shook as she fell to her knees in the deafening roar of impending death and unimaginable dread. She opened her mouth to scream, too, but nothing came out; everything seemed frozen in time. The house began to violently shake, to shudder, preparing to implode or even explode. What held it together was unexplainable. It just was.

In this terrifying moment, Lancelot and Janek stood unafraid. The coming end held no meaning for them. They welcomed the decisive destruction of their secrets and themselves. They welcomed their freedom from their tragic lives of living horror.

Vladamir Janek and Lancelot Strong had waited an eternity of sleepless nights and endless days for this. They would finally escape from their shame and guilt that lived within. Escape from the hatred of each other.

The house's lighting grew dim and hazy. A thick, gray mist came from the walls, the floor, and the ceiling—a swirling mist that hovered about the two men, enveloping them, as Amber watched on in startled awe. Nothing more was said between them, nothing more was spoken. Nothing was heard but a sudden and eerie silence that she would never forget.

Both of them—both Janek and Lancelot—both men and monsters—started to fade away into nothingness. In their remaining moments, they both looked one last time to Amber, spellbound by her angelic eyes and her revealing truth. Whether for comfort or atonement, they together waited for her final acknowledgement. Stepping forward into the mist, unafraid of the unknown that she had become a major part of, she tenderly reached out with both hands and placed one on either side of their fading faces. She felt love; she felt horror. Her eyes filled with tears of happiness and sadness as her heart whispered goodbye.

It was their last chapter as they both disappeared into eternal darkness.

Chapter 25

The stretch limo idled in wait at the entrance of the old, dark house. Jet black in color, it could have passed for a hearse waiting to lead a procession to a cemetery for a burial. But today was not a funeral, not an ending, nor a beginning. Today was a revelation waiting to be shared. And soon it would be, as planned all along.

The sound of its high-tuned engine was all that broke the brisk autumn morning silence. The dampness in the air would soon give way to a brilliant, sunny day. It was as if a large dark cloud that once covered the surrounding property, the house, and everything in it had been lifted and taken away. And it had.

A male chauffeur sat unobtrusively in the driver's seat of the limo, lost in thought, reading a book. Outside the vehicle, a middle-aged woman stood leaning against it looking towards the house, anxiously waiting. Dressed professionally in a fashionable suit and an open tweed overcoat, she glanced at her watch. The time indicated that it was almost twelve noon. The watch had the caricature of Mickey Mouse pointing its gloved fingers to the numbers. She gave a faint smile to herself as she looked at the watch, reliving a brief memory of a special moment in her past. A warm breeze made the woman's open coat move slightly as she put her hand back inside the jacket's pocket while continuing her wait. A few tree branches swayed in the wind, but other than that, and the sound of the purring car engine, everything was quiet. Very quiet. Waiting.

The front door of the old house opened.

And then a woman stepped out of the house's shadows to reveal herself.

But the actual reveal had already been made, but not known. Made for those inside the house to find the truth about themselves, to learn that all of this wasn't real, that it was just a made-up story in one person's fantasy. Hers, His, Theirs. It made no difference. After all, what is fantasy and what is reality? A writer uses both to create and to destroy. All that mattered was that they all now knew the truth. It wasn't her. It never was. It was them. They were Ghosts. And they always would be.

"So, Amber, did you get what you wanted?" the older woman asked.

"You mean, what I came for? Yes. I finished the story."

"So, your book is done. This place, which gives me the chills just looking at it, gave you the ending you were looking for?"

"Yes, and a lot more."

"Another story idea?"

Amber smiled her response. The older woman took a moment to understand the smile.

"Well...as your best friend, as your literary agent, I have to ask..."

"I expected you to," Amber replied.

"Did you see them?"

"Do you mean, their ghosts?"

"Well, they both died the same night, at the same time on their way here over 20 years ago. The place has been boarded up for a long time, but there's been all the talk of strange things..."

"Things that go bump in the night?"

"Yeah, as a writer, I figured you'd say that."

Amber gave no reply, nor any expression of a would-be reply.

The older woman paused to look at the house. It seemed to look back at her. Her body shuttered slightly.

She continued, "Stories, strange things, tales—the place has a lot of 'history.' And you're the first person the estate allowed to step foot inside in a long, long time, let alone spend several nights alone inside."

"Being the great-granddaughter of the original Amber Stone, who once lived here, has its advantages. How could they not?"

"And you're also today's most celebrated horror author," the older woman added. "What a great promo for the planned book launch. Every other living horror writer would love a chance to do what you did—write a historical horror story in a real haunted house!"

"Yes, I suppose. This place certainly has all the classic complexities that qualifies it as a haunted house. But there was something different about this place from everything I found in my research. There was something in here that existed but was not visible until I allowed myself to see it."

"So, did you?"

Amber paused and looked back at the house. She then turned to face her agent.

"Let me ask you a question first. Do you believe?"

The older woman turned her head slightly away to think of the right reply, an honest reply. After all, it was her idea to have her client come here in the first place to finish her book, an idea she had once proposed years earlier to another writer who, tragically, never completed his story.

"In ghosts? Well...yeah, I sort of think there must be some truth to all what people say they see. So, yeah. I guess I do believe."

She paused.

Curious, the agent pressed on, "So, what about you? After several days alone here, did you actually see them? That's why you were here, right? To see if they existed and to have them tell you the unfinished story that they were once going to write about, and give you the inspiration you were searching for to finish your book? So, did you see them? Did you find what you came for?"

It was now the younger woman's time to think of the right reply, an honest reply. After all, she had eagerly agreed to come here to see and feel the presence of her ancestor's past and to stay in the house where two writers had died on their way here to do the same.

"Sometimes the mind plays strange tricks on oneself. Making you believe things that may or may not be actually there. And sometimes they're there for only you to experience alone."

Amber paused and looked at the house for a long moment, then turned to her agent.

"And sometimes it's our memories that are the real ghosts that haunt us."

"Well, that sounds chilling! Make sure you put that in your book."

The older woman got into the car first. Before doing the same, Amber paused and turned back, looking at the house one last time, one long, last time.

Yes, she had the answers; she had the story.

After entering the car and shutting the door to the past days spent here, Amber closed her eyes to take a moment's reflection.

As the limo pulled away from the old strange house, the sounds of stone and gravel crunched loudly beneath the weight of its tires. Amber silently looked up at the windows on the second floor. She saw two faces. Two skulls on two standing skeletons. She saw them, as they saw her. Each staring back at her. One was laughing, one was crying.

A mysterious haunting wind came out of nowhere and raced through the graveyard as though trying to catch up to her and say one final goodbye. But the foreboding wind held no voice, only the sound of a young child's laughter.

Behind the house, in the small family cemetery, mostly overgrown, mostly forgotten, two fresh graves remained open. Two headstones, not as old as the others, but worn from the 20 years they had languished in the changing seasons, faced each other. Two headstones, with the names Lancelot Strong and Vladamir Janek. Between them was another headstone with the worn but visible name, Amber. Across it lay a brand-new white gown, blowing gently in the wind.

The two faces in the window were no longer there. But in the car, Amber gave a wicked smile, as she alone could feel, could hear...

The house screamed.

No one would ever know it...but her.

* * * * *

Ghosts

by Amber Stone
Chapter 1

Once upon a time, two writers walked into a haunted house to have dinner with the devil. Each writer assumed that the other was the devil. It was a perfect assumption because each writer knew the devil personally, having met him in their nightmares and bringing him to life in their writings. Each writer hid behind a smile on the outside and shared the same hatred on the inside. A hatred for each other for what they were and what they had become. Because each writer alone thought they understood the devil's game, they plotted and planned how to beat the devil at his own game. To them, life and death was a game. And in their game, they each used words. It was always the words they wrote, the images they created to protect them, yet hid them from each of their own horrible underlying truths. They each held a secret, and they both knew what it was. It was a simple truth: They each wanted to kill the devil; and they each wanted to *be* the devil. But what neither of them knew was that they were both already the devil. And both of them were already dead.

Do You Believe?

While writing this novel, those who knew about this project all asked me the same question at one time or another, "Do you believe in ghosts?"

The answer is...yes, and no.

Yes, I have experienced some interesting phenomena, including ghost-like apparitions through the years. I have felt some strange temperatures unexpectedly, heard some strange noises, and maybe, just maybe, saw some "things" that happened so fast that I can't explain what it really was. Shadows, shapes, sounds? Spirits of the Dead? Things that go bump in the night? Hmm.

And no, I'm not sure if what I experienced, what I saw or felt were tricks my over-worked imagination played on me, things I wanted to believe I saw or felt, or just a moment in my life that has no tangible proof to once and for all say with certainty, I believe.

But...from all of this, there is something I do believe. And it all came together while researching this book.

My son and his wife live in Denver, Colorado, and during a planned visit he sent my wife Debbie and I on a side trip to spend a night at the renowned Stanley Hotel in Estes Park, Colorado. This is the hotel that world-famous author Stephen King stayed at and got some of his inspiration for his book **The Shining**. The majestic hotel is in an amazing mountain setting and has a history of ghost sightings. It was only natural for me to want to go there as I started to develop the story for this book. Whether it was for inspiration, relaxation, or just to cross it off my bucket list of "been there, done that," I felt compelled to experience it. And once there, I was genuinely intrigued at the opportunity to be there. It was both fascinating and surreal.

I explored the huge place both with my wife and alone. I walked the hotel floors, visited famous rooms that held famous secrets, and sought out the tucked-away hidden areas in search of finding a ghost. There were unusual feelings that I experienced throughout the hotel that are hard to describe. (Yes, I could write a few paragraphs here, but...) Some of these were personal feelings and some of these still live with me today. But here I found my answer, and I sort of knew it all along.

Ghosts do exist for all of us. They really do. Ghosts are our memories.

Good, bad, and indifferent they are always with us and seem to come and go at the most unusual and unpredictable times. Whether we think of our loved ones, family, and friends who have passed or places that we have visited, once or more times, and recall experiences we have shared fondly or sadly, they are always with us, sometimes hidden, sometimes staring at us, but they are always there. Always there for us to see in our imagination, to relive in our dreams, and to think about when, and if, we need to seek them out. Just close your eyes and let your mind drift. Don't be afraid to let these memories in, They're there for you.

They're "your ghosts" just like I have my own ghosts. Ours alone to remember.

So, yes, I do believe in ghosts. And so should you. They have always existed within us and always will. And once you admit to yourself that these memories are the real ghosts in your life, you are one step closer to understanding why. After all, there may be someone, or something, behind you, or beside you right now. Someone or something that is waiting for you as you wait for it. Waiting for us to become a memory, too.

And we will. One day we, too, will become someone's ghosts.

Happy Haunting.

Joe J.

THE NAKED DEAD

By Joe Janowicz

When the clothes come off, the killing begins.

Someone is killing naked people. Paradise Lost, an international naturist resort, is holding a major "bare all" nudist and adult swingers convention. When a celebrity guest is found floating "bottoms up" in one of the luxury outdoor pools, the local police are called to investigate. Another naked guest is found dead in the window display of an on-premise concessions shop. Both victims have bite marks in their necks and are drained of all their blood. Is this the work of a "real life" vampire, or a crazed psychopath pretending to be a vampire?

Detective Jamie Parker and Police Officer Jim McKenna are given the undercover assignment to stay on site as a couple and search for any clues. To blend in, they have to go "au natural" and mingle with the guests.

More mysterious deaths continue as the killer plays a game of cat and mouse with Jamie, intending to make her a victim. Never having been to a nudist resort, let alone walk around in public wearing only sunglasses and a smile, Jamie discovers that you don't need clothes to catch a killer.

Amazon online and selected bookstores
https://www.JoeJanowiczAuthor.com

MURDER ON THE ERIE CANAL

Sequel to DANGEROUS PASSION
Written by Elly Stevens

Do you know a KILLER when you see one?

Sue Gainer starts her career as a private investigator in a hometown detective agency. When a missing person's case is dropped in her lap that ends in murder, Sue faces unusual and desperate suspects and unlocks the clues that lead to the surprising truth—and soon finds herself in deep water with a killer.

Available on Amazon and Barnes and Noble online.

https://www.authorellystevens.com